BLACK CAT TALES

An Anthology of Black Cats

BLACK CAT TALES

An Anthology of Black Cats

Edited by

Francesca Maria & Mark S. Causey

Cover illustration and design by Kealan Patrick Burke

Edited and formatted by Mark S. Causey and Francesca Maria

First Edition

ISBN (paperback): 979-8-9924402-0-1

ISBN (ebook): 979-8-9924402-1-8

Library of Congress Control Number: 2025931111

BLACK CAT PUBLISHING

Pacific Grove, CA

www.black-cat-publishing.com

Printed in the United States of America

DEDICATION

For Agnes

CONTENTS

CONTENTS

CONTENTS

Trigger Warnings: *domestic violence, animal harm*

EDITORS' PREFACE

Black cats are awesome. They just are. Whether you're a fan of the dark and spooky, or a lover of the feline variety, black cats hold a special place in our collective imagination. Why is that? Why have black cats been feared and revered by so many cultures across countless generations? Maybe there is some hidden truth to their mysterious and provocative ways. Maybe beneath their inky, shadowed fur lies a hidden awareness or knowledge that we, as mere humans, are incapable of understanding. Maybe black cats know all the secrets of the universe, secrets that would explode our delicate minds.

These questions along with a mild to moderate obsession of black cats is why this book is in your little paws. We looked around bookshelves and were aghast and shocked to find not a single book dedicated to black cats (of the non-scientific variety) and we aimed to change that.

So we put out a call, and so many answered. We received hundreds of black cat stories and poems from all over the world, showcasing these magical creatures as witch's familiars, harbingers of death, lucky charms, ill-fated victims, beloved pets and so much more. After months of scouring through every tale, we collated our favorite thirteen poems and twenty-six (thirteen twice!) short stories.

In the pages that follow, you will find a mixture of horror, real-life, fantasy, mystery and a sprinkle of science fiction amongst the tales. Some have happy endings, some decidedly do not.

Each author masterfully navigates their own black cat tale; some through heartache, fear, death, grief and loss, while others are just plain fun and may elicit a chuckle or two. It brings us editors great joy to be able to share these stories and talented authors with you. For some authors, this is their first publication and we couldn't be more thrilled to have them see their name in print for the first time in the pages that follow.

So without further delay, sink into a comfortable seat, grab a favorite beverage and if at all possible, a cat on your lap and enjoy.

Francesca Maria and Mark S. Causey, Editors

INTRODUCTION

Black cats have not always been looked at favorably by us humans. All too often in the past, they were judged to be creatures of the devil in one way or the other. Witches' familiars. Demons in feline form. Harbingers of bad luck, when they cross the path of a wandering human. I like to think we've left those beliefs and superstitions in the past. I hope so, anyway.

I love those black wanderers of the night. So, when I saw that Francesca Maria and Mark Causey were putting together an anthology of stories and poems revolving around black cats, it didn't take long for me to offer up this introduction. I was definitely interested in contributing to this book.

I hope all of you will enjoy this collection of tails. Er, tales. Within these pages, you'll be introduced to black-furred felines of all types of personalities and motivations, some friendly, some helpful, some that are ever-vigilant protectors, some just out for themselves, and some, well…some just a tad bit sinister.

Take *Dust and Shadow*, for instance, the opening tale of this anthology. The cats in that story have secrets aplenty, and their motivations are not necessarily in our best interest. Thankfully,…but I'm not going to say more. Cats have their secrets, and those secrets are for them to share, not I.

Jamoca's Last Patrol, on the other hand, is the story of warrior cats, tirelessly keeping a vigil to keep us safe.

Jamoca's heroism is no less than any of the renowned knights and soldiers from our own human history, and their devotion to duty is second to none. For that reason alone, this tale may be one of my favorites of the collection. I love a heroic yarn.

Then, there are cats where it's not too clear if they're our friends, or a beast we need to always keep an eye on, and never turn our backs to, like the feline in question from the story *The Cat and the Custom*.

I mentioned superstitions earlier. *Cross My Heart and Hope to Rise* touches on the old fear of black cats bringing bad luck when they cross one's path, but…well, let's just say that's not necessarily a bad thing.

In my life, I've seen cats that though they were diminutive in size, they more than made up for it in attitude. Memories spring to mind of witnessing a cat chasing a dog who substantially outweighed it down the street, the dog bawling in terror as the little 'tiger' pursued it. *Garbo* brought back some of those memories. Trust me, though they are indeed small, they are not to be trifled with. *Garbo* might be a bit of a tall tale, but there is a very real germ of truth in the tale.

When I was young, I used to read horror comics. Titles from Marvel and DC, the old EC horror comics, and others—sometimes under the blankets late at night with a flashlight for illumination. They had a dark, creepy form of justice where evildoers got their comeuppance, with a ghoulish comment from the narrator. *Elegy for Pilate Hardesty* reminds me of the stories from those old comics, where those who dared to commit dark acts of evil always met a grim end.

Well, I could go on, but if you're like me, the last thing you want to do is read a long-winded introduction. You'd rather dive in and start enjoying the stories. Let me finish by saying there's something for every cat lover within these pages. Sinister cats, playful cats, heroic cats, cats that are bloody damned nightmares, haunting the shadows and waiting for the right time to pounce, mysterious cats, and many others. Time to wrap this up—the felines are growing impatient. They're ready for you to open the book, turn to the first tale, and start reading. Musn't keep them waiting!

S.D. Vassallo
From the heart of the windswept prairie
April, 2025

BLACK CAT TALES

An Anthology of Black Cats

Daniel Roop is a member of the Horror Writers Association and has been nominated for a Pushcart Prize for his work in Will Work for Peace from Zeropanik Press. His speculative fiction has appeared or is forthcoming in publications including Flash Fiction Online, Dark Spores, Black Cat Tales, The Maul Magazine, and Appalachian Places. He is a seventh generation East Tennessean, and his favorite superhero is Kitty Pryde.

DUST AND SHADOW
by Daniel Roop
for Astrid

Once upon a time—well—this would be a good place to stop for a moment, to ensure that you aren't under the impression that this is a children's story. What follows is in no way meant for those little ones, their minds as impressionable as damp clay, clutching their bedraggled blankets, jamming germ-ridden thumbs in their haphazardly toothed maws. You'll soon see, as this story opens, that it is most decidedly *not* for children. So, this very second, if there are any mewling snot-stringers, any syrup-fingered graspers, any feces-laden full-diapered waddlers wailing to stay up just a few minutes more, dash their hopes this instant. Send them all away, whining and grumbling, to their oppressive, comfortable beds. I'll wait.

Are we alone? Good. Now.

Once upon a time, maggots appeared in the kittens' litter box, and that was the final straw. The two sister kittens, Dust, gray as her name, Shadow, as black as hers, could tolerate this neglect no longer. They had been patient and understanding for the entire year that they had lived in the home of their adopted owner, a nine-year-old child, who had acquired them as a gift on her prior birthday, under the strict understanding from her parents that she would be a diligent caretaker. Books on caring for cats were read aloud around the fireplace, lists of chores were written and posted

2

on the refrigerator, supplies were purchased, all in anticipation of that magical day when the family would journey to the shelter and the kittens would be chosen and brought home.

This child, whom we'll call Petunia, had the best intentions, of course, as all children do. Children are *born* with the best intentions, then find the most imaginative ways to turn those intentions into marker drawings on the walls and self-administered haircuts and, as Dust and Shadow were quick to learn, inconsistently filled food bowls, dry water dishes, and a litter box so unattended and foul that any self-respecting cat would never want to sully her paws on its urine-thick clumps.

Petunia, in addition to these betrayals, insisted on calling Dust and Shadow *kittens* even as they neared a full year of age. True, they technically straddled that nebulous edge of kitten-hood and cat-hood, but they certainly didn't want to be belittled by someone who wasn't even mature enough to promptly scoop their droppings or notice the bareness of their bowls.

So, they decided to murder her.

Now there are some old tales about cats, most untrue and unfair, of them stealing the breath from babies and killing them, either accidentally, drawn by the smell of milk on their mouth (in which case they were at worst committing infant-slaughter), or intentionally, out of jealousy for the attention the newborn baby was receiving at the expense of themselves. This is utter nonsense. Firstly, the lingering smell of milk on a baby is rank and unpleasant, far beneath a feline's sensibilities, and secondly, no cat has so little dignity as to murder for attention. There is no truth to these old tales. Cats do not kill in this way, for these reasons.

No, cats only murder people with just cause. How do I know this? Because it's what they have told me, and I have never found an ounce of profit in arguing with a cat.

The evening before Petunia's tenth birthday, the kittens sprawled on her bed while the family ate dinner downstairs. Dust rolled over and said to Shadow, "Sister, this treatment is intolerable."

Shadow said to Dust, "Sister, it is most intolerable, indeed. Shall we murder her?"

Dust said, "I see no other answer, sister."

Shadow said, "No, no other answer at all. We have been most reasonable and patient."

"We surely have. How shall we do it? Claws and teeth tearing the ripe bloodpumps at the throat?"

"Soft paws pressed over mouth and nostrils?"

They paused to groom one another, Shadow licking the elusive patch of fur behind Dust's left ear, until Dust decided fighting would be more fun, and pounced on Shadow. They rolled off the bed and promptly fell asleep in a pile of laundry. When they woke an hour later, Petunia was in the shower, singing loudly, and off-key.

"Paws over mouth and nostrils, I believe, sister," said Dust.

Shadow agreed. They fell asleep again, curled into each other like nautilus shells. When they woke, it was dark. They could hear Petunia's breathing from the bed. They nodded to each other, lightly touched nose to nose, then leapt on padded feet onto the comforter, silent as a feather wafting onto a ball of cotton. Dust crept up the left side of Petunia's body, Shadow her right side. They arrived at her head, and stood over her, right forepaws raised, ready to cut off her breath and avenge themselves most righteously.

Then Shadow said, "Sister, is it possible we are being unfair?"

Dust said, "Many things are possible, sister, but it seems unlikely. We have been patient our whole lives."

"It's true, we have."

"We have been neglected and disregarded in a manner most unbecoming our dignity. We have mewed for food like street animals. We have begged like lowly dogs. How could this restoration of justice be unfair?"

"Sister, you are wise and discerning as always. It's just that I wonder, are we certain her parents truly prepared her for the worthy cause of caring for us?"

Now, cats know many things, things that you and I will never know. But they did not know about the books, about the lists, about the expectations laid down clear as fresh water in a clean bowl. They didn't know the parents were completely blameless, and that Petunia was simply a selfish beast.

"Sister," said Dust, "you are the kindest of cats, and there is wisdom in your words." They lowered their paws.

Shadow, the kindest of cats, said, "Let's murder her parents."

Dust and Shadow eased down the hall, diverting for fifteen minutes to chase, corner and torture a small brown beetle, then paused for a quick nap. They woke and crept into the parents' room. They agreed to murder the father first, as he was the lighter sleeper, and they crouched over his head, right paws extended, ready to snuff him out for his poor stewardship of his ill-prepared daughter. Then Dust said, "Sister, you have shown me new insight this evening, and I feel obliged to ask, is it possible we are being unfair?"

Shadow was eager to press her paw upon his nostrils and stopped at the last second, only out of respect for Dust. "Many things are possible, sister. Do go on."

"Just as perhaps they prepared their daughter poorly, so their parents may have done the same to them."

"You grow in wisdom and empathy every day, sister. This world does not deserve you."

"Nor you, sister."

"Shall we murder *their* parents?"

"We shall."

Now, Dust and Shadow knew very well that, sadly, all four of Petunia's grandparents were already dead. But death was no hindrance to adolescent cats determined to murder. You've likely been assuming that the impending violence in this story is what makes it unsuitable for children, but that's nonsense. Children love violence. They crave it. No, this story isn't for them because it reveals too much of the secrets of cats, secrets children are too unstable to yet be entrusted with.

The most closely guarded secret of cats is this—they can travel through space and time in a way particular to their species. They can traverse vast distances, thousands of miles, in a moment. They can leap forward and backward in time at a whim. How do they do this? They travel by virtue of their names.

This is why children can never know this secret because, sadly for cats, they must use the names they are given by humans, and most often, children are the creatures who bestow those names. This is why cats rarely respond when called by name. They resent being beholden to something foisted on them without their consent.

Petunia, as you have seen, did many things poorly, but she did one thing beautifully. She named her kittens Dust and Shadow.

Shadow could, as you can easily imagine, step into any shadow and emerge from any other. She could stroll into a shadow cast by Petunia's bedroom dresser and saunter out a moment later from a shadow cast by a suit of armor in a Scottish castle hundreds of years in the past.

Dust traveled by the motes suspended in sunbeams or floating in strong moonlight. She could leap into a cloud of particulates, illuminated at Petunia's window seat and land the next moment amidst flecks under a full moon in ancient Egypt, ready to receive her worshippers.

They did these things every night, as do all cats who are able. What, did you believe they spent their evenings scratching carpeted poles and playing with balls of fluff?

These are cats we are speaking of, and they have deeper ways than you know, more talents than I will reveal here.

Some cats, however, weren't so fortunate, named by thoughtless, ignorant children who unwittingly froze them in one time and place. Take a cat named "Mittens" for example. What is a poor Mittens to do to travel? Lay down in a sock drawer and hope for the best? Curl up in the corner of a cupboard and dream of a Narnia-esque miracle? I've already told you, this isn't a children's story. Still, it is true that cats are crafty, with prodigious imaginations that show the poverty of our own. For instance, I once knew a cat named Hazel. In her vast inventiveness, she learned to travel by being gazed upon by someone with hazel-colored eyes, and would then appear in another time and place within sight of another person with hazel-colored eyes. Cats being naturally stealthy, and people being naturally dismissive, it was never questioned when Hazel popped into existence in her new location. She was a genius among her kind, but not all cats hindered by their static names were so gifted. I've yet to meet a wise Mittens, or a resourceful Socks.

Dust and Shadow arrived together, in a cloudy moonbeam, in the shadowed corner of a leather recliner, at Petunia's paternal grandparents. They perched above the grandfather, murderous paws at the ready, when Dust asked, "Sister, is it possible we are being unfair?"

Shadow said, "We must admit the possibility, sister."

So, the night continued, broken by peaceful naps and selfless grooming and the occasional torture of smaller creatures. They leapt place to place, going back generation after generation, from suburban houses to mining camps, from whitewashed farmhouses to shotgun shacks nestled deep in mountain hollows, back and back to thatched huts, and even farther back. They eventually arrived in the shadows cast by firelight in a cave, to dust lit aloft in the hot updraft. They asked one another again, as they crouched with paws upraised to shut off the rotten ancestral breath from the nearly toothless mouth, "Sister, is it possible we are being unfair?"

They answered, "We must admit the possibility." They were impressed, rightly so, with their time-won wisdom, with their time-softened hearts. They turned their backs on the snoring antecedents and leapt into light, into dust and shadow, and stepped out the next moment into Petunia's room.

Shadow said, "So, we'll just murder her then."

Dust said, "Of course, sister. We'll just murder her."

They leaned in over her face, her breath smelling of birthday cake, their right forepaws closing in. They stopped in unison. Shadow said, "There is the matter of the quality of the petting, of course."

"There is that, sister. I have noticed how astutely she focuses on that particular spot above your right eye that you so very much like to have stroked."

"Yes, sister, this is true. Likewise, I've observed how she scratches the fur just above your tail with the perfect degree of pressure."

The paws hung like suspended guillotines in the air as they talked.

"There is the benefit of the homemade toys as well. Many of our sisters in other homes have to be content with poorly crafted plastic toys from human stores."

"This is true, sister. Also, it would be shortsighted to forget the purloined tuna she sneaks us from the kitchen."

The paws lowered. They stared across her face at one another, their eyes slowly closing. They fell asleep, curled against Petunia, her arms wrapping around them reflexively in the cool of the night.

They woke an hour later. Dust yawned and said, sleepily, "Perhaps tomorrow we'll murder her, then?"

Shadow murmured, "Perhaps, sister," and again they slept.

Daniel Bulone (he/him) is a writer of speculative fiction and poetry. He earned his MFA from San Jose State University, and is currently revising his thesis novel about memory, the American Dream, and the hollow Earth. His most recent work can be found at *Eye to the Telescope* and *The Encourager*.

JAMOCA'S LAST PATROL
by Daniel Bulone

This was Jamoca's last day at the Lee Vining Motel. Gold crept along the surface of Mono Lake and tinged the tufa, along with the sleeping, titanic face of the Eastern Sierras. Jamoca's fur bristled. Doom was in that dawning. She welcomed it, as any warrior would.

She summoned up her black cat body from the pool of shadow where she slept under the ice machine and went about her morning business, greeting the ghosts of the motel and hushing them back to sleep.

If Jamoca wanted to be noticed, which she didn't, then a living observer would have seen her stalk along the handrail and pause, peer at a puddle of light in the handicapped parking space and purr. But those with eyes to see (cats, the dead, some gifted living folk, and the Others), would know what business Jamoca was truly about. The purring reverberated below the pavement and pipes of the parking lot to the layer where a westbound family that died in the blizzard of 1887 awoke. The ghosts of the husband, wife, little girl, and baby boy arose and, in the dimension where their spirits could move and clamor, started fixing breakfast and preparing for the passage through the Sierras in their covered wagon. The echoes of eggs cracking and clanking on cast iron and the whinnies and grunts of long-gone horses still sounded in the soil. The little girl's song to her baby brother rippled in the dry desert clay. Jamoca's purr reverberated down, down, down to the space between meaning and matter where the ghosts and memories dwelt, and hushed them. The music of this family piped up every morning, loudest of all of the ghosts, because they had loved and hoped.

The handful of other ghosts on the property stirred with faint bumps and knocks. Hikers, who had conquered Yosemite then miscalculated the dosage of their celebratory recreational substances in Room 8, shook and mumbled. A drifter, who had suffered a heart attack in Room 3, murmured for someone named Arlene. The original owner of the motel moaned for the sea, and Jamoca's purr was close enough to the rumble of the tide to quiet him. Many of their bones had been brought to human resting places, but their echoes remained in the earth, the walls and the electrical wiring.

With the dead quieted, Jamoca slipped to the roof and scanned the world that unfurled itself to her emerald eyes. Shadows of her past self flitted by, and the musical lights of living people's beating hearts flashed in syncopation as they applied sunscreen or watched the news in the motel or rolled along Highway 395. She peered at the shore of Mono Lake and inspected the gate to the Unworld that yawned along its impossible desert waters.

The Mono Lake Unworld gate opened ten thousand years before, when the last black saber-toothed cat on this side of the Sierras, Runhira, had died. The accumulated generations of the hunter-gatherers' dead stirred and then awoke. In their desperate clawing and seeking for their long-gone flesh, they tore a hole in the world. Like rats through rusted mesh wire, the Others sniffed and licked the air, then scuttled through the hole to the twilight spaces of the nearby craters, tufa, and foothills.

The surrounding black cats' territories expanded to encompass Runhira's patrol. The emergent Others had been nipped from their hiding spaces, thrashed, and throttled out of existence before they could accomplish their sinister purpose—but the hole was forever.

It was where Jamoca's doom awaited; it was where Jamoca watched and guarded for one last day. The hours passed as her vision took in the bright desert sun and the dust in the breeze that rattled the reeds and a bag of chips across Highway 395. Reflections on her time as Lee Vining's guardian peeped into her consciousness, but even though black cats can see the past, they don't dwell on it.

Jamoca's vigilance registered a pale nose quiver and dip back into the Unworld. She stretched in the sun and appeared to doze in a shady spot, but projected her essence to the lip of the hole. The essence-projection was herself, seen through wavy desert refraction, feet not quite touching the ground, expanding and refracting the way mirages do. The projection crouched and expanded to the size of a bus, both a shadow and a shimmer that went unseen.

Another nose, several feet away, sniffed the air of the living world and dipped down.

Jamoca didn't allow them to detect her projection. At times, the Others could be scared off by her smell or a visual reminder of her perpetual vigilance, but if two were venturing into the living world at the same time, an example would need to be made.

One nose sniffed while another's body extended bonelessly onto the shore of the lake and lay down in the shadow around a Joshua tree. A couple of hikers scuffed by, oblivious. If the Others could be perceived by the living, they would see what resembled naked mole rats, the size of horses, with veiny, loose-skinned hands like those of an elderly human and six beady, pitted eyes across their faces. Their bald tails lifted up in the air as they palmed their way across the sand.

Jamoca remained invisible as she monitored the motion of the Other that hid itself in the shadow of a Joshua tree.

Jamoca could destroy it immediately, but she needed to decide which was the real decoy—if she went after the one by the tree, the other could lunge out and accomplish the Others' foul purpose.

The nose disappeared for a long time, and the Other under the Joshua tree remained still, believing that it was hidden from Jamoca's post at the motel. Jamoca's essence-projection blinked and then was covered in watchful emerald eyes. She took in the surrounding globe of visual information for a full half hour as the hikers discussed their lunch plans, not knowing what lurked in the shade with them.

Then all at once, the toothy head grimaced out of the Unworld and both of the Others unhinged their jaws, threw back their heads, and attempted to scream.

Jamoca struck at their throats, snapping up the one by the tree at its spine, thrashing until it hung limp. It immediately dehydrated and withered. If Jamoca's essence-projection kept thrashing, the Other's body would disintegrate into ashes, but she cast it back into the hole as an example to any of the Others who had stood by to test Jamoca's strength and vigilance. The Other that had only peeped out wouldn't be screaming anytime soon.

Jamoca ended the projection and checked each of the ghosts in the motel. Many of them were unsettled after the attempted scream but she purred them back down. They would not awaken and tear the world open to unleash the Unworld's teeming hordes. Not today.

Though the heat remained, the yawning enormity of the Eastern Sierra hid the westering sun long before nightfall, and Lee Vining was bathed in the blue of the atmosphere. Jamoca slunk into the motel office and appeared to nap in the lap of the manager while evening game shows wheedled on the TV. As she slept, she projected her essence once more along the hole by the shore of the lake, allowing the

Others within to smell the tang of her patient fury. As the evening's heat decreased, the projection lengthened into more of a shadow than a reflection, stalking along the edge of the Unworld.

A mewl pulled her back. She opened her eyes and sat up from the manager's lap. He scratched her behind the ears, which she liked. She would miss this lap.

She curled around the corner of the door and saw a kitten pawing at the edge of the trash bin. Jamoca leapt up and tightrope-walked along the cinderblock wall behind the bin and locked eyes with the kitten. It matched Jamoca's gaze and stood a little taller. He was young, but he was strong. Jamoca read the smells and particulates on his fur and saw the shimmer of his essence and knew that the kitten had been called by the song of his black-cat-blood from a campsite several days before, to assume Jamoca's patrol.

Jamoca gently touched the kitten on his head with her paw, and the kitten licked it. The patrol was secure.

The shadow of the Sierras loomed long over the lake. A raspy rattle sounded from the Unworld hole, a rattle no living human could hear. Jamoca and the kitten arched their backs and turned toward the shore. The ghosts stirred. Jamoca gave one last look to the kitten, who nodded, then bounded off to purr them back to sleep.

Jamoca loped toward the hole and the rattle grew louder. It was the battle cry of the Others, enraged at the throttled corpse from before, and all the other gruesome warnings that had been cast into the Unworld through the millennia. As she bounded toward the hole, the shadows of all the other past black cats joined her. Time moved differently in the Unworld. It was the doom of all the black cats to rally together on their last day and die, defeating the Others once and for all in their hellish homeland.

As Jamoca ran, she recognized her predecessor, Old Charlie, then Buttons, Bip, Toby, the long line of Tamuas, and Runhira herself, all charging into the breach between living and dead to save the world. Their essence-projections ran alongside each other and leapt into the ragged maw on the salty shore of Mono Lake.

As the kitten purred the pioneer family back to sleep, he looked with sapphire eyes to the shore, knowing that he would join that doomed charge when his final day came. Time was different for black cats too. For now, he curled up in a cozy spot under the ice machine and sent his velvety, leonine essence-projection to guard the dimming twilight as the Milky Way slowly spilled and saturated the sky. The hole was forever, but his patrol had just begun.

William Shaw is a writer from Sheffield, currently living in the USA. His writing has appeared in *Strange Horizons*, *The Georgia Review*, *Daily Science Fiction*, and *Doctor Who Magazine*. He has a healthy respect for all cats, black ones especially. His blog is https://williamshawwriter.wordpress.com and his Bluesky is @williamshaw.bsky.social.

INLAND SELKIES
by William Shaw

You've heard the tales of selkie wives
Who come in from the sea,
How men will burn their skins to bind
The women underneath.

But though they thrive in sealskin wraps
(Shed only while at rest),
For selkies, black domestic cats
Will serve as second best.

The farmyard mouser catches ill
Or else dies in its sleep.
The faithful mistress takes the kill,
A promise still to keep.

The feline body forms a pact
When spirits move beyond;
The woman fuses with the cat
And so the hunt goes on.

You see the black cats gathered round
The homes of dying men?
The ones whose wives were never found,
Who never spoke again?

They all receive a message, scratched
Where none will dare to share it:
There's many ways to skin a cat
But only one *to wear it*.

Richard Lau is an award-winning writer who is published in magazines, newspapers, and anthologies, as well as in the high-tech industry and online. Two of his stories have recently appeared in *Carpe Noctem* (Tyche Books) and *Sinister Century: Capture* (Disturb Ink Books). You can find more of his publications at: https://www.isfdb.org/cgi-bin/ea.cgi?289945

THE CAT AND THE CUSTOM
by Richard Lau

After the freighter *Cornelius* went down, there were four of us in the lifeboat. Five, if you counted the cat.

The two deckhands, Larry and Bart, could have been twin brothers (a uniform of flannel, dungarees, and wool cap topped shaggy, dirty blonde hair). They were also identical in temperament—just plain mean, filling every crack of their narrow frames and even narrower features. I was a mere lad of thirteen, fooling no one when lying about my age to get the job of assisting the ship's cook.

And then there was Akbar, the Egyptian engineer. No one was sure if he was actually Egyptian or even if Akbar was his real name. In his odd way of talking, half-growl, half-hiss, he would say, "You can call me Akbar." Never "my name is" or "I am." If the Captain knew his engineer's real name, he never gave any indication.

What was known about this great big bear of a man, was that he was a terrific engineer, providing miracles with anything metal or mechanical. And that was good enough for both Captain and crew.

Such skill also gained him a perk, a pet.

As I mentioned before, the fifth member of our group of survivors, of rats who had deserted a sinking ship, was ironically...a cat. A scrawny, rough furred, black cat. It never looked like it was fed enough, but I knew Akbar's love for it and given Cook's sloppiness at the cutting board, that cat probably ate better than most of the crew.

In the dark hours of the night, in the middle of the ocean, there had been an explosion.

Was there a collision? Did some overstrained ancient part of the *Cornelius* finally give in and give way? Or was some of the cargo packed and stored improperly? We unofficially carried items of a flammable and combustible nature, items that never appeared on the ship's official manifest, for legal and insurance reasons.

Whatever it was, Akbar knew the seriousness of the situation. He knew there was nothing he could do about it, nothing could fix it. When I saw him hop into a lifeboat with his cat, I knew that the *Cornelius* was doomed. Despite all of the alarms, contradictory orders, and running footsteps, I knew that my best course of action was to join the engineer and his dark-coated companion.

I was slow and clumsy descending the rope into the already lowered boat, which gave Larry and Bart time to also take notice and leap in themselves. They started swinging out the boat before I was fully down the rope. A wave caught me, making the rope slippery, and I slid. Fortunately, Akbar caught me with one arm. His other clutched a black furry ball.

While Larry and Bart weren't my favorite crewmembers, they worried about the whirlpool created by the larger vessel sinking and rowed us away from the ship. And a good thing, too, because there was another explosion, a shuddering felt deep in the bones. For a moment, it was daylight. The entire world exploded into light, blinding us. We felt the burning air on our faces, heard the steel hull scream as it tore like flesh.

Slowly the stars returned, and I could make out the other shadows in the boat with me. The largest one shouted, "Ahoy!" into the darkness, but there was no answer. The smallest shadow simply mewed, as if in mourning.

The next morning's sunrise greeted us. The ocean was empty, as if the *Cornelius* had never existed. The sky was equally empty. If a distress call had gotten out, there should be rescue planes soon. We weren't certain how far we had drifted.

The first day passed with us behaving as professional sailors, taking stock of what we had (fortunately, this included a small barrel of fresh water) and making plans for our rescue (we had rags and matches for signal fires).

"Who the hell packs fishing line with no bait?" grumbled Bart, pawing through a small box.

"You're not using all of your toes, are ye?" sneered Larry. For some reason, his words chilled me in the midday sun.

As the days progressed, hope and good will evaporated like seawater, leaving only salty annoyance and raw nerves behind.

To Akbar, the cat was a representative of Bastet, an ancient Egyptian goddess, and was named in her honor. But to Larry and Bart, the cat was merely food. And they tried to convince Akbar of such.

"C'mon, Akbar, why should we resort to the custom of the sea when we got a good meal right there?" asked Larry.

"And bait, too!" Bart put in, still smarting over the fishing line.

"No one touches the cat," said Akbar defiantly.

Tempers were short and patience even shorter.

"Okay," agreed Larry, the threat in his voice as clear as the sun bearing down from the cloudless sky. "The custom, it is." He made a great show of pulling out five matchsticks and breaking the handles of two of them.

He leaned forward leering, offering the matches to Akbar. "You drawing for the cat?"

With a bear paw swipe, Akbar knocked the matches into the sea. "I'll have nothing to do with your deceitful games and sleight of hand!"

I glanced into the water and saw that all five of the floating matchsticks now had broken handles.

Bart had had enough. He leaped at Akbar, who easily lifted the sailor like a child and tossed him overboard. While Akbar was focused on stabilizing himself and the rocking boat, Larry pulled out a long-bladed knife and attacked the big man's back.

The two men fell upon each other in the bottom of the boat, turning into a squirming octopus with their tangle of arms and legs. Bart was trying to get back into the boat.

"Give me a lift, boy!" he yelled, outstretching a hand.

I don't know why I did what I did. Perhaps it was the chaos of the situation. Or perhaps I didn't like the odds of two versus one. Or maybe I understood Akbar's motivations better and felt more fearful of the other two men.

My response was giving Bart a solid thunk on the head with an oar. Like an old boot, he sank under the dark water. I turned and saw Larry being dumped overboard on the opposite side. He also sank like the boot's mate.

Akbar fell on the forward bench, sitting there, panting heavily, brow and beard drenched in sweat, a red splotch spreading through his never-white apron. In his hand, he held Larry's knife, the blade wet and shiny.

He must have seen the fear in my eyes. "Don't worry, boy," he muttered, tossing the knife to my feet.

Bastet, the midnight coated cat, who had vanished under one of the boat seats during the excitement, reappeared and went to rub against the leg of its defender.

That night, Akbar was still alive but wincing in pain. He spent most of the day and his remaining strength putting the cat in my lap, as if he could force a bond between us. It didn't work. Even now, the cat curled over Akbar's thick thigh.

Neither of us felt like sleeping, so we talked when Akbar could manage it.

"What is this custom of the sea?" I asked.

Akbar was silent for a long moment, and I thought he had fallen asleep. Then he said, "There are things old

seamen don't tell young boys like you. They don't even like to admit it to themselves. Usually, you have to find out..."
Then he started coughing blood.

"The hard way?" I finished for him.

"The hardest way there is," said Akbar, his voice hollow as if he was speaking from the full moon far overhead. "That phrase is a polite way of indicating a time for cannibalism."

"Cana..." the word was a mouthful that I couldn't quite spit out.

"Eating the flesh of other men," he paused and then added for emphasis, "or boys."

Akbar explained that in situations where crews were shipwrecked, survivors sometimes ran out of food. No one wanted to broach the taboo, but eventually someone would mention "the custom." In a fair game, men would draw straws. The shortest straw was to become the meal. The second shortest prepared the meal.

"You mean kill...?"

"Yup. And guts and butchers him. And prepares and cooks the parts, if possible."

My face must have gone as pale as it felt.

"Strong words, aren't they? That's why the act is simply referred to as 'the custom.' Drawing straws allows the consequences to be blamed on bad luck. Not a mob ganging up on one unfortunate, but an honorable sacrifice due purely to misfortune. See the difference? Supposedly everyone can deal with a clear conscience on their full belly. But all of the men I know who participated, still regret their actions and sleep restlessly when they *can* sleep."

Akbar coughed again but managed to wheeze, "But I have seen the way Bart and Larry played cards and dice, how they cheated and worked together to fleece others. Custom of the sea or not, we wouldn't have gotten a fair shake from them."

"I'm sorry," was all I could think of saying.

"Don't be. The threat to Bastet was just a distraction. They had planned on getting rid of me first, one way or another. After that, dealing with you and the cat would have been easy." Right then, I knew I had made the right decision siding with Akbar.

I met Akbar's dark eyes, and he held my attention like a steel trap. "I'm done for. The bastard got me good, front and back. But promise me. No harm to the cat. A shame we lost the other two, but their evil probably tainted their flesh, so even a starving shark wouldn't bite. But I should provide more than enough for both of you until you are rescued."

Neither of us mentioned an alternative.

The next morning, Akbar was dead.

I looked at his corpse, thought about what he had said, and erupted bile into the ocean, losing fluid I couldn't afford.

I made a vow. There would be no 'custom.' The cat and I were going to be rescued or starve.

To deal with the heat, my exhaustion, and the lack of food, I slept more and more and lost track of how long we had been adrift. I opened my eyes and saw the cat had grown, looking fuller, even more muscular. And in the front of the boat, was a big skeleton, as white as bleached driftwood, as prominent as a whale washed up on a rocky shore.

Akbar? But I shoved his corpse into the sea how many days ago? I was certain of it. I couldn't take the sight nor the smell of his decomposition. Plus, getting rid of the body also removed all temptation to participate in the custom. But had he come back? Somehow returned to feed his cat? With his own flesh and organs?

The cat was a pig. There was nothing left for me. Or was there?

I was weak in both body and spirit. I needed food. My starvation had consumed not only my fat and muscle, but also my morals and the memory of my vow.

"Perhaps the time for the custom has come." My fingers weakly fumbled for the pair of matchsticks I had put in my shirt pocket. I didn't remember when I had gathered them, but I knew with each successive hour, I'd been trying to forget that they were there.

I broke one of the sticks and held them so that only the match heads were showing.

"Since you obviously can't choose, I will pick for myself. I am good. I am fair." I was also a liar. I could feel in the palm of my hand which matchstick was shorter. Desperate times called for desperate measures.

Finding the energy to make a big show for my feline audience, I confidently picked the longer match.

"Sorry about..." I looked in horror at the match I was holding. It was the one with the broken handle. I had chosen the shorter one.

The cat started to purr. It grew even larger, growing so heavy that the boat tilted downward toward it, forcing me to brace my feet and grab the sides so as to not slide toward the open jaws and bared teeth of what was now a panther.

I screamed as the claws tore into my shoulder.

"Easy, lad! Easy! It's okay! You're safe now!"

I opened my eyes, struggling to sit up until I saw that it was a human hand and not a paw holding me down. Then I saw I was indoors, the subtle, yet regular hum of a ship's engine reached my ears. A man with a kindly face and a captain's hat looked down on me. After the hard wood of the lifeboat, the bed's mattress felt as soft as a cloud.

"If it wasn't for your cat yowling up a storm, we might have missed you out there in the dark," the Captain said. He suddenly looked down, out of my view. "Why, here's your little savior now."

Before I could protest, the captain stooped and then placed the now familiar black cat on my chest. It was back to being normal-sized but I still didn't want it so close to me after my nightmare. The cat, it seemed, now had no problem expressing its affection. I raised a hand to shoo it away but stopped when I saw the bandages.

The captain continued. "Oh, you must have passed out on the lifeboat. Not surprising considering what you've been through. All that time without food and water. The cat tried to wake you to our presence by nibbling on your fingers. Did a good job, too, according to the doc, but you really must have been out of it."

Then I remembered. While I had made a vow never to participate in the custom, the cat never did.

I looked into the two golden eyes fixed on mine.

The cat licked its lips and purred.

Mary A. Turzillo won a Nebula award ("*Mars Is no Place for Children*" 1999) and two Elgin awards (*SWEET POISON*, with Marge Simon, 2014, and *LOVERS & KILLERS*, 2012, solo.) Her novel *MARS GIRLS* (Apex) features two young Martian women rescuing themselves from Face-on-Mars crazies. She and her husband, author Geoff Landis, live in Ohio with two orange goof-balls that own every lap they find. The cat in "*The Vermin*" is based on our Siamese who once defeated a rat almost as big as she was. Mary's purrfectly delicious story collection *COSMIC CATS & FANTASTIC FURBALLS* appeared in 2022 from WordFire. She is working on a novel called *A MARS CAT & HIS BOY*.

THE VERMIN
by Mary A. Turzillo

Shungita was born with a mission, killing vermin. The goddess Bast had come to her and her mother and let them know this, not with words, but through the magic of Bast's radiance.

It did not matter if the vermin was big or smart or fast. Shungita's purpose in life was to catch it and kill it.

At the beginning of Shungita's life, there was milk and warmth and a very bad place. Mom and Susan came into the bad place and picked Shungita up in their big clawless hands. Susan was a smaller People with a sweet smell, like cream. Mom was a larger People with a perfume smell. Shungita was frightened, but she did not pee in the blanket on which Susan held her.

After a while, Shungita settled her belly down on the blanket and lowered her head between her front paws. Susan's hand crept to her back and petted her lightly.

"She's learned to purr," said Susan.

Shungita, though satiny black except for her paws, was part Siamese, so she understood some People words. Bast had given her this gift.

They took her to a place with carpets and cat boxes and bowls of food and something called yoghurt, that tasted milky. Loud noisy things lived in this place, creatures called the vacuum cleaner, the dishwasher, the clothes dryer. The noises frightened her at first, but she learned to tolerate them, even the high whine and clank of the dryer, which Mom kept trying to fix.

These creatures were not vermin.

Shungita chased flashlight beams and small red dots on the floor, even after she learned she couldn't catch them. These were not actually vermin, but they were good practice.

She slept on the People's feet and their pillows. There were other People there: Dad and Kevin. They were rougher, and at first Shungita was afraid of them.

Shungita found a tiny gray vermin to chase, but she didn't catch it. Later, she grew adept at catching vermin. They were juicy and fun. Dad took them away from her when she brought them up to the bedroom. After a while, the vermin all went away. Shungita had killed them all. She had done Bast's will.

She went out in the yard and chased flying vermin. They were harder to get, but she found one in a nest and played with it a long time before Susan and Kevin took it away from her. They scolded her. Did they not understand Bast's plan for her?

When Shungita wanted something, she meowed at Mom, or Susan, or Kevin. She learned very early that Dad did not hear very well and had to be scratched when she needed his attention.

When Shungita was almost grown up, another animal came into the house, Mephisto. At first Shungita was frightened of how Mephisto jumped on her and tried to mate with her. Later he was more gentle, and she would keen for him when he got locked out of the house and wanted to get in. Once, he got lost, and she woke Mom and Dad up every morning complaining about the absence of Mephisto. She had to jump on the bed and meow directly in their faces, because Dad did not hear very well.

He came back. That time, anyway.

Mephisto and Shungita went to the vet and came home very sore. After that, there were no more mating attempts on Mephisto's part, but he still liked to jump on Shungita and play. She would get exasperated with him and chase him through the length of the house, up and down the stairs, until Mom got a squirt gun after the two of them.

Then Mom and Susan ran away.

Things were strange after Mom and Susan went away. Dad did not try to explain to Shungita, but Kevin did try. "Mom and Susan are gone, Shungita. They aren't ever coming back. I'm sorry. Now I have to feed you and change your box." And he picked her up and squeezed her too hard.

In the days after Susan and Mom went away, clothes lay in heaps on the floor and Mephisto and Shungita slept on them. The noisy dryer seldom made its loud whine and clop-clop noises. The vacuum was quiet. Food stayed for days on dirty plates and pans. Shungita and Mephisto would sample what was in the sink and on the counter and floor. Some days the kitchen got cold because somebody left a window cracked open. Shungita and Mephisto looked out the window. There were nice vermin out there, but now the People wouldn't let them out.

Then Mephisto went away. Just like that. One day Shungita woke up and nothing of Mephisto was left except his dark fur on the bedspread, black as her own.

At first, Shungita went to Dad and asked him with her claws to find Mephisto and bring him back. She asked Kevin with her meow to find Mephisto. Maybe Mephisto had been taken to the vet and kept there.

She herded Kevin and Dad out into the garage to the place in the rafters where Mephisto used to hide when he was planning to jump on her.

But Mephisto was not there now.

Kevin and Dad made signs with a picture of a black cat on it, and the cat looked like Mephisto. There were words on the signs, too. They got a hammer and some nails and took the signs out of the house.

"We'll find him," Kevin told her.

But Mephisto was gone. Maybe some other People had stolen him.

Eventually, she gave up. Mephisto was not coming back, just like Mom and Susan didn't come back. She had nobody to play with. Kevin would try to play with her, but it wasn't as much fun. When the People let her out, she would climb up to the special spot where Mephisto used to hide.

"Dad," Kevin said, "Shungita has forgotten how to purr." He held Shungita on his lap and hugged her. He squeezed too hard, so she gouged him with her back claws, and ran away, to the special place in the garage.

One day the car came into the garage, and Kevin and Dad got out. Kevin was carrying a box. Soft scratching sounds came from the box. Shungita stretched and yawned, then leapt heavily down to follow them into the kitchen.

A pair of orangish ears appeared above the top of the box, then an alert little head.

Out leapt an orange vermin.

Shungita looked at Dad with unbelieving eyes. He had brought home groceries or cat food or something in that box, and a huge vermin had gotten in and infested it. Now it was going to infest the house.

Shungita darted up to the box and looked in, to see what Dad had brought home. There was nothing else in the box except a towel.

The vermin, meantime, was sniffing around the kitchen, looking for food. Surely it would run away when it realized that Shungita lived here. The vermin smelled scared to Shungita, so she hissed at it and glided away, back to Mephisto's place in the garage.

After a while, Kevin came into the garage and called to her. "It's all right, Shungita. We still love you." He stood for a long time under Mephisto's special place, not seeing her. She stayed very still. Finally, he went back in the house. "Dad," she heard him call faintly. "Dad, I think she's sick."

Shungita opened one eye and considered going into the house, where it was warmer and where she might be petted or scratched. Maybe Kevin and Dad would leave some chicken or tuna out, too. But it all seemed like too much work, so she closed that eye and dreamed of chasing Mephisto and of Susan's soft little hands.

When she went to her food dish the next day, the vermin was there, eating her food. She stopped, stock still, and hissed at it. It looked at her stupidly. She hissed again. It approached her, sniffing. She lowered her head and growled, swishing her tail back and forth. The vermin jumped back and ran away. But Shungita's appetite was gone.

It occurred to Shungita that the vermin smelled very much like Mephisto. But the vermin was not black, it was orange, and therefore not at all like Shungita and Mephisto. And certainly not a cat.

She wandered through the house, looking for the vermin. Maybe she would have to kill it after all. The People seemed unconcerned about it, or maybe they didn't know how to kill vermin. She would have to kill it and bring it to them, then they would understand. They would wrap it in newspaper and put it in the garbage where it belonged.

In the living room, she discovered Kevin teasing the vermin. He trailed a lace from his shoe on the floor in front of the vermin. The vermin tried to grab it. Shungita watched for a moment, then yawned. Kevin was a smart People. Dad had no doubt trained him well. He would kill the vermin soon.

But as she watched, Kevin dropped the string and scooped the vermin up in his arms. He held it to his chest and cooed at it. In fact, he kissed the vermin.

Then he said, "Shungita, this is Squeaker. Isn't she cute? You can play mommie now. Squeaker can be your baby."

Shungita was shocked. She turned and ran to Mephisto's place in the garage.

All day she lay in Mephisto's place, her fur fluffed up against the chill. She dozed and dreamed. Her dreams ran mostly to thoughts of Mephisto, Susan, and Mom, but there were occasional flashes of the vermin, intruding his nasty little whiskery face into her dish.

She dreamt that Mom was dabbing that funny smelling spray on her coat, rubbing her fur with just one finger. Mom's finger was wet. Shungita opened her eyes.

The vermin was licking her right ear.

Every hair on Shungita's body stood upright. She didn't bother to hiss—a low grating sound came out of her throat. The vermin's eyes opened wide, and it jumped away.

Shungita rose slowly to her feet. Sudden power came to her hind legs, and she launched herself after the vermin. It scampered toward the door that lead to the kitchen, but the door was closed. It turned and confronted Shungita, its ears sleeked back and its jaws gaping to disclose tiny, inadequate teeth.

She leapt on it.

It tried to push her off with its front paws, but she held it close and went for the throat. It twisted away, pumping with its sharp back claws at Shungita's belly. Now Shungita sprang back, growling like a dog. The vermin fled, but Shungita streaked after it. Using its tiny claws, it scampered up a ladder into the garage loft where Mephisto's place was. It leapt from rafter to rafter.

Inches short of Mephisto's place, it lost its hold and dangled for a moment by one paw, then fell heavily onto the roof of the car. Shungita was onto it, her jaws searching for a hold on its throat.

The vermin screamed and twisted away. Shungita streaked after it, caught it by the neck under the car, rolled and buffeted it, not caring about the grease and dust under the car. The vermin struck out at her with its unsheathed claw, but Shungita was quick. She rolled away, out from under the car, and confronted it again.

Its hindquarters stuck up in the air, its front paws spread for action, terror in its wide eyes, it watched her from underneath the car.

Shungita rushed it.

"What's going on here?" said Kevin. He opened the door to the kitchen just long enough for the vermin to get in. Back in the house, the filthy thing! Shungita streaked after it.

Dad was at the kitchen counter. The vermin ran over his feet, then straight for the cellar door, down the cellar, into the open dryer. Shungita bounded after him, avoiding Dad's feet, down the stairs. She halted in front of the dryer, hair bristling, alert with hatred.

"What's wrong with you guys?" Kevin shouted down the basement stairs.

Dad's voice: "Leave them alone. They're getting acquainted."

The vermin continued to hide in the dryer, so Shungita, bored, left her stakeout and went to munch on dry cat food in her dish. Then she went back downstairs and found the vermin extending a paw as if to get out of the dryer. She hissed at it, and he shrank back into it.

She considered destroying it right then, but it seemed to know its place. She could kill it later.

Meantime, the clothes washer was sloshing away. It was warm on top, so Shungita climbed up on it and fell into a doze.

The vermin woke her up trying to lick her face again, so she chased it back into the dryer and, bored with the game, sauntered upstairs.

Dad stooped to pet her with one hand as he carried an armful of People-smelling cloth down. She glided up the carpeted stairs to the second story, and found Kevin in the bedroom. He was on his bed, reading a book and making marks in it.

"Homework," he said.

She yawned and curled up beside his leg. In the house, various household noises went on. The washer stopped, then began sloshing again. The dryer went whining and clopping.

Another noise underlay it, soft but alarming.

Shungita stood up, stretched, and bounded off the bed. She streaked down two set of stairs, to the basement.

The dryer was running, clop-clopping and whining, all right, but a noise came from the dryer, no less frightening for all that it was very faint.

The vermin was in the dryer, screaming its head off.

Shungita threw herself at the dryer door, scratched at it, then gave up. She ran upstairs to Kevin and meowed at him.

"Stop it! Go play with the kitten!"

She galloped downstairs and looked for Dad. He was in the garage. She threw herself at him, clawing his legs.

"Hey! That's no way to behave. I thought you'd gotten old and lazy." Dad casually scooped her up in his arms. She jumped down and ran into the kitchen. He didn't follow. She threw herself at his legs again. Meowing wouldn't help, he didn't hear very well, or he wouldn't have shut the vermin in the dryer in the first place.

"You got a flea? What's got into you? I bought you a kitten so you wouldn't miss Mephisto so much, and I thought—say, where is that damn kitten?"

She lead him down the basement stairs, to the dryer.

"Oh, shit." Dad opened the dryer door and pulled wet clothes out. Underneath them, screaming its head off, was the vermin.

The vermin looked terrible, even worse than usual. Its fur was wet, its whiskers were broken, it could scarcely stand up. Dad removed it carefully from the dryer.

"What happened, Dad? Oh, no!"

Dad was cradling the vermin in his hands. It cried. "I swear I didn't know. I should have checked. Kevin, I'm sorry."

"He's still alive," said Kevin, petting the vermin's head. "Let's check him for broken bones."

"Or a concussion." Dad tried to hand the vermin to Kevin, but it leapt out of his arms and ran into the dark recesses of the laundry room.

Kevin and Dad searched, but they couldn't find it. "Maybe he got upstairs?"

Kevin was crying. "He's going to run off somewhere we can't find him, just like Mephisto, isn't he, Dad?"

Dad was gruff, but his voice trembled. "We'll find him. Get some flashlights."

But they didn't. Even Shungita could not find it. "We've got to find him, Dad! He needs medical attention!"

While they were stupidly milling around, the vermin must have gotten away. Shungita looked for him too. She even looked in the warm place behind the dryer, where she used to hide from Mephisto. She looked under the bottom step of the staircase, where Mephisto used to hide so he could jump her as she came down the stairs. But the vermin had hidden itself very well.

Toward noon of the next day, the vermin came sauntering upstairs into the kitchen. Its whiskers were still broken, and it had a slight limp. But its fur had dried out nicely.

Shungita rejoiced in her heart. She hunkered down under the counter, rearing her hindquarters for a good start. The vermin looked up from the food bowl. It wasn't quite finished, but it faced her, its tail flicking back and forth. Shungita rushed it, pounced on it, pummeling it with her hind legs. It slicked its ears back and growled, darting its jaws forward for a purchase on her neck. She searched for a tooth-hold. Its huge round eyes narrowed with malicious intent.

The vermin was all right. It ran.

Now she had to catch it. The People were too stupid or slow to kill it. She leapt back, her tail lashing back and forth. Joy, oh, joy. She would destroy it now. Was this not Bast's way?

She had to catch it. She would teach it who was boss!

It was all she could do to stop from purring.

Sumiko Saulson is the Elgin Award and Bram Stoker Nominated author of *The Rat King: A Book of Dark Poetry* (Dooky Zines), Winner of the Ladies of Horror Readers Choice Award for the collection *Within Me Without Me* (Dooky Zines), and the Afrosurrealist Writers Award for "*Balm of Brackish Water*". Their horror romance *Somnalia: The Metamorphoses of Flynn Keahi* (sequel to *Happiness and Other Diseases*) is available on Mocha Memoirs Press, find their horror comic collection *Ghost Cat is Best Cat, The Drain Monster*, and *Other Tales of Terror* on Dooky Zines, and find Sumiko @sumikoska on most socials, @sumikosaulson on Instagram and at https://www.SumikoSaulson.com

HEAL ME WITH YOUR PURR
by Sumiko Saulson

If the Styx ferryman went unpaid
Purrberus never barred the way
For the magic in her humble sound
Was the golden filamentous thread
Uniting them across the veil
The living and the dead

Three obsidian heads, tails dark as night
And from each face glowed radiant light
Three pairs; green, yellow, and crimson eyes
That shone as she cocked three heads sidewise

The injured would appeal to her
To heal them with her wondrous purr
A gentle cantata, a trio, a choir
A song that would aid them
So as not to expire, and lovingly
She'd most always concur

Over illustrious sands, she'd pad
Through backyards her mincing tread
Jet black on petite little feet
She kneads the human flesh like bread

These gifts, she overtime bestowed
Onto the tiny black kittens in her brood
Like shadows on the wall they grew
And shared their purrs with all they knew

Francesca Maria is the award winning author of *They Hide: Short Stories to Tell in the Dark*. She is also the co-creator and writer of the *Black Cat Chronicles* comic book series featuring a mystical black cat. When not writing, Francesca is co-chair for the San Francisco Bay Area Horror Writers Association Chapter, helping to foster horror writers and the love of all things that go bump in the night. You can learn more about Francesca at francescamaria.com.

THE LAND BELONGS TO THE CATS
by Francesca Maria

Dear Jones,   July 15, 1881

I have settled here at the property which consists of a poor grouping of structures, the likes not seen since the dreaded trials in Salem, a mere throw of a stone from here. Each building is maligned with an oppressive dark wood complete with slanted roofs, appearing to be thrown together haphazardly with little to keep out the harsh elements. The heat, my dear friend, reminds me of the tropics, I need not remind you of that misadventure. I hope to settle my late Uncle Philip's affairs and return to the more hospitable habitat of New York post haste.

    In God I trust,
    Your Friend,
    Robert Sinead

Dear Jones,   July 31, 1881

A fortnight has passed and I have yet to be rid of this abysmal land. It seems there is more here in need of repair than I first intuited. And dare I say, to you, my trusted friend, who knows I am not given to tales of the fantastical, something quite odd has rattled these old bones.

While venturing to the barn to replace a section of fallen roof, I heard a loud cry. At first, I thought the hot weather and lack of a decent meal was the cause of my senses deceiving me, and continued about my business. Then the blasted cry echoed again off those damned walls. It sounded like a child, nay, a newborn, searching for its mother's milk. It was a deep cry, one that unsettled me in this isolated and rugged country. As you know Jones, I dismissed the majority of the staff to reduce the exorbitant expenditure that I deemed unnecessary to handle my uncle's affairs. That way I may maximize my profits, taking home a nice healthy sum back to New York, once the property has sold. It is just I and Mrs. Padamoor, the old workhorse, that occupy these vast acres, with not a neighbor or other soul for miles.

I am sure it was nothing, but Jones, it left me unsettled.

Yours in God,
Your Devoted Friend,
Robert

Dear Jones,   August 5, 1881

I am in receipt of your last letter and I am a fool to admit my weakness. Thank you for your concern for my welfare. Rest assured that I have found the culprit! When I found my courage—aided by a shot of strong whiskey—I ventured back into that dreaded barn to complete my work. It was while climbing the loft that I saw movement in the straw-strewn floor. From out of the shadows, two bronze eyes stared back at me. Jones, it was a cat! A black cat, mind you, the kind of which you only see amongst tales of witches and the dark arts.

Its fur was cloudy with barn dust and its body appeared thin and misshapen. Not having many cats in my acquaintance, I was not sure how to judge this mangy creature, but Jones, it felt as if the beast looked right through me, down to the very depths of my soul! As I continued to stare, the feline opened its mouth and let out a cry so loud that I nearly fell off the precarious ladder which shook under my nerves. Oh Jones! It was a horrid sound, horrid! I felt the devilish cry seep into the very fabric of my being. Gathering my nerves, I waved my one free hand at the menace, hoping to chase it away while still gripping the ladder with my other hand, and Jones, the bastard ran towards me! Its tail, bushy with fervor, shook with conviction as the beast swiped at my hand attached to the ladder with remarkable speed and precision. I fell Jones, some twenty feet, to the hard surface below. The pain was immeasurable. I thought for sure every bone in this frail body was shattered! As I strained my head to look up, the damned beast hung its head over the edge looking at me as it cried out again in a long, fetid, maniacal scream that sent me to the very depths of Hades.

I blacked out Jones, I plunged into a pit of my own consciousness that rivaled the murky abyss of the creature's visage. I do not know how long I lay prostrate, but the sun had long set when Mrs. Padamoor came looking for me with a lantern as ancient as she, the poor wretch. When my senses returned, I peered into the shadows, searching for that damned feline and found no trace, other than the deep red scratch that it left me as a parting gift. Mrs. Padamoor later applied a sticky substance that smelled of pine upon the wound which rose in anger. As I write this, my hand is wrapped in a white cloth filled with the same ointment and burns as if I was marred by the devil himself! I will not let it deter me from my endeavors. I will rid the barn of this beast and be done with this cursed land, never to return!

Yours in faith,
Robert

Dear Jones,   August 8, 1881

My dear friend, I doubt you have been in receipt of my last letter as the post, here in the country that time forgot, is less than reliable. I shall not bore you with a repeat of my last correspondence which featured a prominent four-legged fiend, but will endeavor to inform you of a new tragedy that has befallen this cursed estate; Mrs. Padamoor is dead! The steadfast housekeeper of this estate is no more. Her son came to collect her just this morning. No doubt age was a contributing factor as she was older than the first nail and plank built upon these grounds.

Though, the odd thing about all this business, is before I discovered her, I once again heard that mournful cry from the beast in the barn in the early morning before the farm cock had a chance to announce its displeasure at first light. The cry, nay, scream, woke me at some distance Jones, as I am nearly half an acre from the roofless barn.

And as I stumbled to retrieve my shirt and trousers I heard the sound of small feet upon the wooden floor. Mice? I wondered, as they were too slight to be that of a bipedal nature. The sound propelled me to search the rooms traveling through the chambers of my late uncle and then finally down into the lower level towards the servants' quarters (it sounds more grandeur than it is Jones, there are barely five rooms in the house that I now occupy). In each room I crept, listening for the sound of the feet and in each room I was met by only my breath and my uncle's stale tobacco which still clings to the walls.

Then I saw her Jones, poor Mrs. Padamoor, strewn in her nightgown across the floor between her bedroom entrance and the hallway. It was as if she was leaving her room in a hurry as she had only one slipper upon her foot while leaving the other bare, and one hand grasping onto an unlit candle. Her body, already plagued by the rigidity of death, twisted unnaturally, with her torso turned one way while her head turned the other. And Jones, her face! I have never seen a more panicked, frightened look upon any face, even in the Penny Dreadful drawings I am so found of. It was a look of sheer terror, not pain, but fear Jones, that woman was frightened to death! As I bent down to get a closer look, I heard the footsteps once again and while I turned to face them, four black legs scurried down the hall and out of sight. It was that blasted cat, I am sure of it! That ominous creature had something to do with the death of this old woman, I knew it in my bones as I know my own name Jones. I must be rid of it!

Pray for me, Jones as I follow my soul into the abyss,
Robert

Jones,   August 15, 1881

Forgive my shaky writing as the wound on my hand has caused me tremors, making it difficult to bend the quill to my will. Without Mrs. Padamoor and her ointment, the wound has begun to fester and pustulate and the red fever grows steadily up my wrists and into my fingers. Oh that damned cat! Satan himself is no match for that which he has spawned. I have taken to a dusty brown bottle of what I can only assume is whiskey, tucked away in a corner of my uncle's chambers, to calm my nerves and settle the nonstop shaking that now courses through my wretched soul. I fear I am too weak to complete the necessary work on this blasted land and may need to return to more hospitable climate and abandon this silly endeavor altogether Jones. For I fear, I am defeated.

Every night since dear Mrs. Padamoor met her maker, in such a dreadful display (Jones it still causes me nightmares, seeing her face frozen in terror), I have been hearing cries from within the walls! That blasted cat must have multiplied or gathered up its brethren, for I now hear them echoing back and forth to each other, as if to surround me like a poor mouse, about to be preyed upon. Their sharp little nails scratch constantly against the wooden floors and I can hear them ripping something from the interior of the walls. When I go to investigate, all I can catch are quick glimpses of black paws, sometimes a swishing tail, then nothing, as the beasts are experts at hiding amongst the shadows. I have never seen more than one at a time, but there must be a dozen of the creatures coming in and out. I cannot find their means of entrance and have taken to closing up all doors and windows, despite the stifling August heat.

I did, however, find my uncle's rusty blunderbuss and trust that I will put it to good use.

Pray for me Jones.
Yours in God,
Robert

Dearest Jones,   August 31, 1881

Thank you for your last letter and offer to help rid me of this plague of demons that now haunt me without rest. I would not want to take you away from the city that we both love, nor curse you to the foul country I find myself in. But Jones, I do not know how much more I can take! I have been in a terrible state, my body and mind racked with fever from that accursed wound that has now swollen my arm so egregiously, that I can scarce use it to accomplish the simplest of tasks. Even now as I write this, I am full of pain, having also depleted my uncle's supply of spirits, I have nothing to ease my suffering. A few days past, the local doctor, (a primordial statue, a few breaths away from the grave with the poorest of eyesight and deaf as a mole rat), prescribed an ointment and gave me a tonic that tasted like soil and bitter root, I daresay it was a weed he pulled in the front of my very own yard on his way into this damned place! Needless to say, I feel no affects from his 'treatment' and am dubious as to whether he is even a doctor by our modern standards!

Though as wretched as I am, it does not compare with the torture I endure hourly from the cursed beasts! They have taken to sucking my breath while I sleep Jones! I am sure of it! I often wake from nightmarish visions of amber eyes and a weight upon my chest, so great that it sends me into a gasping fit, only to hear the unmistakable thump of the four-legged creature as it hits the floor having stolen the very life force out of me.

I am too weak and unsteady to use the blunderbuss and have taken to waving a large broom with my one good arm to try and ward off the demons. But I fear, it is of no use. Jones, I need your steady hand, as I dread I may be losing my grasp with reality. Please pray for me as I may be too feeble to make the journey back to New York, where sanity reigns and ghastly apparitions are reserved for parlor tricks.

Your trusted friend,
Robert

Dearest Jones,   September 5, 1881

Oh Jones! To hear of your upcoming arrival has put me at such great ease! I am beside myself with gratitude. I know you will vanquish the black foes at once! For Jones, the last several nights I have seen the beasts upon me! They cry such a horrible pitch that it somehow paralyzes me where I lay, unable to move, blink or breathe. I thought for sure they would take my last breath while I slept. Jones, last night, as I once again woke to the screeching cry, it is a banshee's cry, for no natural beast can create such a sound, I stared up at the ceiling above my bed to see the black cat, the same one from the barn, the same one that infected me with its claws, hanging from the ceiling, claws outstretched and locked into the planks above with its tail dangling towards me. The head of the demon twisted unnaturally upon its body, much like that of Mrs. Padamoor's corpse, and looked at me with such evil while it hissed and bared its bloody tongue spitting red droplets upon my face. Terror froze me in place as I watched in the dim candlelight the creature run backwards, tail first across the ceiling, down the wall and disappear beneath the floorboards! When the paralysis finally subsided, my own screams joined in a hideous chorus with the beast and we both screamed into the night until I had no breath left and exhaustion took over.

Come soon Jones, do not delay.

Your desperate friend,
Robert

From the desk of Henry Jones, Jr.

Dear Ms. Abernathy,   September 15, 1881

I regret to inform you of the death of your uncle, Robert Sinead. I came to his aid while he endeavored to prepare your great Uncle Philip's estate for the solicitor. I received several incoherent letters from your uncle and rushed to meet him as soon as my business dealings freed me enough to grant me the opportunity.

Upon my arrival, not three days past, I found the abode closed up and had to forcibly let myself in as there was no answer from within after several attempts to call out to your uncle. Once I breached the front door, the smell was unbearable. Forgive me for being insensitive, but I must be honest with you for your own sake and safety for you now are the sole heir of your family's estate and I would not want you to go into the property without proper warning.

As I called out to your uncle and received no response I felt a great dread wash over me. He had complained about a black cat that had been haunting him and a scratch administered by the beast became infected. I suspected he was hallucinating, based on his ravings, but upon my arrival, I felt there might be some truth in his madness, for every inch of the place, every floor board, every wall, even the ceiling, was covered in deep gashes. It was as if tiny knives, in groups of four, completely scoured the rooms, marking them as their own.

I searched every room and found the same scratches on chairs, tables, paintings, books, I could not find one surface that was not affected by these scorings. Even in a madness, Robert, could not have done all of these on his own.

Brace yourself Ms. Abernathy, for what I am about to tell you may haunt you in nightmares as it has in mine every night since. When I discovered your dear Uncle Robert, his body too had been littered with these markings, shredding his sheets right through to his bedclothes. I could make out tiny red slashes through the torn fabric. His left arm, the one infected by the scratch, was three times the size of the other, pink and bloated and covered in a foul smelling puss, the likes of which I have never seen in all my years. As I stood in astonishment at the state of my friend, he stirred and I ran to his bedside. I shouted his name, "Robert, Robert, it is Jones, I am here!" but his eyes did not meet mine and were glassy with a milky haze that I had not seen since my own dear mother passed ten years ago. Then his chest rose and from it came a low growl that turned into a high pitched scream as something internal moved up from his stomach, to his chest and throat, like boa constrictor regurgitating its prey. Something black, I could not tell what at first, jutted out passed his teeth and directly out of his mouth growing in size as the screams grew in intensity. A black tail, fat like a dust feather, protruded straight out of dear Robert's mouth, followed by one back paw then another, a torso of slick black fur, covered in the remains of your uncle's insides, then another pair of paws until finally, a wet cat head emerged. Its head faced me, ears pinned back, mouth open screeching as it exited out of your uncle's mouth and yet its body faced the opposite way.

I ran out of the home, abandoning my oldest friend, leaving him there, unable to bring myself to help him as the steadfast friend he took me to be. I left the estate immediately and sought shelter at an inn, an hour's ride away, to rest while I pondered my next move.

With the light of day and a fresh meal, (and not a nights rest for I did not dare to close my eyes), I gathered my courage and returned to the estate with the local undertaker a Mr. Whitticker. On the ride over in his carriage, he relayed the strangest tale to me of the history of the land your estate now sits upon. Before the first English settlers laid claim to the land, the area was plagued by unnatural beasts, ghostly spirits that would appear in the guise of cats, black cats more specifically. The land your great uncle built upon was home to hundreds of these cats and with few predators as cunning as themselves, they thrived and multiplied covering the fields and the forests beyond. When your great Uncle Phillip built his estate, he would leave out poison and shoot cats with his ancient blunderbuss until it was thought he exterminated them all.

When he grew ill, Mrs. Padamoor told Mr. Whitticker that she had begun to see black cats appear on the property line, as if they were waiting for old Phillip to die so they could retrieve their land once more and take their revenge on their slain brethren.

I daresay that when your Uncle Robert moved in, the cats, both alive and dead, must have mistaken him for your Uncle Phillip and began to haunt him, torturing him into madness. But, I am just speculating as to the nature of cats, which is in itself a mystery.

When Mr. Whitticker and I arrived at your Uncles' estate, we were dumbfounded to find a clowder of black cats, no less than seventy five, of all shapes and sizes, stationed in, on and around the property. When they saw us approach, they began a hellish, low growl, all in unison at first until they each broke out in a terrifying cry, screeching into the air like nothing I have ever heard of before in my forty-three years. If hell has a sound, it was this. I felt as if my ears would rupture and clasped both hands upon them in a fruitless effort.

The horses, at the sound and sight of the cats, reared and took off past the property with us in tow, nearly crashing the carriage and leaving us there deserted. We luckily escaped back to the inn, but I am afraid I was not able to retrieve your Uncle Robert's body. Forgive me as I have failed him and you and I will regret that until my last dying day.

Please heed my warning and do not consider venturing to the estate, it has been reclaimed.

The land belongs to the cats.

With the greatest sympathy and regret,
Henry Jones, Jr.

H. T. Martineau grew up reading fantasy stories and playing role-playing games, and she has translated that love into her YA fantasy saga, *Tales of Ambergrove*, which includes the *Dragonwolf* trilogy, the *Hammer and Flame* trilogy, and two Dungeons & Dragons companion books—so far. This is her first published short story. As a survivor of domestic violence who leaned on her cats as she healed, she wrote this story for survivors who've felt the comfort of a cat in their arms when they thought their world was ending. You can find H. T. Martineau at https://www.talesofambergrove.com and on social media @talesofambergrove.

CROSS MY HEART AND HOPE TO RISE
by H.T. Martineau

Glass shards and wooden splinters littered the floor around the young woman. Wracked with uncontrollable sobs, she dug her nails into trembling arms as she hugged herself. The door to her apartment was open, and she listened numbly as he peeled out of the lot and sped away. She kept her eyes squeezed shut, fearing that if she opened them, he would still be there, standing over her, still destroying everything within reach.

The terror-stricken woman heard voices at the doorway and then felt a gentle touch on her shoulder. She jerked and squeezed her eyes shut more tightly.

"It's okay." The other woman withdrew her hand. "My brother is out watching for him in case he comes back."

What if he comes back? she thought. She opened her eyes and looked at the damage around her. People always said the most dangerous time for a survivor of domestic violence is when they leave. She'd survived this time because her neighbor had interrupted him as he turned to her after he stopped destroying the apartment—but what about next time?

As her neighbor helped her clean up the pieces of her shattered apartment that afternoon, the woman pondered what would help her with her shattered life. She dreaded the idea of sleeping alone in that apartment, knowing he might come back. She couldn't get a dog because she was too busy to care for it properly, so the woman decided she was going to get a cat, and she wasn't going back home until she did.

A shelter brought pets to the local pet store for adoption, so the woman decided to just pick one of those. There were six cats there that day, all wandering around in the same enclosure. There were three adorable tabby kittens tumbling around in a hammock together, two young calicos tussling over a toy, and one smoky, black blob lying under a blanket at the bottom of the enclosure. She looked at the name sheets and found him. Then she knelt in front of the old cat and wagged her finger through the bars.

"Batty?" she murmured.

The blob made a *murp* sound as he lifted his head and looked at her. Seeing his face, she stifled a laugh. He had two large fangs that were too massive for his head, and the look he gave, with those angular cheekbones and bright green eyes, was absent of all thought. Innocent. Precious. He stood and approached, and when he did, his foot caught in the blanket, and the older cat stumbled. The pitiful look he gave made her laugh out loud. She scratched his chin, and he purred loudly.

"Do you want to see that one?" a man behind her asked.

The woman turned. The employee gazed at her with a raised brow. "Why are you looking at me like that?" the woman asked him slowly.

"It's just—no one has wanted to see that one the whole time he's been here. I mean, look at him. He's just spooky. He scares little kids and adults alike. He's a senior cat, and the shelter told us if he doesn't find a home soon, he'll probably be put down," the employee replied.

Then he shrugged apathetically, opened the enclosure, and picked up the cat. When the man placed Batty in her arms, he wiped his hands on his shirt as if the cat were something nasty. The woman, on the other hand, felt the softness of the cat's fur and the light vibration of his purring. Batty reached a paw up to touch her neck, and he bumped his head against her chin. She looked down at him and scratched his cheek, and she knew that this black cat was the one she wanted. He needed her just as much as she needed him.

She completed the adoption paperwork and prepared her apartment, and to her surprise, she was able to go back and get Batty that same day. Another employee gave her a cardboard carrier for him, but she found that once he was truly hers, she didn't want to let him go. She held him in her arms as she drove back home, comforted by his warmth and presence, surprised he was so content there with his head tucked into the crook of her elbow. When she brought him inside, he spent a few minutes looking around while she sat on the couch, and then he hopped into her lap and stretched his body up her torso, tucking his head under her chin and resting his paws on her chest.

She took one slow breath and then another, and then the storm of fear and anxiety within her begin to clear. Over the next few days, it cleared further. Batty's antics were a source of constant joy. He was always getting himself into trouble and crying pitifully to be rescued. It did the young woman good to have someone who needed her—a place to direct her warmth and focus her energy on positive goodness when so much pain and darkness had dominated it for so long.

She'd always thought that the superstition surrounding black cats was unfounded, but her time with Batty had shown her that, not only was he not *un*lucky, but he seemed to bring her luck and happiness. At least, that was how she felt—lucky and happy—until her monster came calling once more.

As she lay on the couch one night with Batty tucked up against her, the young woman dozed off and dreamed of her monster. She thought of the things he said to draw her in and the things he used to keep her trapped for months as he desecrated her body and crushed her soul. She saw herself still with him and felt the fear pounding in her heart at the idea of him standing there once again, heard the thumping as he destroyed the furniture in the apartment when the downtrodden woman had finally stood up for herself.

She jerked awake, sweating, and flung out a hand to search wildly for Batty. He wasn't beside her, but as his person started to panic, the cat hopped onto the couch and tucked himself up against the woman's stomach for her to hold him like a teddy bear. As she clutched her cat and tried to slow her breathing, the woman heard the thumping again. Only this time, she was wide awake. Her monster had come for her.

Horrified, the woman faced the window and saw the glow of a phone through the thin curtains. That dreaded name appeared as her phone's ringing cut the air, and she held Batty more tightly. When she didn't pick up, she heard the man growl, and he sidestepped over to the door and thumped harder.

"I know you're in there. Pick up your phone. I just want to *talk* to you," he said.

The man's voice was all honey, and the woman knew that trick all too well. It certainly wasn't the first time he hurt her and came back with warmth, apologies, and promises. She held onto Batty and stayed silent. He called again a few times, pleading with her each time. After the sixth call, there was a pause. Silence. No thumping. No calls.

After a forceful sigh, he said, "Listen. If you tell me you're done with me and you just want me to leave, I'll go, but I need you to tell me we're done and you don't want me here."

The woman looked at Batty and then over to the window. Maybe it would work. Maybe this was her chance. She opened her mouth to speak, but nothing came out. She was too afraid to make a sound. Still holding Batty, she reached out a hand and picked up her phone. She couldn't breathe as she typed the message and pressed send.

I don't want to see you anymore. Leave. Leave and don't come back.

She watched through the thin curtain as his phone lit up and framed his face with light. She watched the anger burn in his eyes and his brows knit together as he read her message. Then he threw his phone and roared, "How could you do this to me?"

As he slammed his fist into the door again, it changed from a thumping to get her attention to a beating in earnest—a feverish need break through that door to get to her. The woman knew then that if he got in, she would not survive without help. She'd never been able to fight back, and in all the time he'd terrorized her, she'd never felt a fear so immobilizing as in that moment.

She did the only thing she could. She called 911.

"911, what is your emergency?"

She stammered as the pounding persisted. "I-I need help." *Slam.* "My ex is here, and I think he's going to kill me." *Slam.*

The dispatcher got her address, her name, and his name, and before she could say anything else, the door burst open, and there he was. His eyes blazed. The shock of the door slamming open into the wall spooked Batty, and the cat lurched out of her arms and ran toward the back of the apartment.

She was alone.

The man strode forward and grabbed the woman's hair, pulling her up from the couch. "After everything, you think you're just going to leave me?" he hissed dangerously.

He threw her by the hair into the wall and then clawed the TV stand and wrenched it over, bringing all its contents crashing to the ground. He stepped over the debris and came toward her, and when he passed the end table by the couch, he grabbed the table lamp and thrust it against a wall as well.

"P-please," the woman stammered.

She backed away into the kitchen, and he strode forward and shoved her against the stove. She reached around desperately and grabbed the frying pan from the stovetop.

He glanced down at it and sneered, "Really?"

He ripped the frying pan from her hands and grabbed one of her wrists, bodily dragging her toward the back of the apartment. She struggled against him, and he tossed her to the floor in the doorway of the back room. There she lay, looking up at him, and she felt the same hopelessness she had all the other times she'd seen him looming over her. At the beginning, she'd frozen when he'd abused her, unable to believe it was really happening. As it continued, she fawned. She just did what he wanted because that was the only way she could see to survive.

She couldn't run anymore. She couldn't fight. Nothing she could say or do dimmed that murderous flame in his eyes. So, she froze. She froze as she had so many times before, and all hope drained out of her as he came at her for the last time.

Suddenly, Batty ran full tilt out of the bedroom and darted in front of him, and the monster before her tripped over the black blob in his path. With a shout, the man was thrust forward, and his head slammed into the doorframe beside her with a devastating crunch. His body twisted as he collapsed, and she looked into his open eyes as the savage fire in them dimmed and went out. He was still.

All was silent for a moment. The woman released a long, slow breath, and then Batty yowled. She glanced at the cat and then back to the limp form of the man who had terrorized her for so long. Batty trotted forward, stepped into her lap, and stretched himself up as he had when she'd brought him home. As she felt his paws on her neck and he bumped his head against her chin, she looked down. He rubbed his cheek against hers and purred.

"I guess it's only bad for a black cat to cross your path if you're a bad person," she whispered, more to herself than to the cat in question. Then she laughed despite herself, and she gathered Batty into her arms, held him tightly, and began to sob, releasing the pain she'd held and the man who'd caused it. A man who would never be able to harm her again.

When the police arrived, they found an impassive woman sitting on the floor in the back of a ravaged apartment holding a black cat, the blessing that had ridden her of the darkness that once consumed her. They carted the man's body away and took the woman's statement, and she held Batty tightly all the while. If black cats hold any kind of magic, they passed it to Batty that night, and all it took was unconditional love for a black cat to bring luck, happiness, and freedom to the woman who crossed his path—and death to the evil who'd crossed hers.

Author's Note

Based on a true story, this was a mash-up of true events. There really was a cat named Batty, a senior cat whose fangs and blackness scared little kids, and who was in danger of being put down before someone saw him and decided to love him forever. A young woman really did survive her abuser trashing her apartment and brought home a cat for a companion as soon as she could, though it was a different cat. Her abuser really did come after her in the middle of the night. Fortunately, when she called 911, help arrived before he could get through the door. He has yet to cross a black cat, but maybe one day.

The black cat, Batty, is the only character I've chosen to name for this story because this sort of violent occurrence happens every day all over the world. You might find the woman in your friend, your neighbor, or yourself. You might be the neighbor. You might know the man. If I give them names, they become characters—and they are—but they're real too.

John Russell is a member of The Authors Guild and the Academy of American Poets. He has authored three multi-award-winning nonfiction books on the paranormal, all of which are available at all booksellers online: *Riding with Ghosts, Angels*, and the *Spirits of the Dead; A Knock in the Attic*; and *20 Ways to Increase Your Psychic Abilities*, which was the #1 best seller on Amazon in Ghosts & Hauntings, and it was also a bestseller at Barnes & Noble, hitting the Top 100 Bestselling Books list. He's completed writing his fourth nonfiction book on the paranormal (to be published in 2024), *The Crying Tree and the Magic Rock*. In addition to being an award-winning author John is an internationally known psychic and paranormal investigator.

THE BLACK CAT
by John Russell

She watched me from the ledge
of the window, devoid of glass,
Queen of the abandoned store
which daily I would pass.

Her eyes were unfathomable
some might even say so strange
they hid a depth of feelings
of emotions so wide a range.

Her expression gave me chills
but I overcame my fright
and late one chilly evening
I took her home for the night.

She didn't seem to protest
but made herself at home
then she crept into my closet
and her mouth began to foam.

THE BLACK CAT *by John Russell*

She had thirteen kittens
the mere memory I still dread
for every single ball of fur
possessed a human head!

Ash Fanglore (he/she/they) is an autistic queer originally from the moody Appalachian mountains but now residing in a small parish village in England with his husband, kitties Agatha Rose and Harrowhark, The Squirrel, and chow chow Xióng Tea.

In their free time, Ash runs D&D for teens at the local library, plays computer games, tries new foods, and tries to gain access to as many libraries as possible on the Libby app.

This is her first published piece, but you can still find more of Ash at https://ashfanglore.wordpress.com/ and Instagram or Twitter @ashfanglore.

MARROW
by Ash Fanglore

She built me, piece by piece, around the one she loved. She connected the circuits too soon—I felt every screw she tightened, every black spray-painted panel she welded together, every break of the Old One's bones when her hand slipped. It hurt so badly to be brought to life over the corpse of someone you were meant to replace, but the Builder loved the Old One, the Old One loved the Builder, and I began to love, too. When she was done, she flipped a switch and I blinked for the first time.

"Persephone?" She looked afraid. I didn't know what she was asking, but I could tell it was important to her, so I meowed. With that single sound, her face widened in a grin that made her look less like a hollowed-out waif and more like a childish cherub, which was a better look for her round face. The Old One's bones within me yearned for that smile, enough to push me to my paws and rub against her legs for the first time. When her hand tentatively reached out to stroke me, it felt right. We were always meant to be together, forever. She was mine.

We spent several days in her hovel, just the two of us. I curled on her lap while she cleaned and assembled her gun. When she slept at night, I cuddled her over the blankets so my black metal body wouldn't make her colder than she already was. I loved her fiercely, and she loved the Old One, which was close enough to loving me. I was content.

Eventually, she needed to work again. When she opened the door, dark braids coiled around her scalp and her gun strapped to her back, I darted out too.

"No, Persephone. You stay home. You know this."

I did not know this, considering she had never left before, but I did know I could not leave her alone.

"Go inside."

I did not. She tried several times to grab me and put me back, but I evaded capture at every turn.

"Please, I can't lose you again."

I didn't understand—she had never lost me. I'd been with her since the moment of my creation. After half a click passed, she gave up, though I could tell by the hunch of her shoulders that she was displeased.

"Dumb cat," she muttered tearfully, stomping into the amber night with me following a few paces behind. The bones inside my chest rattled.

I learned quickly that she was an errand-runner, picking up parcels in one location and delivering them to another, sometimes to people, sometimes to empty space. Some of the parcels ticked, some of them tocked, some of them squelched, some of them cried, and some were so utterly silent that they cloaked the clunk of her heavy boots against the cracked pavement. She never opened them. This is how we spent our days, one after the other, until a package was addressed to her.

"Shit," she said, crouching over it while orange raindrops pelted her latex cloak. I twisted around her ankles in comfort, curling my long inky tail around the hard muscle of her thigh.

Your thigh is my thigh, I thought. *You are mine.* The skeleton of the Old One shuddered against me, seeming to forget that I had no lungs for its ribs to puncture. Inside the box was a silver rapier, a plastic card, and a note on real paper. She read the paper several times with a grimace before snapping her fingers, igniting a gentle flame from her wristpip. Gingerly, she pinched a corner of the page and held it until it caught, green fire licking up the edges. She watched the fire burn to her fingertips, then flicked it into a puddle to stutter and die. When she swiped the card against her wristpip, it lit the screen with blue trails and a throbbing X that she hissed at.

"This is it." Her voice was so quiet I wasn't sure if she was talking to me, herself, or whoever sent the parcel.

While her focus was elsewhere, I sniffed the parameter of the box to ensure there was nothing overly suspicious before lithely jumping in to investigate the rapier. It smelt of ice and its tip was sharper than my fangs.

"Don't touch that," she said abruptly, lifting me out as I mewed in protest. "It's dangerous." Despite the proclaimed danger, she lifted it out carefully, cradling it like a baby, sparking jealousy in my circuits. When she looked at me, there were tears in her eyes. All I knew to do was prop myself with paws against her knee and stretch to lick the salt from her face with my sandpaper tongue of needles and steel. Against the hurtling rain, she finally stood, sword in hand, and held me in the crook of her neck.

"I love you, Persephone." She spoke to the Old One, not me, and it hurt.

I love you. More than you could ever know. A warmth diffused through me, starting where a heart might have been and spreading through my limbs. It heated the metal plates containing my wires and the Old One's corpse jumped to her skin, turning it a puckered pink. I tried to pull away—the last thing I wanted to do was harm her—but she held me tightly, only releasing her grip after the burn branded my pawprint onto her cheek. I landed on my feet, rainwater hissing into steam around me.

"I love Persephone." She had more lines on her face than someone her age should have. The bags under her eyes used to be light and puffy, now they were hollow and purple. The black braids she'd worn for so long turned silver halfway up. How long had we been making deliveries? Days? Years? Decades? What is time to a machine?

"I love Persephone. But you're not her, are you?"

I stared at her, black eyes meeting black eyes as she clutched the rapier away from her body. Orange rain dripped down the blade like citrus juice. I could not tell what inscrutable thoughts were happening inside her skull when she spun on her heel and stalked down the streets we'd traversed so many times before.

She walked as dawn lightened the sky to mauve, and the rain petered out into the occasional violet cumulus wisp. We finally stopped when we reached a hollow glass spire reflecting the stars' glare so strongly, that I had to shutter my lenses with a second lid. We stood, steel to skin, shoulder to shin, as the morning light travelled from the base of the tower to disappear amongst the ether at the top.

"You deserve your own name," she said abruptly. "You have been a good cat."

My purr rattled the Old One inside.

"Your name is Marrow." She raised the rapier above her head then hesitated to cast a small smile at me. She brought the blade down, its tip slamming into the glass structure to create infinitesimal cracks from the point of entry that swiftly spread across the spire's surface.

After a suspended moment, glittering knives of glass exploded from the tower, the sword fell from where it had pierced the spire, and in the iridescent beauty of it all, I lost sight of her. For a moment there was only me, the body I carried inside me, the sweet tinkle of shattered finery, and the glare of a hundred stars reflected on a million mirrors. When the sky cleared, she was lying on her back, pointing a bloodied hand towards the base of the destroyed structure. I followed her direction, glass turning to sand beneath my paws as I made my way to the centre, curiously clear of debris. In the very middle where the tower had stood was a sapling with golden leaves, slowly yet surely growing before my eyes. Around the tree, the air smelled different, like sweet water from an unopened bottle instead of what pooled in the city.

I turned to see if this made her smile, but she hadn't moved. The rapier had fallen to the ground, appearing rusty and chipped next to the glistening pile of glass that surrounded and pierced her. Crystalline rubies of blood spilled from a surplus of gaping slices across her flesh. When I curled myself atop her breast, I already knew my purring couldn't save her. Her breath rattled too much and the wounds would not clot.

"I love you, Marrow," she wheezed, crimson bubbling from her lips. I purred harder than I'd ever purred in my life, though no amount of my whirling cogs could stop this. I kept purring, even when her chest didn't rise again, through the next night, while the tree grew taller than her, while the wind scattered particles of glistening glass, while the blood crusted her clothes and her limbs stiffened, I purred. When I thought I could purr no longer, the Old One shook in the same tempo until it, too, fell silent.

I couldn't leave her there. She had built a new body around the one she loved and now I would do the same. I elongated, popped open the seams of my exoskeleton and stretched myself wide, the Old One's remains tangled inside my circuitry. I yawned, jaw cracking wider and teeth pushing out to match the rapier that I pressed into my silicone gums. I was so gentle as I laid myself on top of her and took her inside of me, consuming her delicately, barely tearing her cold flesh as I folded her body deep inside my crevasses and closed my form around her into a new, grotesque shape.

We were always meant to be together, forever. The three of us: the Old One, the Builder, and Marrow. I will never be lonely because I am always with me and we love ourselves very much.

Joanie Brittingham (she/they) is a writer and soprano living in New York City. Brittingham is the Associate Editor for *Classical Singer Magazine*, the author of *Practicing for Singers*, and has contributed to many classical music textbooks. Brittingham's writing has been described as "breathless comedy" and having "real wit" (*New York Classical Review*). Brittingham is the librettist for the opera *Serial Killers and the City*, which premiered with *Experiments in Opera*, and will be a part of *New Wave Opera's Night of the Living Opera*. On Instagram and TikTok: @joaniebrittingham.

THE GOLDEN HAIRBALL
by Joanie Brittingham

Dermot walks home from Costco, having lost his driver's license in his third DUI. He has a chicken in a bag—he hates the new bags. It's leaking, a steady drip drip drip of chicken juice onto the hot pavement. He's trying not to think about how little money he has left, and how he has to stretch this chicken for three days. He hears a meow, but keeps walking, chanting "one day at a time" under his breath. Then the black cat crosses his path.

He stops. He's not superstitious, or at least would tell himself he's not. He'd laugh if someone else told him about stopping in the middle of the sidewalk when a black cat crossed their path. Nevertheless, he's stops. The cat meows again, that plaintive "purr—ow" where the second syllable goes up in pitch. The cat looks at the bag of chicken, and then looks at him.

The cat is so thin, he thinks. His life is such a mess. He bends down onto the hot pavement, the motion hurting his knees and his sciatica. He opens the bag and takes the chicken out, places it on the grass next to the sidewalk. It doesn't occur to him to give the cat only part of the chicken. He presents his offering to the cat. He trudges to the Costco and buys another chicken. He gets a soda too, drinking half of it in the store, and filling it back up before leaving. He won't have money to buy a bottle of schnapps from the liquor store now, but that's ok, he won't drink today. His sponsor will approve.

He returns to the place on the sidewalk where he fed the cat. It's been a half an hour or more—getting through the parking lot without a car and across the highway twice ate up most of his time. He sees the carcass of the chicken, picked entirely clean. Poor kitty, it was so hungry. There's no sign of the cat. He looks around and calls for it softly. The feline comes out from some scraggly bushes and meows at him again.

"You only get one whole chicken today!" he admonishes her. The cat rubs against his cargo pants, the fabric stiff from days of sweat, leaving black fur sticking to the caked on filth. He needs to wash his clothes. The creature claws at the pants, and climbs up him. He almost drops his drink and leans forward to balance himself, pain shooting through his leg. The cat climbs up his back, and as he straightens, settles on his shoulder.

"You can't come home with me." He looks at the black animal, furrowing his brow. She stomps her front paw, right at the neck of his t-shirt, as if to say, "onward."

He starts walking, telling the cat it can't come home with him, the second chicken in one hand, Pepsi watering down in the other. She sits on his shoulder and chirps back at birds along the way and occasionally rubs its face against Dermot's head, sweat co-mingling with the feline's scent glands.

The two arrive home. The cat jumps from his shoulder, and, rather than exploring, settles into Dermot's aging recliner in front of the television.

"I suppose you think that's your chair now!" The black mass of fur does not respond, she's asleep.

He goes to the garage and finds the kitty litter he keeps for de-icing the stoop in the winter. He finds a box and sets up a temporary litter box in the bathroom. It'll do for now.

He looks in the mirror, sees an old drunk. He's sweating, it's dripping down his face. The chicken should last three days if it's him alone, but he has to feed the cat. He has very little money left, having drunk himself out of a job months ago. Unemployment ran out.

He can't run the AC, he's only a few weeks away from the electric bill and he won't be able to pay it. He needs work, but without being able to drive, how will he get to a job site? He'll walk to the library tomorrow, use a computer. Look for work. Ask the librarian. He'll get cat food with the last of his cash. He shakes. He wants booze. But the cat—who will take care of it? It's his problem now.

But he wonders, will the cat keep me sober? He doesn't want to wake up covered in blood again. He doesn't know whose blood it was last time in the alley behind O'Donnell's—the regular barstool a distant memory. He woke up curled in a ball behind the dumpster, covered in his own sick with blood on his face and hands. He had no cuts, so it wasn't his. He walked home, a frightening figure in the day.

He could beg tomorrow—he's stood by the exit from the interstate with an old paper coffee cup, scrounging enough cash to go to the bar or to buy the cheapest schnapps at the counter. Or cat food. A better litter box. Some cat toys. When the chicken runs out, he'll need to feed himself too. The computer at the library would tell him what churches have food drives. Sometimes the librarians know. They offer the information before he asks, as if they see the hunger in his eyes. The desperation. How did it get this bad?

He'll be homeless if he can't pay the tax bill in the spring. By the time they take the house, he'll have no power and water anyway. The streets are no place for a cat, he thinks. He does not think about how the streets are no place for Dermot. He cares more for the feline's welfare than his own. He washes his face, dries it on a musty old towel. He goes to a meeting while the cat is still curled up in his chair. When he returns, she stretches and yawns. He feeds the cat some chicken, and pours her a bowl of water. He then pours himself a glass of water and eats from the chicken. He feeds himself and her with his fingers. He talks to Kitty, the first time he's spoken in this house since—he doesn't want to think about that, so he tells her what he's going to do tomorrow, and that he knows, "Kitty is uninventive, but that's your name now."

And he does those things. He starts the day eating more chicken with Kitty. He cleans up the kitchen, too. Washes the dishes in the sink. Not the ones piled on the countertops, those can wait, but for now, the sink is empty. He looks at his pet and says, "I guess we need to clean up this whole place." The cat grooms herself in response.

He gathers the laundry—the worst of it—and puts it into the washer in the basement. He starts the load, knowing he won't be able to run the dryer, something that stopped him before. It's hot enough to hang the laundry outside. He has a line somewhere in the garage he never put up. He finds it, takes it outside and sets it up between two trees. He wonders if he should let the cat outside. He thinks about how he needs to take her to the vet.

Back inside, Kitty is already in his chair. He goes to the library, emails the power company about being a senior and needing an extension on his bill. The cat knocked the bill off the kitchen table that morning, and when he picked it up, he saw the notice. He hadn't known that email was an option. He asks the librarian about finding a job. She tells him there's a session later in the week, gives him all the information, and shows him a website to apply for jobs from the city. He buys cat food, a real litter box, and more litter. He struggles to get it home in the heat. He's out of money. There's only a little bit of chicken left, but at least the cat won't go hungry today.

He opens the door, calling for Kitty. He fills her dish; she sings to him. He gets the last of the chicken out of the fridge, sits down to eat. She leaves her dish of cat food and meows at him, slow blinking. Before he takes his first bite, he gives a little bit of chicken to the cat. She gobbles it up, head butts him, and returns to the cat food. He finishes the chicken, thinks, I could make broth, stretch out the bones another day. He finds the stock pot, rinses it, fills it with water, the chicken bones and fat, sets it on the burner on low. He putters around the house, cleaning, folding the crisply dried laundry. There are still so many piles, old bottles, and cans. Maybe he could recycle some of them, get a few dollars tomorrow. He gathers it up in the rolling trash can, which he can wheel to the recycling center tomorrow. It's a few miles away. A hard walk with only broth to eat.

Dermot wakes in the morning to the sounds of the cat retching. He jumps out of bed, calling for her. He finds her in the kitchen, a mess of puke and hairball on the floor. "Oh, Kitty. Poor Kitty." He gets a towel, cleans it up and finds something hard and cold inside it. He takes it to the sink and rinses it off. He holds up a solid gold coin.

"Well, Kitty, you've bought yourself more chickens!" He laughs, picks up the cat and sings to her. She purrs happily, jumps from his arms, and returns to what he now thinks of as her chair.

He takes the coin to a pawn shop first thing. The owner looks at him warily, weighs it, checks the rates of gold.

"I can give you eighteen hundred in cash, take it or leave it." Dermot knows it's worth more than that, but that's enough for the electric bill to run the dryer and the AC at the same time. To pay the bills. To get a bicycle, so he doesn't have to walk in the heat. To maybe celebrate with a little drink.

He takes the cash, stuffs half of it inside each of his pockets and the rest down his sock. He's wary, because he knows what it looks like to leave a pawn shop. He stops at the bank, deposits half of the cash. He goes to the library, pays the electric bill in full. Pays the water bill, too. His last stop is Costco, where he gets two more chickens, plus other groceries for the week. He's got a large, heavy box and he is already across the highway and halfway home before he realizes he didn't buy any liquor. He can celebrate at O'Donnell's!

He takes the groceries home first, feeds Kitty from the fresh chicken before putting it in the fridge. Getting out the broth and flour, he makes chicken and dumplings. He feeds the cat again before he eats. A little bite of chicken, plus her cat food. He gets out a pad of paper and writes "call veterinarian" on it.

He continues cleaning the apartment. It's starting to look livable. He rolls the recycling bin to the curb, full of bottles. He doesn't need the few dollars, it's not worth the walk. The coin settled him up, and he'll be ok while he looks for a job. He can even enjoy a few drinks tonight. He goes back inside to get the cash and walk to the bar. The cat wraps herself around his legs, meowing. He picks her up and carries her to her chair. She jumps onto him as soon as he puts her down. Hisses. Stays on the arm of the recliner, back arched.

"That's not like you, Kitty." He sits down in the chair. She stops hissing and climbs into his lap, falls asleep, purring.

"I see, you don't want me to go out. Probably for the best." He turns on the TV, stays with the cat for a few hours, then carries her to bed, where she falls asleep again at his feet.

He wakes up in the morning to the same retching noise. He finds a fresh gold coin. Staring in awe at the cat, he cleans up the mess. He can't go to the same pawn shop. They'll have questions. He looks at the cat. "Well, two blessings aren't so bad."

He walks to another pawn shop on the opposite side of town. When the dealer offers him two thousand dollars, he asks how much it would be if he throws in the bicycle he sees for sale. The owner shrugs and says he can have it, it won't sell. He takes it outside, walks it to a bike shop down the street. It takes fifty to get the bicycle in working order. He pays another forty for front and rear baskets—one for groceries, one for the cat. He rides to a pet shop, picks up a harness and leash. A carrier. Asks for vet recommendations.

Every day, he wakes up to a new pile of vomit in the kitchen, with a new gold coin. Soon he's cleaned up the entire house, made repairs he could never afford to do. He takes the cat to the vet, where she hisses at the mention of spaying. Dermot refuses, but gets her all of her shots. She sulks that evening, even when presented with an entire chicken leg. She still coughs up a gold coin the next day.

Dermot stops looking for a job. He has a vague sense of unease about the coins, but the cat is happy, and so he is happy. His eyes brighten, his skin becomes clearer. He goes to a physical therapist for his sciatica. He meets other seniors at the library, talks to them about their cats. Opens up to a handsome woman his age named Mary, tells her about how the death of his wife made him lose hope and start drinking. How Kitty saved him. The cat doesn't get mad when he goes out for their first date, or for their second, or when Mary comes home with him on their third. She waits till after breakfast when Mary leaves to cough up a coin. Life begins to feel good again.

Late one night, as he and the cat sit in the recliner, watching television, there's a knock on the door. A banging, really. The black feline jumps from his lap and growls at the door. Dermot answers and she goes into the kitchen, out of sight. It's Vinny, a man from his "before Kitty" life, before the gold coins and the home improvements and Mary and hope. He'd done off the books work for Vinny, desperate for money and booze. Many of the fights he'd been in, the nights he'd come home with blood on his hands, were at the behest of Vinny.

"Where you been, Dermot?"

"Sober." Dermot stands in the doorway. He isn't going to let Vinny in. He suppresses a shudder at the idea of what Vinny would do to Kitty.

Vinny is younger, bigger, than Dermot. He pushes his way in, nearly knocking Dermot over.

"The thing is, people have missed seeing you fight. When you hit the blackout point, there's no telling what you'll do. It's entertaining. People miss their entertainment."

Dermot regains his composure. "I'm not fighting or drinking anymore."

"I think you will. See, you put the last fellow in the hospital. And we both know you need the money." Vinny sits in the recliner.

Kitty saunters into the living room, and seeing Vinny in the chair, her chair, she hisses at him. He waves the cat away. She comes closer, growling and hissing. She looks bigger, her black fur bristling on end, Dermot thinks. Vinny kicks at the cat, his foot just barely connecting to the cat's mid-section. Dermot calls out, but it doesn't matter.

Kitty has had enough.

And the cat is not really a cat. The black feline shifts and groans and grows, an amalgam of the various forms it has taken over centuries. When she is done, she reclaims her now blood-stained recliner, and grooms herself. Dermot cleans up. He has a lot of experience cleaning up blood. He finds a shovel and the lawn lime in the garage, gets the bleach from under the sink. He digs up the remnants of his late wife's rose garden, and a deeper hole. He vows to care for the rose garden, long left abandoned and wilting, so there's never a reason to dig here again and find what remains of Vinny. He gives the cat an entire chicken breast.

She purrs.

They are safe.

Years later, Dermot buries his second wife, Mary. Her granddaughter, Sarah, holds his hand when they arrive back at the house after the service.

"Sarah, I need you to take the cat. I can't take care of her anymore, not without Mary. I need you to listen, carefully. There's a rotisserie chicken in the fridge. You're going to give it to Kitty, and wait, but don't watch. She'll eat it whole. Then you're going to pick her up and take her home. Don't look back. Don't look behind you. Don't look into the rear view mirror, not once. Look forward, onward. That's what Kitty wants. Take her home. I've got a bag of supplies and her carrier ready for you. Give her the first bite of every meal. She'll hack up a hairball in the morning. Call me when she does, when you find something in it."

Sarah does as he says, willing to humor her adopted grandfather, and more than happy to take Kitty. She loves that cat. The cat loves her, more than all of the other adult grandchildren. She drives away in the car Dermot bought her for graduation from the college Dermot paid for with Kitty, purring in her carrier.

Kelly Matsuura is an avid short story writer, with a focus on fantasy, horror, and literary fiction. She is the creator of *Insignia Stories* (Asian fantasy anthologies) and has had stories published with *Black Hare Press, Iron Fairie Publishing, Wolfsinger Press, The Sirens Call Ezine*, and many more. Kelly lives in Nagoya, Japan with her geeky husband. She loves traveling, knitting, cooking, and of course, reading. You can find her at
https://blackwingsandwhitepaper.wordpress.com.

PRIZED BLOOD
by Kelly Matsuura

Little black cat,
why don't you bleed?
Can't you see,
That I must feed?

I cut you once, knife deep in.
Prized blood I seek, from veins within.
I still find none, so cut again,
I slit your gut, reach in and then—
Fingers dry, not wet, not sticky.
Just a lick! I won't be picky.

My stomach growls, my anger soars.
I slit your throat—I have just cause!
But there's no mess, no red on white.
I cannot gain strength tonight.
I drop the knife, sink to the floor.
There's no point to try once more.

Fangs bite deep into my neck,
Blood spurts quick and bright.
Ah, 'tis *you* then dear kitty,
Not I, who feasts this night.

Ken Hueler teaches kung fu in the San Francisco Bay Area, where he also co-chairs the local Horror Writers Association chapter. His work has appeared in *Weirdbook*, *The Sirens Call*, *Weekly Mystery Magazine*, *Andromeda Spaceways*, and anthologies such as *"The Cozy Cosmic"* and *"Tales for the Camp Fire"*. He is an assistant editor at *Space & Time* magazine and, with Frances Lu Pai Ippolito, co-edited the game fiction anthology *"Winding Paths: A Playable Reading Experience"*. You can learn more at: https://kenhueler.wordpress.com/

A BABY'S BREATH WREATH, A HEART FULL OF THORNS
by Ken Hueler

I pursue the cat over the boy's front lawn, past a rosebush, a mailbox, and then across a street and around a house. His black fur burrows into the night, but not his white paws. Two blocks later, he disappears in the thick weeds of a vacant lot. I stay to a straight line—he has a destination.

We both do.

Only he knows where it is.

I emerge in a cared-for backyard and spot the cat pulling himself onto the top of a wood fence. The body I have borrowed is too small to jump that high. Instead, I shadow him as he walks the narrow rail. To my right is a tree I could climb, but it might cost losing sight of him. I sprint, dig my claws into the bark, and cross a drooping limb onto the fence.

Where is he?

I skitter along the fence, scanning all directions for where he dropped down. He's black against dark, but I have enhanced vision. Then I see him, crossing another street. He lights up, a horn blares, tires scream.

No!

Twenty years of searching...

The car stops short. I push to catch up. We dart past a recycling bin, down a side alley, around a corner, and he slams through a cat flap.

by Ken Hueler

So do I.

Before the chase, sitting on a sill outside the open window, I had watched him creeping across the bed. A boy slept, heavy and limp, half out his sheets. He appeared dead, but if he were, the cat would not have eased white forepaws onto that gently rising chest. From my perch, I finally saw what a different cat, thirty years ago, had done to me.

I held in my fury. And waited.

Once through the door flap, I'm in a kitchen with six other cats, all with fur as black as mine. Slippered human feet approach. A woman enters, counting her familiars. She looks younger than Mamma, but the clarity in those clear blue eyes is stolen, as is the shine of her cushiony skin. I slink from the room. Behind, I hear a faucet and then a metal bowl set onto the floor. Her cats must return thirsty from running, as mine must be, but I don't risk going back.

That kitchen, a tiny doorless bathroom, and this living room-bedroom is all, in this tiny subdivided house. More cats, curious about me, lie atop the woman's bed, but I slip underneath it and wait. Muttering grows louder, and a faded robe hem and slippers swish into my vision.

I dearly want to bite those ankles.

A BABY'S BREATH WREATH, A HEART FULL OF THORNS

by Ken Hueler

I was a spite ghost—not by design—created from my death, its unfairness, and, above all, a mother's grief. But twenty years ago, I willed myself to be stronger than that, because while spite wallows, vengeance acts.

So I am a vengeance ghost.

Twice more during the night, the woman counts her cats, and then, satisfied, she squats not far from me. All the cats—the lounging, the dozing, the tussling—gather. One opens its mouth. Out floats tufts as white and scattered as a gust of dandelion seeds. The woman snaps with her mouth and scrabbles with her hands, shoving each one into her mouth. Another cat, and then another, do the same. On the fifth, a mote escapes and drifts toward the bed, toward me, and the woman chases. I narrow my eyes to slits and don't move. I am dark fur deep in shadow, hard to see. That is why she chooses black, after all.

More cats disgorge wisps of stolen life. Finally, the woman stands. I hear bristles against enamel, a deep plunk and a flush, a soapy gush of faucet.

Soon, Mamma, your daughter will be back. I am so sorry for leaving.

Mamma and I, we had fallen into patterns. For example, in our kitchen each morning, Mamma would talk to me and I would stand near the pantry or the sink or the door— wherever her eyes pointed—to listen. And whenever Mamma was sad and quiet I would jabber all the words I was learning from her, from visitors, from the television. I would sing. Anything to fill the house with me. She couldn't hear me, of course, but I think she felt me.

We lived that way until the year I should have turned ten, when Mamma planted a burr into my heart, "You stopped breathing several times," she said, and I scurried so she

by Ken Hueler

would be looking at me. "We moved you into our room. That last night, I woke up suddenly. Something slipped off your bed and jumped out the window. It was a black cat, I'm sure of it. After that you never breathed again. I'm sorry, baby girl, but I knew you were gone. And, well, Mamma knows things, and I did what was needed to keep you with me. For the company. And for that I am sorry."

With each retelling, Mamma's heart seemed less heavy, but inside mine the burr grew bigger. More painful. I sang louder. More often. Nothing helped.

I drink water, for my cat, and then eat dried food from a bowl. I don't taste anything.

Back in the main room, I jump onto the woman's bed—I do not need stealth, not with so many cats wrapped around her. I wonder at how she stops them from leaving—I hold onto mine because I never sleep. Her sternum is occupied, and much of her outline, but I find an open spot beside her neck. I watch her slack face—so untroubled, even innocent—and I let go of vengeance.

I will myself to be a hungry ghost.

I oppose her breathing, inhaling as she exhales, and one white speck floats out and then down into my lungs. Then a few, then so many. Unlike her cats, I am a ghost. My boundaries span two worlds. I cannot be filled.

She coughs, wakes too late. Her eyes have filmed. Her skin is sagging and thin. All she can do is rock, moan. She is terrified. Everyone knows they are going to die, but she doesn't. Not until this moment.

A BABY'S BREATH WREATH, A HEART FULL OF THORNS

by Ken Hueler

Back at the boy's house, I enter the window and creep up the bed. The woman's cats visited other children tonight, ones who will die days, months, or years before their time, but I do not know who they are or where. I spread my jaws and a thick fluffy fog encircles the child's face. Down his throat slips the stolen life force. Any strays I catch and spit back until he's taken every one.

Done, I exit my cat, who begins exploring the room. Maybe the family will keep it.

I bring my lips to the boy's ear and whisper: "You have extra life. Do all the things we wanted, be all the things we could not be." The boy can't hear me, but maybe he will feel me, like I hope Mamma did.

Mamma.

I should go home to her. That was my plan, to go home. But, for the first time, I feel at peace. Without spite or vengeance or hunger, I have no purpose. And returning to Mamma would just rekindle her grief, wouldn't it?

In the boy's front yard I choose a rose bush: trimmed grass, a weeded circle of bare dirt, buds and blooms. Leaning in, I can't smell anything, but I substitute memories: sweat, puréed carrots, Tide, strawberries, cigarette smoke. I lie so the rosebush rises from my heart. I can't feel the thorns, of course. Nothing hurts. Nothing at all.

I am a dying ghost.

And that is good.

Paul A. Freeman is an English language teacher. He is the author of *Rumours of Ophir*, a crime novel which was taught at 'O' level in Zimbabwean high schools and has been translated into German.

In addition to having two novels, a children's book and an 18,000-word narrative poem (*Robin Hood and Friar Tuck: Zombie Killers!*) commercially published, Paul is the author of scores of published short stories, poems and articles.

He is a member of the Society of Authors and of the Crime Writers' Association, and has appeared several times in the CWA's annual anthology.

He resides and works in Mauritania.

A MEWLING MADNESS
by Paul A. Freeman

Haunted! I'm haunted! No other word can convey the situation that's caused my state of nervousness, an acute anxiety created not by anything tangible, but by a supernatural entity—or so I believed at first. And none is to blame but myself for the apprehensions attending me, the ghostly apparition of a yowling black cat included. Yet I get ahead of myself, perhaps attracting along the way scepticism and a suspicion that I am no longer of sound mind, which may well be true. So, to the beginning.

The black cat, an unhealthy-looking, mangy brute that in appearance was little more than an overgrown yet undernourished kitten, began lurking about my lodgings one autumn evening. Slyly she skulked about the front yard of the apartment building, searching, I supposed, for someone gullible enough to feed her, to take her in, perhaps even to adopt her. This in a country where the retention of a pet was rare because owning such an animal was a burden on a person's monthly income, especially if one had extended family to attend to.

The cat's mewling was worse than the beggary of mendicants in the central souk, its aim to tug at the heartstrings of naïve idiots who had more money than sense. Her whining was doubly strategic, for the ear-splitting noise only started up whenever a kind-hearted-looking mark was at hand, done, I presumed, in an endeavour to elicit a maximum amount of sympathy.

The chubby fool upstairs, a new resident who seemed to have materialized out of the ether, readily fell for the feline's trickery. "Here, Sooty! Here, Sooty!" he cried, punctuating his words with an irksome clicking of the tongue and an equally irritating kissy-kissy sound through his ugly, puckered lips.

In the evenings he thought nothing of placing a saucer of milk and a bowl of sloppy, gelatine-dripping, tinned cat food opposite my front door, beneath a small, much fronded palm tree festooned with dates. He then proceeded to sit on the staircase, leading upstairs to his own abode, watching the scabby beast feasting on the offerings. The weather was still hot for that time of year, the autumnal coolness being unaccountably delayed. Any milk that remained soon became rancid and the food stinking and flyblown. My upstairs neighbour was in no hurry to remove or clean the affronting saucer and bowl, leaving them instead to offend my eyes and nostrils with their unsightliness and their stench.

I can't but admit that I became unhealthily fixated on my new upstair neighbour's comings and goings, both to his place of occupation and to the nearby grocery store. It was as though he was mocking me, rubbing my face in my relative poverty with his gainful employment, his fine attire and the excessive amounts of luxury purchases his situation could afford him. Jealousy's a horrid word, but I suppose I felt just that. He was showing off, ridiculing me as he paraded past my apartment on his way to and from work or to the grocer's shop. He had more than he needed, more than he deserved. The excess, which he spent on feeding that flea-bitten abomination of a cat, bothered me immensely. As days passed by, and as my envious malaise deepened, I also became aware of his sneering lip and a particular way in which he angled his head to look arrogantly down his nose as he passed by my flat.

Then there were his irritating habits, the worst of which was the constant rearranging of his furniture, dragging chairs and tables and whatnot across the tiled floor, at any time of the night or day, the sound reminiscent of a schoolmaster's fingernails scraping across the surface of a blackboard. In response, all I could do was grind my teeth and feel a giddiness close to swooning, another of the symptoms of weakness afflicting me that were the fault of that flabby fiend upstairs.

But let me get back to the ever-wailing cat. On an evening, as I sat outside my apartment in the tropical heat, unable to sleep under the indoor air-conditioning unit I couldn't afford to get repaired, that thing—I couldn't bear to call it 'Sooty'—watched me with its malevolent eye, mewling triumphantly on occasion, letting me know she had found her cash cow in the guy upstairs. She was going to milk the dullard for everything she could and there was nothing I could do about it. By this time, she was no longer feral, wandering the neighbourhood. Instead, she was spending her days and nights curled up asleep at the base of the palm tree, stretching herself at times on the hose-pipe watered ground, in the coolness of the shade, while I sweltered in an insomniac's fevered reality, fretting over how to obtain even the most basic life-sustaining requirements. And where was the fairness in that, a newly domesticated creature that was treated better by the capricious whims of Fate than I?

And to make matters even worse, when she wasn't napping the day away, she was choosing her moment to cross my path, to infect me with a black cat's bad luck, to press me further into the mire of poverty. The situation was becoming more than intolerable.

Meanwhile, from my garden chair vantage point in the evenings, I also became engrossed in watching a pair of fruit bats that had taken up residence somewhere in the immediate vicinity. At sunset they would flit about in the sky, flapping their leathery wings before alighting in the fronds of the palm tree and screeching to each other as they nibbled away at the dates. I no longer tried preventing them from doing this. Let them have their fill. I attempted to stop the thieving little monsters a couple of weeks earlier and one of them bit into my index finger to the bone. I learned my lesson, and now we had an understanding—the bats and I; we left one another alone. But not so the cat, and chubby upstairs. They were getting in my way, getting on my nerves and needed to be dealt with.

They had to go.

From the apartment complex garden shed, after much consideration, I selected my weapons of choice, the implements by which I would set myself free. A spade for the cat, I decided, and a garden fork for the portly pleb in the flat above.

The feline, with her incessant mewling, was the easier of the two to despatch. She thought she had one over on me, that I'd perhaps accepted her status as Queen of the Yard and that I had already meekly capitulated, scurried away and would leave her alone. But as she slurped at the long-rancid milk in the saucer, I crept up on her from behind. A sixth sense told her something was awry however, and she leapt around on all fours, her back arched, her hair on end, and managed a single hiss before I steeled myself and bashed her brains out.

Mr Corpulence must have heard the kerfuffle below, for he came waddling out of his apartment, descending the stairs at high speed, doing that kissy-kissy, tongue-clicking routine, straight into the prongs of the garden fork. Gasping, he fell to the ground, and before he could catch enough breath to scream out and denounce me as his assassin, the garden spade had done its magic a second time.

I grabbed the dead cat by its tail and tossed it in the direction of the palm tree. The body slapped against the trunk of the palm and slid down to the ground, ready to be buried in the soil at the tree's base. As for Fatty, I grabbed him by the ankles and manoeuvred his corpse, with difficulty, towards the garden shed where a chain saw and dismemberment awaited him. Soon I would be free from those two banes of my miserable life and be able to chart a course towards an unimpeded, prosperous future—or thus I told myself.

With His Porkiness in six pieces (limbs, trunk and head), I returned to my own apartment for some black garbage bags. It was at this juncture that my life was forever changed by the arrival of two men in uniform, one on the slim side, the other somewhat musclebound. They came through the front gate of the complex, saw me in the garden and made a beeline for me. In the palm tree the bats were squawking and squealing, like hecklers in the peanut gallery, betraying me, pointing me out to the newcomers in their mumbo-jumbo, echo-location language. Adding to their treacherous chorus, I heard too the mewling of the black cat, high-pitched and accusatory, testimony from beyond the grave as to my cruelty.

And that's when I experienced for the first time in a month, a moment of lucidity, a moment of clarity. The two men were not policemen, as I had imagined in my paranoia. The badges sewn onto their serge uniforms identified them as our neighbourhood animal control officers. Perhaps they had been sent here to free me from the haunting presence of the cat that was still wailing away in my head even though it was stone dead.

But I was mistaken.

"Bats!" the slightly built officer said. His eyes were focused on the palm tree, squinting, searching, ignoring the carcass of the cat. "There's been an outbreak of rabies," he continued. "We've identified bats as the main carriers and there are reports of bat inhabitations in this district. Just one bite, and if it remains untreated, it's certain death."

Recalling my bat-bitten index finger, I tensed up. My mind swam, my legs grew wobbly and I felt light-headed.

The second, more heavily built officer, at first seemed perplexed by my pale, sickly appearance. But then the look in his eyes grew cunning. Nonchalantly, he took a small bottle of water from his trouser pocket, unscrewed the top and melodramatically sipped from it, all the time observing my reaction as I cringed, salivated until I was frothing at the mouth. I suddenly felt as if my head was about to burst open from all the racket the dead cat's restless spirit was making.

The animal control officers were not taking any chances. The heavier one kicked away my legs and had me on the ground in seconds, front first, while his partner zip-tied my wrists behind my back.

"He's symptomatic," said the second officer, as if I weren't present. "He's got hydrophobia and he's hallucinating. A hopeless case. He's doomed." He took a closer look at the dead feline. "This cat's called Oliver," he continued, "He belongs to that little old lady who lives upstairs."

By now the first officer had spotted the blood trail to the garden shed and was following it to where my harmless, cat-loving upstairs neighbour—my real upstairs neighbour, whom my rabid condition made to seem a large and threatening interloper, lay dismembered, her body parts stacked in a neat pile.

At last, it had all come back to me, along with the knowledge that because of a bite from a bat, my days were numbered. There was no fat guy upstairs. There was no black cat called 'Sooty'. There had however, been an old lady, Mrs de Silva, and her jet-black cat, Oliver, who in my deranged state I had hallucinated as being ill-willed masqueraders.

"I didn't mean to kill the old girl," I cried, more out of pity for myself than out of guilt, as the mewling in my head reached a crescendo.

I looked towards Oliver, lying at the base of the date palm. He was plump and glossy-coated—a picture of health if he were not dead. And then, according to the workings of my misguided mind and vision, he began squirming, resurrecting himself, while in the background the rabid bats, the architects of my demise and living on borrowed time themselves, chattered and laughed at me.

Amelia Gorman lives in Eureka where she spends her free time exploring tidepools and redwoods with her dogs and foster dogs. Her fiction has appeared in *Nightscript 6* and *Cellar Door* from *Dark Peninsula Press*. You can read some of her poetry in *Vastarien, Utopia Science Fiction,* and *Strange Horizons.* Her first chapbook, the *Elgin-winning Field Guide to Invasive Species of Minnesota,* is available from *Interstellar Flight Press.* Her microchapbook, *The Worm Sonnets,* is available from *The Quarter Press.* Find her online at https://www.ameliagorman.com/.

IN THE BOTTOMLESS FALLING PIT
ALL CATS ARE BLACK
by Amelia Gorman

Black as comfort, black as kind. Velocity
is as disobedient as a kitten down here,
So familiar friends
fall near
      and fall far
like the weather

I have reached the depth
where I unrealize the difference
between open eyes
eyes closed

The pit starts to feel normal
except for the storm of cats
endlessly falling alongside me
and the wind-whistle
that could be a voice

Hell wishes it could drill
as deep
as this loneliness

IN THE BOTTOMLESS FALLING PIT ALL CATS ARE BLACK

by Amelia Gorman

But solace lies in the
shadows
that meow
and scratch

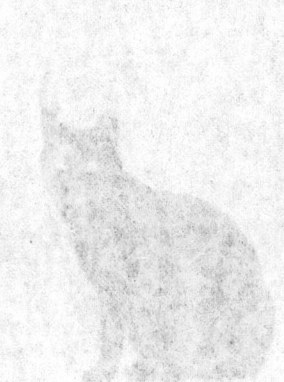

A frequent contributor to Mystery Magazine, **Edward Lodi** has written more than 30 books, including six *Cranberry Country Mysteries*. His short fiction has appeared in anthologies published by *Cemetery Dance, Murderous Ink, Main Street Rag, Superior Shores Press*, and most recently *Hungry Shadows Press* and *Black Widow Press*. His story *"Charnel House"* was featured on *Night Terrors Podcast*. He is a member of the Short Mystery Fiction Society. He can be contacted at edwardlodi@hotmail.com.

DARK STRANGER
by Edward Lodi

The morning after Laurie moved into the old farmhouse she'd bought on a whim a month ago, she wakened to find bright sunshine streaming through her bedroom windows and a stranger in her bed.

All night long, frightful dreams plagued her sleep. Dreadful, shape-shifting phantasms, like resurrected corpses or demons loosed from Hell, floated above her head. They swirled around the bed threateningly, as if probing for weak spots in her psyche through which to enter and seize control.

Maybe *he*—the stranger that lay in her bed—was a fragment of that dream.

Laurie closed her eyes, rubbed them, counted to ten, and opened first one, then the other. The stranger was still there. Not *under* the covers, as she'd first supposed, but curled up on top of the counterpane at the foot of the bed, peacefully dozing. That is, he appeared to be dozing. She felt that somehow, despite his eyes being closed, he was staring at her.

She sat up in bed waiting for the cobwebs to clear, then smiled. Why, she asked herself, did she keep referring to him as a stranger? When obviously he was no stranger at all, but only a cat—a sleek cat, black as midnight, with short thick fur, black nose, and green, penetrating eyes.

None of this made sense. How could she know his eyes were green if they were closed? And how did she know *he* wasn't a *she*? It was all a puzzle.

The bright light hurt her eyes. She could kick herself for forgetting to pull the shades down before turning in.

But how did he—the cat—get in? She'd had the house inspected before signing papers. It needed work, a lot of work, there was no denying that, but basically it was in sound shape for a two-hundred-year-old house that had been abandoned for decades.

That's what the real estate agent told her, that the house had been vacant at least thirty years. Before that, its only occupant had been an old recluse with a mean reputation who kept to himself, or so the neighbors claimed—those who were still alive. One day he'd simply disappeared and was never heard from again. Or so they said. Eventually the town seized the property for unpaid taxes, and The Town put it up for sale. There were no takers. Until Laurie came along.

Okay, then how could the house have remained in such relatively good condition all those years? No termites, no mold or rotting boards, no leaky roof, no bats in the attic, no rat holes through which a cat could squeeze. The fields, fallow all those years, showed no signs of abandonment. No trees had sprouted, taken root, and grown tall. No weeds had taken over. Not even wild flowers.

Truly a mystery. There must be something wrong. With the house. With the fields. A reason why the handful of neighbors in the area seemed to shun the place.

No way was she about to look a gift horse in the mouth. The asking price was ridiculously low. And the house was exactly what she'd dreamed of, ever since she was a little girl. An old house with plenty of land on which to roam and keep chickens and plant things and do whatever she wanted, where she could spend all the time she needed to write the poetry that, she hoped, would someday make her famous.

It was hers now. She owned it. And along with the house, it seemed, a cat.

Laurie glanced at him. His eyes, open now, were calmly contemplating her. She'd been right. They were green, with just a streak or two of yellow. He was a tom, of that she was certain. His head was too big for a female's. And he had a conceited look about him, typical of many of the males she'd known.

"What are you doing in my house?" she asked. "And however did you get in?"

This is my house.

"Your house? Don't be absurd. I bought it. I have the deed to prove it."

It's my house. But you're welcome to stay.

She swung her feet onto the floor. Here she was talking to a cat. And imagining he was talking back. If she didn't watch out she'd find herself talking to the ceiling fixtures. It was time she got dressed, brewed a pot of coffee, and fixed herself breakfast. Caffeine along with an egg and cheese omelet would dispel any nightmares that still clung, like leeches to her fogged brain.

A full day's work lay ahead. The hardest part would be deciding which of the many tasks to undertake first.

The cellar.

That made sense. She'd cleared out the attic before moving in but hadn't tackled the cellar yet. She'd begin with that. She slipped into a worn blouse and pair of faded jeans and headed into the kitchen. The cat followed her.

As she stood in front of the refrigerator he rubbed against her legs, purring.

"Oh, so you want to be fed," she said. "Well, I don't have any cat food. How about leftover chicken?"

Chicken will do. And a saucer of milk.

Coffee. She must have coffee. Either that or she needed to see a shrink. She'd been working too hard, that was it. Her mind was playing tricks. Or maybe those phantasmagoria haunting her dreams last night had taken possession after all.

They haven't yet, but they will if you don't heed my advice.

A cat that could talk. A cat that could read her mind. What was going on? She didn't use drugs. She hardly ever drank alcohol, just a glass of wine now and then.

Overwork, that was it. The past month getting the old farmhouse in order had exhausted her. Why worry? The cat didn't actually talk. How could he? She didn't actually hear a voice, feline or otherwise. His thoughts, if that's what they were, merely entered her mind.

A mind she might lose if she didn't get a grip on herself.

Laurie got the coffee going, presented the pesky feline with morsels of takeout fried chicken left over from last evening's supper and a saucer of milk, and made the omelet. After the first cup of coffee she felt better.

"Where did you come from?" she said to the cat. "What's your name, if you have one?"

Like an ordinary feline, the cat chose to ignore her. Licking the saucer clean, he sat on his haunches, and with a fastidious paw, wiped his whiskers.

Everything's copasetic, she reassured herself. Back to normal. What a little coffee and a full tummy can do to restore one's sanity! Humming a tune from the musical *Cats*, she piled the breakfast dishes into the sink, added soap and hot water, and left them to soak.

She had a daunting task ahead of her. The cellar was dark, dusty, foreboding, cluttered with bric-a-brac and detritus from generations of farm families. She'd ventured down there only once, having entered through the bulkhead outside, remaining less than a minute before hastily retreating into sunlight. There was something ominous about the cellar. She'd felt unwelcome there, as if someone—or something—resented her presence.

Foolish, of course. No doubt her fear stemmed from a sense of isolation. Her nearest neighbors lived more than a mile down the road. A road which dead-ended in front of her house. Beyond were fields bordered by dense forest.

The cat sat before the door, the way cats do while waiting for someone to let them through. "Eager to get started?" she said. "I suppose you intend to supervise while I do all the work."

Yes.

If she was being delusional, so be it. Children have imaginary friends. What harm could there be in her having an imaginary cat?

"Meow."

The meow was audible. Maybe he was a real cat after all.

The key to the cellar door hung from a hook on the wall. Laurie hesitated, then took the key, inserted it into the keyhole, and opened the door a crack. Like a bolt of lightening the cat slipped through and bounded down the steps. Emboldened, she swung the door open, found the light switch, and snapped it on.

Stirred by the current of fresh air, dust motes danced in the dim light shed by the low-watt bulb that hung, like a phosphorescent bat, from an overhead rafter. Laurie peered down the well. The cat—a silhouette cut from black crepe—sat at the foot of the stairs looking up at her. Beyond the cat lay shadows. The feeble light that filtered through the narrow dust-coated window panes set just above ground level gave the illusion of impending night.

Laurie placed a tentative foot on the top step. Was it her imagination, or did the shadows beyond the cat shift position? Closing the door behind her, she took another step down, then another, then another, inching her way to the bottom where the cat awaited her, all the while fighting panic, telling herself there was nothing to fear. It was after all only a cellar.

When she reached the dirt floor the cat, purring, rubbed against her leg. "Now what do you want?" she asked, grateful that she was not alone, even if her sole companion was a black cat with an attitude.

The cat made no reply.

"I think I may be sane after all," Laurie said to him. "Now if you'll get out of my way I can get started."

She found a string attached to a bare bulb dangling from the center of the rough-hewn ceiling and pulled it. The jaundiced glow made the cellar seem even gloomier. She threaded her way through a maze of amorphous objects to the bulkhead. Feeling her way up steep steps she thrust the bulkhead doors outward. They flopped open, landing with loud clangs that startled her.

The cat, who had trailed behind through the maze, seemed unfazed by the clatter.

Sunlight streamed in through the opening, transforming shadows into everyday objects: a chest of drawers missing knobs, a Victorian-era baby carriage with a torn canopy, a box piled high with discarded china, a half dozen milking cans.

Just ordinary junk. To think only moments ago she'd been afraid.

You have reason to be afraid.

Laurie stared at the cat. He returned her stare with impassive eyes. She shook her head. "I refuse to be intimidated, to give in to delusions. You, mister, are just a cat. A plain, run-of-the-mill black as midnight house cat. There's nothing—I repeat, nothing—in this cellar to make me afraid."

Follow me.

Without waiting to see whether she obeyed, the cat wended his way through the clutter toward the far end of the cellar, holding his tail erect, like a tour guide leading a group of sightseers. At first Laurie ignored him. She'd be damned if she'd take orders from a cat. But in the end curiosity won out.

A strange thing about the cellar—the lack of cobwebs. Or spiders to spin them. A cellar abandoned for decades should be festooned with cobwebs. And populated with beetles and sow bugs and other creepy-crawly creatures. There didn't appear to be a single living thing in the cellar. Or in the rest of the house for that matter. Just her and the cat—if the cat was a living thing and not a creation of her mind.

Laurie dutifully tagged behind the cat, whatever he might be. The cellar was much bigger than it appeared. Either that, or the cat was leading her around in circles. No way of knowing, there was so little light. The farther they got from the open bulkhead the murkier the atmosphere became. The air grew heavy, as if oxygen was being siphoned off. She found it difficult to breathe.

The cat came to an abrupt halt. Laurie nearly stumbled over him.

"Okay, Buster, now what?"

My name's not Buster.

"What is your name?"

Dowell. D-O-W-E-L-L.

"Dowell? Strange name for a cat. Is it because you do well?"

No. Dowell comes from Gaelic meaning Dark Stranger.

Laurie felt faint, as if a noose was being tightened around her neck, making it impossible to breathe. Here she was, gasping for air in a virtual dungeon, conversing with a cat who might not even be real. And there was something else. A presence. Something vague, but real. Something baleful.

She looked at the cat. Dowell. Dark Stranger. In many parts of the world black cats were believed to be evil. She was not superstitious, but—

Open the door.

Laurie glanced around her. "What door?"

In the wall in front of you.

With misgivings, she extended her hand. She saw and felt it at the same time, the reason why the cat had stopped—a brick wall where the cellar ended.

Miraculously she found herself able to see in the dark, as if she'd donned night-vision goggles. She looked at Dowell. He wore that smug expression cats assume when feeling especially superior.

"You've lent me your night vision, haven't you." She glared down at him. He returned her gaze with feline impudence. "What kind of cat are you?"

He ignored the question. *Take care. Evil lies within.*

"I see the wall. But I don't see any door."

Look closely.

She looked. At first she saw nothing but bricks. Then she noticed that some of the bricks, rather than being staggered, had been laid one atop of the other in straight lines. That must be the door. She pushed against it. It didn't budge.

"How does it open?"

Rather than answer Dowell meowed.

Despite her fear, a sense of impending doom, not to mention her difficulty breathing, Laurie couldn't resist taunting the cat. This whole thing was a dream, anyhow. It had to be. What else could it be? "What's the matter?" she asked. "Cat got your tongue?"

Dowell rubbed his flank against the base of the wall.

That's when she saw it. A brick in the bottom row that was not flush with the others. It protruded a few inches. She bent down and grasped it. It felt loose. She tugged. At first it resisted, then gradually slid out, revealing a metal pedal on the floor.

Step on it.

Laurie shook her head. "I don't trust you," she said. "How do I know what's in there? How do I know it's not a trap to entomb me alive? I can't breathe. I need air." She backed away from the door.

The cat fixed sea-green eyes on her. She felt unable to move, like an insect pinned against a board.

Those phantasmagoria that haunted your dreams. He sent them. Leave now, and they will return, night after night, until they find a weak spot and infect, not only your mind, but your soul. You must resist. Now, before it's too late.

She hesitated, then before she could change her mind she brought her foot down hard on the pedal. With a creaking, grating sound, like a ponderous lid lifted from a stone sarcophagus, the brick door swung inward. Fighting against mounting panic Laurie peered inside.

Whatever it was she'd expected, this wasn't it—a cramped room, illuminated by a phosphorescent glow whose source she was unable to determine, walls draped in purple velvet and carpeted in plush red, the overall look being that of a cheap bordello. On the wall opposite the door stood a shrine set into an alcove shaped like an upright coffin.

The black cat slunk into the room, ears slanted back, fur bristling, issuing a low sibilance not quite a hiss. *Follow me.*

Laurie shrank back. "I'm not going in there."

You must. Before it's too late. You must destroy him.

"Who? Who must I destroy?"

The evil mage who once dwelt in this house.

"This is absurd. There's no one in there."

The manikin.

Laurie poked her head into the vault. A fetid stench like something long dead assailed her nostrils, causing her to gag. Ink-black shadows swirled around her in eddies, like the phantoms that had polluted her dreams. Through veils of darkness she saw a manikin, a foot-high miniature man, standing on a pedestal in the shrine like a pagan god in a heathen temple. At its feet lay a miniature cat. A black cat with luminous emerald eyes.

"You!" she exclaimed.

Only a porcelain icon of what I once was. Take the mage, and with a hammer or rock smash him to smithereens.

"What about the porcelain cat?"

Leave it on the altar. Intact.

"I don't trust you."

Having come this far, you have no choice.

Laurie stood glued to the threshold. This reek of death, these shadows that threatened—what had she unearthed? That evil dwelt within this crypt she had no doubt. But what of the cat? Did he represent good? Or evil?

She moved toward the alcove. As she drew closer the shadows that churned and roiled, gathered and thickened, coalescing to form a dark shroud that hung above her head like the wing of a gigantic bat. It hovered a moment, then without warning dropped to wrap itself around her, engulfing her in a tight cocoon. Screaming, she struggled to free herself but was bound tight, unable to move.

The shroud bunched itself into her mouth, forming a gag, and inserted itself into her nostrils making it impossible to breathe. Deprived of air, she began to lose consciousness. As she struggled to keep her balance, she faintly heard the cat give off a shrill screech, then felt its body slam against her. The blow sent her lurching forward into the alcove, where her head came into contact with the manikin, knocking it from its pedestal. As she blacked out, the last thing she heard was the manikin crashing onto the brick floor.

When Laurie came to, she found herself lying in bed, sunlight streaming through the windows and the cat curled at the foot of the bed.

Had it all been a nightmare? Of course. What else. Only the cat was real.

She got out of bed and was fully dressed before she noticed something on her nightstand that had not been there the night before—the porcelain figurine of a black cat with emerald eyes. Where had it come from? Who put it there?

A chill ran up her spine. She had to know. The last thing she wanted to do was return to the cellar. But she had no choice. She couldn't remain a day longer in the house without knowing.

"You coming?" she said to the cat.

He ignored her.

"Okay, I'll go by myself. She grabbed a flashlight from the closet, went into the kitchen, unlocked the cellar door, switched on the light, and hurried down the steps before she could change her mind.

Aided by the flashlight she quickly crossed to the far wall. There she played the beam over every brick but found nothing resembling a door. All the bricks were set in staggered lines, and no brick protruded from the others.

She returned to the bedroom. The black cat was still there, as was the porcelain figurine.

"Hungry, Dowell?"

With a soft meow the cat jumped off the bed and trotted into the kitchen. Laurie dropped pieces of leftover chicken into his dish and filled a saucer with milk.

Dowell never "spoke" to her again. But he remained with her the rest of her life. He would have been just an ordinary cat except...

Though years passed and Laurie married and had children, and then grandchildren, Dowell never aged. He remained the same inscrutable cat. Every now and then a line of poetry would enter Laurie's head, seemingly from nowhere. Whenever that happened Dowell, looking particularly smug, would pester her by pawing at her arm as she attempted to write, knocking the pen from her hand, and otherwise annoying her until, giving in, she trudged off to the kitchen and tossed him a succulent shrimp, his favorite treat.

Another strange thing—when Marcie, Laurie's favorite granddaughter, was a little girl, she claimed that Dowell could "talk" to her by reading her mind. "He tells me secrets," she confided. "He told me that he once saved your life? Is that true, Grammy?"

After 20+ years traveling the world for the U.S. government, **A.H. Plotts** (she/her/ella) has a lot of scary stories to tell. A.H. is an active member of the HWA and her local writing community. She writes screenplays and makes short films, teaches writing workshops and designs horror-centric events for local libraries. Music, books, and food are some of her (many) other vices. Connect with her on IG: @ahplottsthecoast, on X and Bluesky: @ahplotts, and at her own website: www.ahplottsthecoast.com where she writes about life on the California coast. This is her first publication.

CATS JUST DON'T CARE
by A.H. Plotts

I sit and watch the house burn and all I can think is that I'm hungry. Cozy and warm from the heat of the flames licking the sky, and from the tongue in my mouth slick on my own black fur. It is good, like when My People stroke me. My People watching, waiting out here with me. Not the people screaming in the building on fire.

My People said, "We'll always come back," and they did. Obviously. "Don't worry," My People told me at the door to The Outside. Scratch, scratch, scratch under my chin where it is good to feel. "We'll come back. We'll always come back for you." And The Outside took them.

The Inside was quiet and dark. I waited. I'm always waiting for something good to eat. Unless I'm on the hunt. Me and my tongue. I tasted the air where the barest flavor of Man and Woman still lingered. My own smell and theirs was everywhere I walked or slept. I stayed where my own smell was strongest. Curled into a tight ball in the warm blankets fighting the cold. Sounds and flavors in the air I didn't recognize came and went. Things Inside moved around me and went away. Other things—*other people things*—replaced them. I hid then, in the dark, cool place, below the footsteps. My People's smells and flavors left me. Just like when My People were swallowed by the hole to The Outside.

One Little Woman found me, in the cool dark place. It cooed to me.

It smelled delicious.

"Oh Kitty, Kitty," It said. "Pretty Kitty. Don't be scared." It left me food for my tongue, and I ate it. It wasn't enough.

Some Big People came and talked about me not to me.

"It must have been their pet, the people who lived here before us."

"It must be hungry, all trapped down here for so long. Should we bring it upstairs?"

"Black cats are bad luck. Better leave it down here."

I made the Little Woman speak for me. I'd already brought It under my spell. "Can't we keep her? She looks so scared. So alone."

But I was not alone. I was waiting. My People were coming, like they said they would. "Kitty, Kitty, don't you worry. It's just a short trip," My People said, before The Outside took them. "We'll be back. We'll always come back for you." So, I stayed, to get whatever morsel My People might bring back for me.

How long has it been? I have no sense of time. It doesn't matter. Light-dark. Sleep-awake. Sleep some more. Piss and shit. Hunt. Hunt. Feed. That's what matters. The Little Woman treated me like the Good Kitty that It thought I was. It brought me food for my tongue, and I ate it. And waited.

One day it happened. I think it was day. At least they *looked* like My People when they came down the stairs. They also looked like the Other Things that flit around me all the time. The Things that crawl up the walls and fly through the ceiling. Those things I'm most afraid of.

My People couldn't touch anything. Not stroke my shiny black fur. Not talk with their mouths but they could show me that they were angry with the Other People upstairs. My People needed me to do what they couldn't do themselves.

What did I care? Those People upstairs were not My People. That Place was not their home. Not that any of it mattered to me, except for the promise of food for my tongue. I could sense My People thinking their slow, sludgy thoughts that amounted to the same conclusion.

Why it was so dark upstairs I do not know. It was easy to push the candles over. One tap with my paw and it was done. Every candle in the house fell so easily. Thump thumped so silently down on the crinkly papers that sounded like bones breaking when I walked on them. That sound made my tongue and my mouth wet even before the flames came.

Now I'm in The Outside. I'm not eating so I'm bathing and watching That Place burn to the ground. My tongue tastes the smoked wood and roasted meat in my dark fur, and I'm hungry. My People must be excited, too. They shimmer and quake in the light of the full moon, like the shiny things they used to dangle in front of me to play with. I thought the screaming coming from That Place would never stop but I'm glad it's done. The wait is over.

Jordan King-Lacroix is a Jewish writer from the Blue Mountains, just outside Sydney, Australia. His first book, the non-fiction *Ugly: A Bikie's Life*, was published by Penguin-Random House in 2021, and his short story, *"The Last Chosen"*, in the *Jewish Futures anthology* (Fantastic Books, 2023), was well-received by critics. When not writing, he can be seen gigging around Sydney in his punk band, *The Limited*.

JUDGE

by Jordan King-Lacroix

I have this cat,
this big black cat,
this big black three-legged cat,
this big black three-legged cat that I adopted
from a rescue shelter.
He was already named Judge when I got him.

He's a stately beast,
         with claws the size of butcher's knives.
Even with his missing limb,
he could probably take down a polar bear.
I'm pretty sure he already has.
He comes home with blood on his claws,
and a new scar,
no word at all of where he's been.
        But something died in the night.
        I can hear them dying in my dreams.

He was run down by a delivery van,
the vet took the leg to save his life.

Now he sits on my couch's armrest,
seeking revenge in the night.

And occasionally begging for treats.

Cailín Frankland (she/they) is a British-American writer and public health professional based in Baltimore, Maryland. Their literary criticism has appeared in *The First Line Literary Magazine* and their flash fiction has appeared in *Flash Frog Magazine and Black Hare Press's Dark Moments* series. They live with their spouse, two old lady cats, a rotating cast of foster animals, and a 70-pound pit-bull affectionately known as Baby. You can find Cailín on X at @cailin_sm or contact them via email at cailinfrankland@gmail.com.

SCHRÖDINGER'S DINNER
by Cailín Frankland

It all began when I fed your grandfather to the cat.

I know it sounds strange now, but at the time it felt like the perfect solution—I had a dead body in need of disposal, and had just ran out of Schrödinger's wet food that morning. You remember Schrödinger, don't you? With the black fur and that darling little white spot on his chest? He was probably a kitten the last time you saw him, now that I think about it. Anyway, it was already past his dinner time, a fact of which he had no qualms reminding me in a series of ungodly wails—Schrödinger has many virtues, but patience was not among them. I knew he was about ten minutes from tearing apart one of my pillows in protest, and the closest pet store was closed for the holiday. What was I supposed to do, feed him the emergency stash of dry kibble? I'm not a monster.

Never mind where I got the bone saw, that's not important right now.

Unfortunately, my good-for-nothing husband of fifty years decided to inconvenience me one last time by dying in the living room, his corpse splayed out on that hideous white shag rug he insisted upon when we moved in. Don't get me wrong—I'd take any excuse to rid myself of it, as it had already picked up its fair share of wine stains and Schrödinger's endless shedding dyed the thing a blotchy grey despite my best efforts to keep it clean. But a bloodstain would hardly improve the look, I didn't have a replacement handy, and no man dead or alive would catch me with bare floors.

All this to say that I dragged the body to the bathroom.

It took longer than I anticipated to get Grandad cut down into manageable chunks, and even longer to solve the puzzle of getting all the pieces into my freezer without a stray foot or finger blocking the door hinge. And then there was the matter of bleaching and scrubbing the bathtub down, all while Schrödinger perched on the lid of the toilet seat nibbling on the cheek fat I'd given him to tide him over. He seemed to enjoy the spectacle of it all, or maybe he was just judging my technique—cats are inscrutable in that way, with their big yellow eyes and questionable motives.

By the time I had finished cleaning up, the sun was setting and I could hear trick-or-treaters laughing out on the street—I picked up the bowl of chocolates I had left by the door that morning and headed out onto the driveway to greet them. And so that's how I spent my first evening as a widow—curtsying to little princesses and feigning fear of toddlers in little pointed hats, children with eye patches and plastic swords. It was only after all the fun was over that it occurred to me that I had forgotten to take off the apron I had been wearing all afternoon, stained red and brown with dried blood and various other bodily fluids.

It's unbelievable, the things you can get away with on Halloween.

It took a long time to run out of Grandad—he sat there in my freezer resolutely for months on end as I gradually wore his mass down, one muscle group at a time. Schrödinger seemed to take well to his new diet, and God knows I appreciated the peace and quiet, the extra space in the bed where my pet food once snored next to me. All was well, and I'm big enough to admit that I got complacent— perhaps even a little smug in my ingenuity.

When I got down to the last appendage—a big block of thigh tucked at the back of my bottom-most freezer drawer—I decided to start weaning Schrödinger off the man meat, mixing some of his old wet food into his dinner in increasing proportions. He didn't seem to notice at first, but around the time about a third of his breakfast was back to chicken he stopped eating it, nibbling at the edges before pushing the bowl away or knocking it over. More disturbingly, his fur started to change—his white spot seemed to be getting bigger, encroaching on the sea of black that covered the rest of his body. He started sleeping more, following me around less—sometimes I would walk into the kitchen to find him staring at the freezer longingly. He'd push the contents of his bowl away as if the poultry was tainting them.

There was only one thing for it—I had to kill again.

It's one thing to dispose of a corpse, it's another thing entirely to plan a murder. In retrospect, I had lucked out with your grandfather's death—he was retired and had little in the way of family and friends, as you well know, so a few well-placed emails and text messages effectively wrote him out of the living world without so much as a phone call (as much as I would have liked to hear from you and your mother during my so-called bereavement, but that's neither here nor there). I knew that I wouldn't have the advantage of knowing my next victim's passwords and habits, and at the rate of Schrödinger's appetite I didn't have time to do my research. I needed an accomplice—someone close enough to the victim to know their movements, but aggrieved enough to want them dead.

And that's how I found myself browsing the marital records of sex offenders in my zip code. Depressingly, I was spoiled for choice.

It all actually went pretty smoothly from there—I approached my target's wife in the supermarket, invited her over for wine, and soon enough she was spilling her whole life story out on my kitchen table. It was dawning on me that Schrödinger's dietary requirements had the potential to do the whole neighborhood a public service. I sat with her all night, wiping away her tears and refilling her glass (eventually we switched from wine to the hard stuff). By morning we had hatched a plan.

I'll spare you the gore here, but it's safe to say that by Schrödinger's standards, that poor woman's husband was delicious.

Now from there I figured I would simply wait until Schrödinger got down to our most recent victim's last limb before even bothering to plot my next kill, but it seems life had another plan for me. Only six weeks had passed since my accomplice's widowing, when I found her cousin standing on my doorstep, biting her nails and glancing behind her every few seconds in the way women tend to do in a world of men.

I was furious at first. I had given my last accomplice explicit instructions not to speak of our little arrangement. And yet here was a perfect stranger at my door recounting every detail of my crime back to me with a humble admiration that would have been disturbing if I weren't so easily flattered. I realized with a start that this woman had no intentions of turning me in—she was requesting my services.

I had plenty of good reasons to say no—it was too soon, her relationship with my last accomplice could arouse suspicion, there was barely any room in the freezer. But the woman seemed so desperate, and quite frankly, she knew too much for me to turn her away and hope she drove somewhere other than the police station. So I let her in, and soon enough her husband's body was lying in my bathtub waiting to be carved up.

Your mother always called me a pushover—I guess she was right about that.

So now you see that I never intended to get into this line of work—I don't consider myself particularly entrepreneurial, and I'm not so much violent as I am pragmatic. But word of mouth is a powerful thing, and the demand was there—from the women and girls who found their way to me through whispers exchanged behind closed doors, and certainly from the soot-colored feline yowling at the freezer all hours of the night. It stopped feeling like a crime, really. More like a hobby, or a chore.

You probably have questions. How many men have I killed? I lost count a while ago, but you could dig up the bones under the deck and do the math if you want. How have I never been caught? The police are bad at their jobs. How do I sleep at night, knowing that if I hadn't run out of cat food one Halloween ten years ago, dozens of dead men would still be very much alive? Soundly. I sleep well.

The doctors told me I had six months—if you're reading this, they were actually right for once and I'm rotting away in my bedroom as Schrödinger tucks into an eyeball or two. Promise me you won't get emotional about it, because I'm not upset in the slightest—everyone dies eventually, and quite frankly living is an exhausting task at my age. I'm on borrowed time, and after playing the reaper for so long, I'd quite like to meet her for myself.

The house is yours now. You'll find a spare key under the planter sitting on the left side of the back door—the lock is a little stiff but if you give the door handle a firm shake you shouldn't have any problems getting in. The garbage truck comes on Tuesdays, recycling is on Thursdays, and the electricity and water bills should come in the mail at the end of each month. It's a lovely neighborhood, really, especially this time of year—when Halloween comes around I highly recommend pulling a chair out front to meet the trick-or-treaters. If they ask, tell them I'm on vacation.

I have no intentions of haunting you, but I think it's important that you know the truth—you can do with this information what you wish. My only request is that you keep the front garden neat and the driveway clear, since nothing depreciates a house's value quite as quickly as squandered curb appeal and I don't want a penny spent on this house going to waste. I hope you enjoy your inheritance!

Oh, and don't forget to feed the cat.

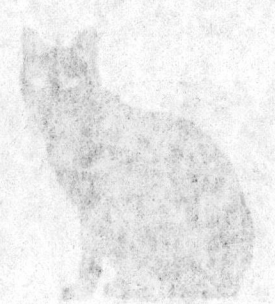

Loren Rhoads is the author of almost thirty stories about Alondra DeCourval. Those stories have appeared in *Best New Horror, Strange California, Occult Detective magazine, Weirdbook,* and others, including Loren's short story collection *Unsafe Words*. She is the author or co-author of five novels, including the *As Above, So Below* duology about a succubus who falls in love with an angel. Loren lives in San Francisco with Nocturne and Amulet, only one of which is a black cat. Her latest book is the nonfiction guide *222 Cemeteries to See Before You Die*. Follow Loren's adventures or learn more about her work at lorenrhoads.com.

BLACK AS SHADOW, RED AS BLOOD, WHITE AS BONE
by *Loren Rhoads*

The zoo's parking lot was nearly empty when Alondra DeCourval stepped out of her cab. She walked past the shuttered ticket window and paused at the unattended entry gate to allow a family of five to exit before her. The parents looked at her strangely, so Alondra wished them, "Good evening."

"Evening," the father answered as the mother hustled the curious kids past. No one asked why Alondra was going in after closing time.

She picked up a map from the entry kiosk and traced her path with a fingertip. As she wound her way through the zoo, long shadows chased away the last of the sunlight. An eerie roar echoed through the gathering dark, a shattering growl of power that was copied and amplified by other big cats. An atavistic shiver rolled through Alondra's body. She paused to listen, breathing deeply, fighting the instinct to turn and flee.

Since the accident several years earlier, the zoo had completed a highly advertised remodeling. No longer could visitors lean over the grottos to look down on the big cats. Now bulletproof glass separated all the predatory animals from the crowds.

A peacock screamed in the twilight. The bird stepped into Alondra's path, shaking loose its magnificent tail. When

Alondra didn't offer him food, he paraded onward into the shadows.

Eventually the twining path led Alondra to the big cat enclosures. She found a knot of keepers gathered on the terrace outside. One of the women, dressed in a zoo-branded jacket, stepped forward to greet her. "I'm Dana Faison. Thank you for coming."

Alondra smiled. "That roaring is really impressive. Do they do that every night?"

"Yes. It's one of the ways they bond. Everyone is checking in with each other as they settle in for the night."

"How much longer before the haunting begins?"

Dana winced, but checked her watch. "It shouldn't be long now."

The keepers ceased chatting. Alondra realized that the lions had also fallen silent. The lion she could see crept on his elbows behind a boulder and hunkered down. As the last of the afterglow fled the sky, the temperature dropped and a chill wormed down her back. It was beginning.

Four partially transparent young men strolled out of the darkness, shouting and laughing and shoving each other.

An animal roared like nothing she had heard so far. The hoarse vocalization skated down five tones, settling into a rumbling huff that Alondra could feel in her bones. The sound was so loud, so close, it was impossible not to feel like prey. She breathed deeply, grounding herself. The keepers huddled closer to each other.

In contrast, the semi-transparent young men burst into raucous laughter. One of them, dressed in a hoodie depicting a snarling orange bear, growled back at the shadow of a large cat pacing in front of the cowering lion. The black jaguar growled even louder than before. The lion—the only creature alive inside the enclosure—shrank backward from the shadows like a kitten, making itself small.

The jaguar seemed to be half the size of the lion, lean and lithe, but his coloration made him flicker in and out of the darkness. His skull looked powerful and over-muscled, with a predator's jaw capable of crushing a skull like a walnut shell. His lengthy tail thrashed, whip-like.

The shadowy echoes of the men slouched over to the jaguar's enclosure. On the far side of the moat that separated them, the black cat paced across the grassy area from one wall to the other, wheeled, and trotted back the way he'd come, as if he was measuring the distance.

One young man roared at him again. He was bigger than the others, broader in the chest as if he lifted weights. Alondra judged him to be twenty-two or -three, slightly older than the others, and therefore had to act tougher.

The jaguar halted, staring at the invaders with eyes like glowing jade.

"Oh, shit, Walker," someone said. "You made it mad."

"Fuck it. Which one of us is in the cage?"

One of the keepers said, "I can't watch this."

Alondra's attention was yanked from the haunting to the knot of zoo staff clustered outside the enclosure's thick plate-glass wall. She wondered if any of them had watched this event play out before. How many had heard the stories but hadn't believed that it would happen again? As she regarded the zoo staff, wondering if she should say something to reassure them, the keeper who'd spoken up strode off into the deepening night. A moment later, a pair of women jogged after him.

Trapped in the replay of events from three years ago and oblivious to the interruption, one of the young men drank deeply from a tall can of beer. The jaguar roared again. The man flinched, spilling beer down his orange sweatshirt.

BLACK AS SHADOW, RED AS BLOOD, WHITE AS BONE

by Loren Rhoads

His friends laughed at him. Things might have gone differently if his manhood hadn't been insulted. Without a moment's consideration, he hurled the beer can. It passed through the bullet-proof glass as if the barrier wasn't there—as it had not been on that fateful night. The beer can crossed the moat and struck the jaguar's shoulder. It foamed over, spewing a puddle at his feet.

As if he sensed what had been coming, the youngest member of the transparent quartet said, "Fuck this." He ran through Alondra. She shivered at his touch. His spectre passed through—rather than among—the remaining knot of keepers, picking up speed as he sprinted toward the zoo's front gate.

The zoo had gone silent except for the echo of his retreating footfalls. One of the zookeepers unlimbered a tranquilizer rifle. He held it to his chest in both white-knuckled hands. Alondra wondered what good he thought that would do against the ghosts. Maybe the gun was his security blanket. Maybe he wished he'd been there, three years ago, and could've prevented what had happened.

A spectral young man's voice shook with adrenaline when he asked, "Where'd the panther go?"

The ghostly men shoved each other, shouting that someone had to go to the enclosure's edge. Someone had to look for the jaguar.

Before anyone could gather courage, the jaguar's paws grasped the top of the moat's wall. He hauled himself up silently. Clenched in his teeth was the crumpled beer can.

One of the men straight-up screamed. Two of them panicked and bolted—in the wrong direction, toward the back of the zoo where there was no exit to the street. The third froze in place, a rabbit before the jade green gaze of the big black cat.

The beer can dropped from the cat's jaws, clattering as it landed. Alondra readied a spell in her fingers, preparing to protect herself and the remaining zoo staff. Instead, the jaguar's gaze slid over her without seeing her.

The zookeeper fired his tranquilizer dart, but it passed through the cat without drawing his notice.

Instead, the cat sprang after the runners. He caught the hindmost man and rode his back to the ground. He seized his victim's skull in his mouth—the crunch of skull that followed made Alondra's heart stutter.

The noise was enough to galvanize the frozen man into a sprint. Either his whimpering or the motion caught the jaguar's attention. He abandoned his first victim and went back on the hunt.

The cat took the second man down by sweeping his legs from under him with one razor-tipped paw. The man twisted over as he fell, flailing, unable to coordinate a defense. When the jaguar roared into his face, he fainted. The cat swiped at him, shoving his limp head back and forth with its claws. It tore his cheek open to the bone but got no response.

Without a challenge, the jaguar lost interest. He rose from the prone man, stretched leisurely, and loped off after his final victim.

When the screaming finally, blessedly, stopped, Dana told Alondra, "This happens every year on the anniversary of Balam's escape."

Alondra nodded for her to continue. Dana wiped the tears from her face and drew a shaky breath. "They aren't ghosts. Brad, the kid that escaped before Balam attacked, is still alive. I mean, you saw him leave and heard him running away. He's alive to this day. And Henry…well, he's alive, too. Severely disfigured and he lost an eye. He'll never recover, but he survived."

BLACK AS SHADOW, RED AS BLOOD, WHITE AS BONE
by Loren Rhoads

"This is a residual haunting," Alondra explained. "When something traumatic happens, sometimes the emotions can imprint on the surroundings, like a recording on an old-fashioned tape. Those hauntings play back under a variety of conditions."

"How can we stop it?" an older man demanded.

"This is Christopher Matthews, our general manager," Dana explained to Alondra.

"We tried an exorcism last year," Matthews said. "Father Gabriel came down from St. Mary's. Nothing changed."

"There's no one to exorcize," Alondra said. "There are no spirits. No ghosts. Just emotions."

"So how can we 'erase' the tape?" Dana asked.

"When it happens in a house, sometimes a residual haunting can be cleared by remodeling, by moving the walls or replacing the staircase. Wherever the haunting occurs must be radically changed," Alondra suggested.

"We've already renovated Balam's enclosure," Matthews protested.

"Did you remove all the plants, all the dirt, all the stone?" Alondra asked. When no one responded immediately, she knew the answer was no. "That would be a start, but since the majority of the events take place out here, outside the enclosure, this terrace needs to be majorly altered, too. I wouldn't guarantee that will clear things, though. That night was so traumatic...and not so long ago. The haunting hasn't degraded at all. Nothing, not even the jaguar's eyes or the beer can, have lost any color."

Off across the zoo, the howler monkeys began to hoot at each other, building in volume before tapering back to silence. The peacock screeched again.

"What do you suggest we do?" Matthews demanded. "The neighbors hear the screaming every year. People always call the police to report it. The city is threatening a noise abatement lawsuit every year until we get it under control."

by Loren Rhoads

"Balam was an Amazonian jaguar, right?"

"Yes. But he was bred and born in the U.S., at the San Diego Zoo."

"That doesn't matter." Alondra fished her phone out of her jacket's heart pocket and opened the recording she had cued. A Mayan chant filled the silence. She let the recording play until Matthews shifted in irritation.

"That's Roberto Cocom," Alondra said. "He's a shaman who lives in Miami. You could try playing his recordings on a loop every night from sunset to sunrise. His prayer may be sufficient to change the vibrations here. Of course, you'll want to contact him, tell him what you're doing, and find out what kind of licensing fee he'd like."

"He a friend of yours, then?" Matthews snapped.

"We haven't met." Alondra looked up at Matthews. "It's okay that you're upset by this," she said. "Watching those young men die is awful."

"Upset!" Matthews repeated. "What upsets me is all this mumbo jumbo. Father Gabriel shouted himself hoarse and it made absolutely no difference."

"And then he suggested you call *me*," Alondra said calmly. "I doubt he would consider us friends." She gazed at the general manager, waiting for an apology she knew wouldn't be coming.

"He said you could fix it!"

"I've told you how."

Matthews stepped closer, looming over her. Alondra did nothing until he grabbed her arm. Then she released the protection spell she'd prepared earlier. An explosion of white light flung him backward, onto the recycled plastic surface of the terrace.

"You're assuming that because you paid me to consult on your haunting, I owe you anything more than my expertise, Mr. Matthews. I don't appreciate being threatened, menaced, or bullied. I'm not a charlatan and I've given you my recommendation, but you're not obligated to institute my suggestions. What you choose to do does not make my time any less valuable."

Matthews scrambled to his feet, shaking the hand that had touched her as if it had been burned. Behind him, Dana stifled a smirk.

"I could sit and meditate here for the next year and see if I can alter the atmosphere enough to erase the residual haunting, but I don't think that either of us would be happy with my being tied here," Alondra told him. "I believe you will get more satisfying results if you bring in someone with a hereditary connection to Balam's place of genetic origin. Of course, if you don't want to put your faith in my advice, go over Father Gabriel's head and bring in another exorcist. I'm sure the city—and the neighbors—will wait while you explore all your options."

Matthews had enough sense to act chastened, even if he didn't apologize. "You said you think the shaman *may* be able to help."

"When it comes to something like this, there are no guarantees," Alondra said, "other than if you do nothing, the haunting will repeat next year and the year after that and the year after that. Closing the zoo will not make it stop. Building apartments here will not make it stop. There are still Roman legions marching through York or, for that matter, Civil War skirmishes still being fought at Gettysburg."

Alondra scrolled through the numbers on her phone. She held it out so that Dana could copy Cocom's number into her own phone.

"I want you here next year," Matthews said. "If this shaman doesn't fix it, I want you to disrupt it somehow."

"I can try." Something occurred to her. "What happened to Balam's body after the police shot him?"

Matthews turned to Dana, who said, "The pelt and the skeleton went to the Field Museum in Chicago."

by Loren Rhoads

"Are they on display?"

"I don't know. I don't think so. I think they went into their specimen types collection, behind the scenes."

"Okay. If you can request them back, I can assemble a burial ritual that might drain some power from the haunting. If the jaguar spirit can reclaim its energy and rest, that might tilt the balance enough that the haunting will evaporate. I would start Cocom's chant sooner rather than later, though."

"All right," Matthews said, "let's start there. I'll call the Field curator and Cocom in the morning."

Flashlight beams crisscrossed the darkened zoo, drawing nearer. "We're over here," Dana called. Four armed and heavily armored police converged on them.

"Everything all right?" one asked.

"Same old, same old," Dana said.

"There were fewer calls this year. Either people are getting used to it or…"

Matthews coughed.

"…or they know to be away from home on this night."

"We're still trying to fix it," Dana promised.

One of the police raised the visor on his helmet. "I see you finally called Alondra."

Alondra smiled. "It's been a while, Officer Okello. Everything still quiet?"

"Thank you. Yes."

"You vouch for her?" Matthews asked.

"She cleared up some trouble in our locker room downtown. She'll fix your problem."

Alondra was grateful for the vote of confidence. She just hoped she could live up to it.

by Loren Rhoads

Alondra set the shovel aside when the grave was about two feet deep and three feet long. It didn't need to be deep. Either this was going to work or it wasn't, but if she had to dig things up later, she didn't want to have to go six feet down.

She arranged the turquoise pebbles in a starburst pattern. It wasn't the way a shaman would do it, but she was a witch and she had her own ways. She strewed herbs across the stones: bright yarrow and sharp-scented laurel and long sprigs of lavender. Then she lit the charcoal in her incense burner, blowing on it until the flame sunk in, and added three pearls of copal.

She turned to the shipping box at her feet. After she wrestled it open, she discovered when she lifted it from the tissue paper that the jaguar's pelt was not entirely black. Alondra saw the hint of rosettes beneath the shadows. She stroked the fur and said, "I'm sorry they taunted you. I'm sorry they insulted you. I'm sorry you were killed trying to protect your home."

Alondra placed the pelt gently into the newly dug grave. She tore a cardboard flap from the shipping box, then used it to fan the smoke rising from her incense burner over the grave. The sweet, earthy scent reminded her of another predator she'd encountered far from his home and family. She hoped he was at peace now.

Sitting at the edge of the grave, Alondra unwrapped the tissue from the jaguar's skull. Its ivory fangs were as long as her little fingers. With a shudder, she remembered the sound of the young man's skull being crushed in those teeth. She took a deep breath and shook herself.

From her messenger bag, Alondra took a large round stone as big as her fist and blacker than the jaguar's pelt. She fit the jet orb into the skull's mouth. She set the skull on her knee as she sorted out the red embroidery floss, then wound the floss in a web that would hold the jaw shut.

Finally, she turned the skull over in her hands and placed it upside down in the grave. She repeated the layer of herbs, then cast salt gathered from the Bolivian Salar de Uyuni across it all. Then she picked up the shovel and filled in the hole.

"Be free now," she said. "Be free." She repeated it until the sun was gone from the sky and the lions in the enclosures on either side of her began to roar their bedtime ritual.

The last step was to shove the grave marker into place. Using the shovel's handle as a lever, she rolled an unevenly shaped boulder atop the grave. Matthews told her that they were going to put a pair of fishing cats in here next. They should not be strong enough to uncover the grave.

When Alondra had finished the burial, Dana waited outside the enclosure with a bottle of Chilean Carménère and two coffee mugs. "I thought you could use a drink."

"Thank you." Alondra brushed off her hands and sat on the stone bench that faced the big cats' enclosure. After the lions settled down, she heard the low chanting of Cocom's prayer, played on a loop every night from closing time until dawn.

"Will it work?" Dana asked as she poured Alondra a hefty mugful of the deep red wine.

"I think so," Alondra said. She supposed they would find out for certain on the anniversary of Balam's escape.

Meredith Gladwell is a blogger and writer of poetry, short fiction and spiritual non-fiction. Her non-fiction work has appeared in *Sage Woman Magazine*. The culture, land and history of her native North Carolina inspire her work and her life. Meredith lives in Durham with her husband, son and, of course, cat. She is currently working on her first novel.

THE FAMILIAR
by Meredith Gladwell

In shadowed streets of cobbled stone,
A black cat prowls, but never alone.
Her mistress watches from her distant bower,
Their bond unbroken by mysterious power.

Nightly she hunts with fang and claw,
Keeping vermin in check, a silent law.
Yet fear breeds fast in ignorant minds,
As new-come monk dark purpose finds.

He speaks of evil in feline form,
Of witchcraft bringing a deadly storm.
The villagers heed, their hearts grow cold,
Forgetting protection centuries old.

They seek to end the cat's nightly prowl,
But death cannot claim this shadowy soul.
Nine lives are nothing to one so blessed,
Immortal, unscathed, though put through the test.

THE FAMILIAR *by Meredith Gladwell*

Locked away, the witch can only weep,
As rats run free and shadows creep.
The plague arrives on quiet feet,
Claiming lives down every street.

In emptied homes and silent halls,
The cat still prowls as darkness falls.
Two hearts still beat when all is done,
The witch, her familiar, and setting sun.

Andrea L. Staum is the author of the *Dragonchild Lore* series, *The Attic's Secret, Rogue's Kiss,* and has contributed to several anthologies. In order to avoid the mundane, she creates worlds and destroys empires in her mind and eventually translates them to the page. She lives in south central Wisconsin with her husband, children, and their overlords...err...cats.

JANIS AND NOODLE

by Andrea L. Staum

Tree branches slapped against the unlatched shutters as the wind howled. The horn panes had blown out several seasons ago allowing the draft to chill the cabin. The storm was getting worse and the clouds gave a dusk-like appearance to the day. The thatch was pulling from the roof, widening the already present holes.

Inside, the cabin's lone occupant struggled into an oversized backpack. Groaning as he settled the weight across his back, he forced his legs to straighten so he was standing at his full eight inches from the floor. Noodle lifted a tentative foot and immediately set it down without stepping forward.

Must get stronger. Noodle's legs buckled under the weight and he felt his belly hit the floor. Squirming his way out of the makeshift straps, he managed to pull himself free. His black tail swept back and forth as he stared at the travel sack stirring a tiny tornado of dust into the air. *Perhaps I don't really need so much.*

He considered his options as the wind picked up once more and a few droplets of rain landed on his whiskers from above. Swishing his tail in agitation, Noodle jumped to the table top and put his shoulder against a pot. Even though his limbs were sore from packing, he put his entire body into shifting the iron vessel under the new hole that was starting to form. He was running out of containers. There was getting to be more repairs than one cat could keep up with. Hopefully he could leave once the rain stopped, but not if he couldn't carry his pack. That was why he tried to maintain the cottage—without it, he had nowhere else to go.

Noodle finished setting out a few more pots and bowls to keep at least the ingredients and books dry. He had long given up on keeping the entire floor dry. He had a few paths that allowed him to keep his paws from getting wet, but the longer he stayed, the harder that was becoming. He curled up on the bed when it became too dark to make out the shapes outside the windows. Even his cat vision couldn't pierce the darkness of the forest in this storm.

What did I do to deserve this? He grumbled before covering his eyes with his tail and closed them. *Maybe tomorrow.* Something told him that he would be able to leave on the morrow, even if the exercises with the pack greatly countered that logic. He put the thought aside and tried to focus on the darkness and sleep.

Quality sleep hadn't been very common since Janis had left him on his own. Noodle missed the warmth from the fire and the occasional scritches to the back of his ears. He tried burrowing deeper under the blanket to avoid the chill that permeated his once cozy home, but his claws ripped the thin sheet causing straw to pop out. He sneezed at the mold and dust that puffed into the air. Once the dust settled, he wiggled into the straw for more cover and sighed. It was scratchy and stuck to his fur in odd places but it was a bit of insulation, so he willed himself to rest.

Warmth. That was hard to come by now. He wished he could get a fire going in the fireplace and stretch out on the stones in front of it like he always did when Janis was home. The bed gave him some relief, but it was nothing like fire warmed stones. It didn't matter inside or out, the chimney was always the best part of the cottage. It was what had drawn him here all those years ago.

It had been a day similar to today with the howling wind and blinding rain. He had been separated from his mother and littermates when they were moving to a drier home. The log they had been staying in near the creek, had flooded before sunrise. As a result, the five of them set out into the forest together. Usually their mother would have carried them singly but there wasn't time for that. He had been the runt and his mother chose to carry one of his sisters instead of him and he found himself trailing behind. The leaves were weighed down and showered waterfalls over the cats as they moved. His dark fur was soaked through in short order and he was miserable soggy shadow as they continued. It didn't take long for him to lose sight of his brother's white tipped tail. The smell of rotting vegetation and dirt were all that came through the rain. There was no trace of his mother's scent. He didn't know where or if they had turned off the path. All he could do was keep moving forward along the path he thought they had started on.

The trees soon receded as a clearing opened before him. He continued on until he came to a tower of rocks and wood unlike anything he had seen before. His mother had cautioned them about unusual structures and caves and he was hesitant to approach. Lightning struck a tree near him and he dashed to get away from the branch falling out of the canopy. He ended up against the stone tower, heat radiated from it and he curled up against it in exhaustion.

"Wha' 'ave we 'ere?" a voice cut through his sleep. Kneeling beside him was a creature unlike anything he had seen before. She was round like a bear, but the wind ruffled the fur that flowed off her shoulders as if it were a second skin. Her face was nearly naked of fur except for above her eyes and a few stray hairs on her chin. She opened her mouth in a snarl, but the teeth were hardly menacing. Picking him up by the scruff of his neck they stared into one another's eyes for the first time. "A wee kitteh? Thisn't the place fer yar kind."

He tried to swipe at her with his front paws, however, she had him at a disadvantage with his hind legs dangling in the air.

She chuckled and rubbed beneath his chin causing him to relax. "Thar ya be, limp as a noodle. Le's get ya inside." She tucked him into a pocket in the front of her strange coat and pulled the large branch that had scared him away from the stone chimney. She did a walk around the strange wood den, moving a few other fallen sticks and branches before opening a strange slab and stepping inside. A thick haze hung in the air of the small room they entered. "Good thing tha' branch blocked the chimney or ya mightn't 'ave made it. Tremblin' worse than a lass in her weddin' bed."

He could barely get his legs beneath him when she set him on the wooden platform surrounded by dried herbs and leaves.

"Jus' relax, ya lil noodle," the creature stated as she threw some logs into the stone area on the side of the odd cave. "Guess I'll just call ya Noodle. I'm Janis. Bah, ya can't understand wha' I'm sayin', now can ya?"

After she had sparked the fire up within the stone tower she returned to the table and pinched some chalk between her fingers, crumpled a leaf before spitting in her palm, and mixing it all with a drop of tree sap. She warmed the ingredients in her palm before rubbing a bit on his ears and mouth. She did the same with the remaining paste to her own cracked lips and ears. "Tha' should help. Can ya understand me now, Noodle?"

The kitten cocked his head to the side as the strange garbled words became much clearer to him. He opened his mouth to hiss. "Get away from me, monster!" he squeaked then cowered at the strange words that came from him.

"Ah, worked well." She ran a heavy hand over his back. "Now, jus' relax, Noodle, and tell ol' Janis how ya ended up here?"

He tried to arch his back to appear larger as she reached for him again, but the long strokes felt surprisingly nice. Almost like when his mother had licked him dry. He mewled, "Water rose moving to higher ground."

"I see. Been a right wicked storm," Janis said as she pulled a pot down from a higher shelf. "Lost track of yar mum, did ya?"

Noodle lowered himself to lay flat on the table. "Yes."

"Well, ya can stay with me until the storm passes and ya can look for her," she said as she busied herself with cutting some meat, tossing him a couple trimmings as she filled the pot with other ingredients and ignoring him most of that night except for offering him some broth and a little pile of moss to sleep in.

He had eyed the little pile oddly and tried to get comfortable in it. Even with the fire, Noodle found himself missing the warmth of his siblings and mother. Crawling out of his mossy haven, he ventured to the strange wooden structure Janis was growling in. His paws sunk as soon as they touched the soft blanket but eventually he made his way along her sleeping form to curl up in the crook of her neck.

Something in the air was tickling his nose. It was familiar and strange at the same time. A sneeze built and woke him from his memories. Another followed and he saw a fire burning low in the fireplace. Smoke was billowing off of the wet logs and a small form huddled over them. The figure turned while he was having his sneezing fit.

"Oh! Hello, kitty." The firelight haloed her, masking her features from him. The flash of a smile was followed by a relieved chuckle.

The way her shoulders relaxed when she saw him, should have put him at ease, but his back arched as he stood. He couldn't believe the creak of the door hadn't woken him. He hissed. "Who are you? Why are you in my home?"

The light flared as more of the white of the girl's eyes caught it. "You can talk?"

Noodle stepped back in surprise. His back legs slid off the edge of the mattress and he had to scramble to try to regain his position. "You can hear me?"

She nodded. "Not with my ears though."

The cat lost his battle with the edge of the bed and slid down to the floor. He crawled through the cobwebs beneath the bed and joined the girl at the hearth. "Ah, then the original spell has worn off, but not the telepathy."

"Telepathy? Are you a witch in hiding?" she asked as she reached down and removed a piece of web from his ear.

Noodle shook his head. Before he could explain, another sneezing fit overtook him.

Janis would have been very upset at the condition of the cottage. It had seemed disorganized but that wasn't the case. Everything had a place within. All the ingredients were carefully set on shelves or hung from the rafters. She never labeled anything but always seemed to know where everything she needed was. If there was ever a spiderweb or dust speck it was intentionally kept. The old woman even kept a family of mice for a short time within the walls so she could use their whiskers. "Everythin's useful," Janis explained as she mixed an ointment to clean one of the scrapes along his back. "It don't matter if anyone else can see it as long as I can."

In time Noodle began to understand the system. Originally he only meant to wait out the storm and then search out his mother and siblings, but the storm lasted nearly a week and all scent or imprint was long lost. He was saddened by the loss, but Janis was kind to him. She seemed to enjoy having someone to talk to. She wove those few spells and Noodle was able to talk back to her. There were two different spells in place. One gave him a voice while the other opened his mind allowing his thoughts to go to other beings. She called it telepathy.

"Tha's a good kitteh. Now ya won't feel so lonely when I'm gone. Can find a new friend."

"Gone?" Noodle asked as he swatted at a passing fly. "You are leaving?"

"Not anytime soon," she responded as she closed her book and settled in her rocking chair. "Some day though."

They never spoke of it again. Even when the time had come for her to leave him, Janis kept her spirits jolly and kept him from worrying. She just assured him that one day he'd have another friend. In the meantime he should keep the mice away. They had become quite demanding, wanting repayment for their whiskers.

"Oh!" the young woman said, for now that he was closer, he could tell she was not a child. Her pale blue eyes continued to sparkle in the firelight, but she seemed to be ignoring tears that were welling in the corners. She took a small brush from the pile of things she had set out to dry on the hearthstones and started to brush the dust from his fur. "What lush black fur when you're not covered in dust. I'd have sworn you were a ghost with as light as you were, but no wonder you're wheezing."

"I could only clean so much. I put the books up." He replied as indignantly as he could, but Noodle couldn't stop the purring that rumbled in his throat.

She looked around the room, noting the dried flowers and herbs hanging from the rafters and the mortar and pestle covered in dust and cobwebs in the center of the table. "This was the hag's cottage, wasn't it? Were you her pet?"

The purring stopped and the hair raised along his back. "Janis Wolfstrider was not a hag and I was no pet!"

She paused in her brushing and smiled sadly. "I'm sorry. The villagers referred to her as a witch or hag."

"Witch, maybe," Noodle conceded. "Hag, no."

"So she is dead?" Her head bowed and her chestnut colored hair fell forward. "I suppose we all knew that. When she stopped coming to the market a year and a half ago, we thought perhaps she had. I just hoped, perhaps, it was just that she had been sick too. Maybe she heard about things and was working on a cure."

Noodle hung his head. He didn't count time in years like the humans, but a year and a half sounded about right.

Janis' some day had come and gone nearly six seasons ago. Noodle sat at her side and retrieved whatever Janis asked him to. She had two spells she wanted to complete and he traveled farther into the forest alone than he had in a long time to find the ingredients.

Thankfully in the thirty-three seasons they shared together, Janis had taught him about the forest and explained how there was more to the world than their little cottage. She refused to take him with her to the market saying he would merely be underfoot despite his protests, however, she made sure he understood how to take care of himself in nature.

"Now Noodle, I can tell we're goin' our separate ways soon. These bones of mine won't suppor' me much longer. Been a long time comin'."

He placed a black paw on her wrist, the cool pads provided very little relief to her fevered skin.

Janis gave a crooked smile and set her other hand on his head. "Don' be sad, Noodle. I 'ave one last gift to give ya. Ya have a lot of skills and can use them for some good. This spell will make yar mind jus' as strong as a human's. Couple that with yer feline brain, no one'll be smarter." She cackled softly before coughs racked her body. Janis' hand tightened on the back of his neck to keep him in place.

Noodle's ears flattened against his head with worry as he waited for the coughs to subside. "Janis?"

"I'm a'right. Now be bit hard fer ya to manipulate things." She paused and flipped a few pages of her spellbook. "Ah, yes. May as well move things with yar mind as ya can speak with it." She snatched up a couple of things from the table and hummed to herself before shoving the paste between his teeth. "Chew that."

The vile glob stuck to the roof of his mouth and he had a hard time chewing it. Eventually it broke down and he was able to swallow it. His throat felt blocked by the thick sludge, but he eventually felt it settle heavy in his stomach. He twitched his tail in disgust and a few pages turned in her book.

Janis nodded. "Ag'in."

Noodle tilted his head and the book closed completely.

"Good," Janis said as she settled into her bed and closed her eyes. "That'll make up for not having thumbs." She gathered the ingredients for the second spell and laid them out. Her chest rattled as she breathed and she had to sit down several times. "Now it might take a bit to set in." She poured the liquid into his bowl and watched as he tentatively licked it up.

Noodle began to feel his mind unlock everything that he learned from Janis. All the incantations made sense. He understood now that she had always meant to do this for him. Her lessons had been subtle over the years, but it was very clear as the tincture warmed his stomach. He hadn't been a common cat for quite some time, but now he was something greater than he was. He would have asked Janis to explain, however, she was focused on gathering some more items. Looking at her he began to understand what she meant by leaving him and he pawed at her sleeve. "Maybe we could figure out how to make you better now that I'm smarter. I could help you."

She grinned her familiar grin as she mopped her forehead with a cloth. "There's one last spell to put in place. Just got to finish getting everything in order. We'll finish after a nap."

She pointed to the spell on the page and for the first time Noodle understood what all the squiggles meant: *Decompose.*

It would be the first spell he would do by himself when it was clear Janis was not going to awaken from her rest.

The woman pulled him onto her lap and settled closer to the fire. "I was hoping Janis would take me as her apprentice," she sighed, then straightened as if remembering something.

She looked into Noodle's green eyes. "I'm Eloise but most call me Ellie."

"Noodle," he replied. "No one ever journeys out here. The woods aren't very safe."

Ellie shrugged. "No one would miss me if something happened to me."

"No one?" He tilted his head.

She shook her head. "My parents died when the sweating disease swept through our village. I thought maybe the old ha—Janis—would be able to teach me something so I could help the sick should it happen again. I hoped she already knew about it and maybe had a cure to help the few who survived the first bout."

Noodle's ears perked. There had been some gossip among the crows that food was overly plentiful in the surrounding area, but it tasted funny. "You are all alone?"

Ellie nodded.

"Janis was my family." Noodle nestled into her arms. "I am alone too."

A thunder clap shook the walls of the cottage and Ellie buried her face into Noodle's back. The cat looked up at the falling rain through one of the ceiling holes. Yes, there had been a similar storm when Janis had claimed him. Maybe someone was looking out for him and Ellie after all.

Tears ran down Ellie's cheeks and her grip tightened on Noodle. "I guess I'll have to go to the next town to find someone to teach me."

Noodle licked at one of the salty tears to get her to look at him. "What if I taught you? I know what's in every book in this cottage and while my magic is a little different than witchcraft, I'm sure I can explain it to you."

Ellie pulled back to look at him, "You could?"

Noodle purred, his chest puffing slightly at the thought, as he moved his head to her forehead and rubbed it. "If a witch can teach a cat, a cat can teach you."

Chris Opyr is a neurodivergent writer of horror and science fiction and is the author of the *Wishing Shelf* award-winning, psychological horror novella, *Calling Mr. Nelson Pugh*. Through their fiction, Chris explores issues of otherness, anxieties, and neurodivergence. After a brief career in television story-producing, they repented and returned to writing prose fiction. Currently, Chris lives in North Carolina with their wife, daughter, and a menagerie of obstinate animals, including their three cats, John, Margaret, and Mr. Cat. You can find Chris Opyr on X @cwhutton and on Instagram @chrisopyr.

ILL LUCK
by Chris Opyr

"Come here, Zuzu." I pat a cozy spot on the mattress. I know better than to bark commands at him like a dog, yet I do so anyway. Perhaps I've grown lonelier of late than I am wont to admit. There is a comfort in hearing a voice in the house, even if it is only my own.

My cat simply stares at me from the doorway. He perches on three legs, his remaining front leg canted towards his center of mass to maintain balance. The vet said he'd adjust quickly to the loss of a limb. Apparently, she was right. After cancer took that left leg, I had viewed each day with Zuzu as a blessing. Four years on now and he gets by better than me most days and is far more fit than I, still lean and agile as ever. Sure, I'm lean once more, but I've slowed considerably.

I prop myself up against my pillows, content to watch him. His eyes squint at me and I smile. I read somewhere once that when a cat keeps its eyes half-closed it is a sign that they are relaxed and comfortable in your company. I squint my eyes back hoping to convey the same to him.

If I didn't know better, I'd swear he was much younger. His fur, however, betrays the passage of time. He still wears a fine black coat, but the finish does not shine as bright as it once did. Even more obvious a tell, that fur has thinned on his face. I can't see it from here, but I know it. Age, I fear, has set its sights on both of us. I hope, however, that he might yet have a few good years left in him.

I pat the empty space beside me once more. There is plenty of room for him, it is a large bed, much too large for one person alone. Even so, I cling to the right side of the mattress out of decades of habit, leaving a good four feet of space for the cat.

"Time for bed, Zuzu."

His black brows furrow. This isn't a squint of comfort, but something more judgmental. Some say he has an evil eye, but I say Zuzu possesses a discerning glare, one that quickly surmises the measure of a person. The neighbors may believe otherwise, but they are wrong about him. They always have been.

As I wait, he holds steady in the doorway, his tail swishing back and forth. For a moment, I think that maybe I am wrong. Perhaps he is cross after all.

I pat the bed again, but Zuzu does not come. No matter. He will come when it suits him. Rolling to my side, I click on the lamp and pull a novel from my nightstand, then slip on my reading glasses. The book's an old tattered affair, the spine creased and the edges of the cover faded from years of thumbing the pages—a prized copy of Mary Shelly's *Frankenstein*. I've read it times beyond count, and yet one more won't hurt. One more read may be the best for which I can hope anyway.

I part the spine flipping to my marked spot and finding myself upon the final chapter. I choke back a faint chuckle. Lowering the book ever so slightly, I peer over its pages to my friend, Zuzu, still swishing his tail in the doorway.

"Appropriate," I whisper, uncertain if I am talking to myself or to him. He is my only real company now, save for the occasional visitation from my son when he and his husband come down from the ranch. Met himself a cowboy in college and never had a chance. I'm not bitter that he left;

I'm happy for him. I have Zuzu and my books to keep me company, and if my joints aren't hurting too badly, there is always the garden out back. The wild encroaches upon it once more, weeds and vines strangling out years of maintenance, but I manage to keep a patch clear for tomatoes and a pepper plant or two.

Billy should be landing in the morning. I had offered to pick him up, but I knew he'd refuse. He'll be renting a car at the airport or maybe catching one of those Ubers. I'm not sure if Robert will be coming down with him, but I suppose it doesn't matter.

I attempt to return to my book, pushing aside all thoughts of my son. We're in the cemetery now, Dr. Frankenstein and I, pledging our revenge. As we finish, that whisper parts the night and the monster is made known, but we all know the true monster of the story. I can't focus anyway. There is too much at stake.

Zuzu is my best friend, perhaps my only friend left.

The afternoon sun stabs down, blinding me as I tilt my head up and wipe the sweat from my brow. I wince and curse and drop the rotary tiller as I do. The handle whacks me in the knee as it falls, and I curse some more.

From the deck, Margaret yells at me.

"Two for the swear jar, Lee!"

"Christ's sake, Margaret," I yell back.

"Make that three."

I mutter under my breath making sure she can't hear me this time. Billy is sixteen years old now and I'm certain he has both heard and said worse. Hell, I'm not even sure where he is. He's made himself scarce ever since we moved. Still, whether he is here to hear it or not, a deal is a deal.

Margaret wants me to tone it down and I told her that I would.

"Sure, honey," I call back, massaging my knee and casting an angry glance towards the sky. "Three it is," I say, then return my gaze to the work at hand. I've pulled out and hacked away most of the weeds in a five-by-five patch, but now I have to break up and loosen the soil if it's ever going to make a decent garden.

The clink of ice in a glass sounds behind me and I know that Margaret is pouring herself some sweet tea. I think that I might take a break and join her, and so I heave up the rotary tiller, catching it by the center of the pole, ready to haul it off to the garage.

That's when I spot him.

The cat tiptoes along my backyard fence with a graceful ease, the sun shining off of his black coat. He pauses for a moment, his eyes locking with mine, and I hold very still, hoping not to scare him off. He bears a slightly too small frame and I fear that he may not be well fed.

Slowly setting down my tiller, I kneel and cluck my tongue a few times, then tap the dirt patch at my feet. He makes no move towards me, but I can see him weighing the option.

"Shoo!"

My new neighbor, a hairy man with a stout frame and a thicker head, barrels over shouting and waving his arms at the cat. I don't know his name yet, but I can tell instantly that I do not like him.

"Shoo," he shouts again, and the cat bolts away.

"It's just a cat," I say.

"Bad luck is what it is."

Yep. That confirms it. I do not like this man one bit.

"What ya got there," he asks motioning towards the patch of dirt that I've cleared, but I'm not having it.

"Just finishing up." I say, and leave him behind, taking my tools to the garage.

When I return, Margaret reminds me that I need to make nice with the neighbors, but if that is any measure of their character then I'd rather be a social pariah. As she tries to explain the intricacies of neighborly decorum, a movement catches my eye across the yard.

"What do we have here?" I kneel again, as the cat inches out from behind a bush.

"Ps, ps, ps," I call and the cat inches closer still. Behind me, Margaret stops and watches as little-by-little the cat approaches. When he comes within a couple feet of us, he flops down and rolls over showing his belly. Yes, he and I are going to be fast friends. Tentatively I reach out, and, when he shows no sign of running, I softly scritch his belly. He pivots into the motion, shifting and arching his back in the dirt.

"Lee, don't you dare."

"What?"

"You know what. We are not adopting that cat."

I raise my hands in defeat. What Margaret wants, I give. The little guy has a collar anyway, and collars mean owners.

He slips to his feet and head boops my leg, not yet done with attention.

"Of course not, dear," I say as I run a hand over his side, feeling his ribs all too clearly. I shift my other hand to his collar searching for a tag. There I find a name engraved: Zuzu. On the back is a number.

"Let me just make a quick call."

That call resulted in an automated 'this number is no longer in service' message. After a few questions around the neighborhood, however, Zuzu's situation became clear.

Everyone in Pine Hills knew Zuzu. They still do. More, my thick-headed neighbor, who I later learned was named

Erik, was not the only one to believe that Zuzu was a harbinger of ill luck. Zuzu's last owner died of unknown causes and the more superstitious lot within Pine Hills had taken to blaming the cat. Even those that didn't buy into such lunacy still seemed reluctant to take the boy in—but of course, there was more to Zuzu's story, even if I did not know it then. So, the kind-hearted souls of Pine Hills let Zuzu run wild, but they did not feed him and they did not welcome him.

Me, however, well, it only took one storm until I installed a cat door to my sunroom. By the next storm, I found Zuzu curled up and content on a cat tree I brought in on the off chance he accepted my offer of shelter. Within a few weeks, he had settled in and claimed the room as his own.

I ease my bookmark in place and glance towards the doorway. Frankenstein has arrived at his ship amid the icy north. Zuzu, on the other hand, has abandoned his post, the doorway now empty.

"Ps, ps, ps," I call. Usually he is quick to bed, but tonight he seems more reluctant than usual. Perhaps he is not the only one.

I rise and make my way downstairs to the kitchen, half expecting to find Zuzu waiting at his bowl. No luck there. The bowl sits empty, and I should remedy that, but first I need to satisfy my curiosity. Moving slow and quiet, I ease into the living room where I find Zuzu sitting upon the windowsill staring out into the night. He turns as I enter, but his black coat blends into the shadows, just a darker shade amid the endless night, so that all I can make out are his two golden eyes, wide and alert, staring back at me from the darkness.

I pause to observe and a second later he returns his attention to the window and the yard beyond. I can tell he misses the freedom of being an outdoor cat. Zuzu was never meant to be caged. At the time, however, it was the best that I could do for him.

I hang up the phone with a perfunctory I love you. I say the words, and I mean them, but Billy and I don't speak much lately. A great tension lies between us now. Margaret tells me I need to do better, and I want to, but I don't understand. I know times are changing and social norms with them, but the world doesn't make sense to me anymore.

Margaret's disappointment reads clear on her face. She's told me to accept Billy for who he is, and I'm trying, but it isn't enough. My shoulders sag, and I let out a deep sigh as I prepare for the argument that is coming.

Only the argument never comes.

An evening breeze blows through the house, our windows open to the autumn air, but this breeze brings with it the smell of smoke. At first, I suspect Erik next door has forgotten to extinguish his burn pile, leaves still crackling from the pit out back, but then I notice the amber hue outside and the flicker of flames. Perhaps he did fail to extinguish the leaves, but this fire has grown greater than a fall burn.

I doubt there is much that I can do, but I speed down the stairs, nonetheless. I can hear the sirens approaching. Logically, I should stay back. I don't even like the man, but he is my neighbor.

In moments I am in his yard yelling his name, careful not to get too close, the heat of the flames licking uncomfortably near. The fire engulfs the whole house, dancing through the upstairs windows and straining towards the stars. I cannot imagine anyone surviving.

Other neighbors start to gather as well, the street filling with a bleary-eyed community. I call again and again, but no answer comes. By the roadside, a commotion begins. A small clutch of neighbors stand, some pointing, while others turn their faces away, as if to shield themselves from some horrible sight.

I know that I shouldn't look, that whatever they have witnessed, it doesn't bear seeing, but I look anyway. Around the corner of the property a door hangs ajar, just off Erik's garage. Here too the flames feed on the now charred and rippling siding, but it is not the flames that draw everyone's gaze.

A few feet away Erik lies face down in the dirt, his skin crisped and bubbled, a sickly scent of barbeque in the air. Beside him lies Zuzu, snuggled against Erik's outstretched arm. He cocks his head back, as if sensing me, then licks Erik's arm and rises in a great arch of the back and forward stretch of the paws before bounding my way.

My gut twists. I am sorry for Erik, but I worry more for my cat. The neighbors won't forget this. Zuzu will have to stay inside moving forward. I can't let him out again. I can't risk them hurting him.

Not my Zuzu.

I leave Zuzu at the window, returning to the kitchen and scooping a cup of dry food into his bowl. Instantly he is there, ready to eat. He seems happy, but still, I worry about him.

Dropping the scoop back into his bag of food, I lean over and check the cat door. The flap swings open then shut as I tap it. This door leads from the house proper to the sunroom, but the cat door to the outside has remained closed ever since the fire. Another has been installed as well. This third door leads to his cat run, which I have painstakingly built over the six years since Erik died. The neighbors want it taken down, but I know what they really want. They want Zuzu. Well, I don't have an HOA, so they can kiss my ass.

Assured that he has free reign to reach his catio and enjoy the night air, I return to bed and the waiting pages of my final chapter. This time Zuzu follows me, hopping up beside me as I lay down, and snuggling into the crook of my arm.

The doorbell rings, but I don't bother to rise. I am lying on the futon in the sunroom, Zuzu nestled on my chest. The afternoon light cuts through the window and lands on Zuzu's glistening fur. He purrs and makes biscuits with his paws as he basks in the warming light.

The doorbell rings again, but still I do not rise. Margaret will get it if someone must. Billy is off at college now. It's his junior year and he and some kid from Montana are rooming together in a little apartment just off campus. Robert something. I can't quite recall the boy's name. It can be hard to focus lately.

The chemo has ravaged my system, though I suppose not as much as the cancer. Either way, exhaustion clings to every ounce of me and I have no will to rise.

The doorbell rings once more, and then at last I hear the door open.

"Yes?" Margaret asks. I can tell by the tone of her voice that she is less than happy to see our visitor. The moment I hear his voice, my mood sours as well. Erik.

"It's about the cat," he starts. I try to focus, but the sun is so warm and my meds are kicking in. I need my sleep.

A moment later I stir again. The voices in the foyer echo louder now. I fear I better get up and I am about to rise, when I catch the retreat in Erik's voice.

"You should know," he says. "That's all."

"That an old lady died and another lady adopted her cat. That's called life."

"It's called death, ma'am, and it follows that cat wherever he goes."

Sounds ominous, I think, but it also sounds like B.S. The door closes and I try to relax once more, Zuzu still on my chest. My body aches all over, and I worry about what is ahead, but Zuzu is here with me now and he has made the pain of the past year so much more bearable.

Victor and his monster face their final confrontation and my final chapter draws near to a close. I should finish, but my eyes grow weary. As if sensing my exhaustion, Zuzu rises from his nest in my arm and hops onto my chest. Every day I am still amazed at how well he has recovered from the loss of his leg. He settles on top of me and I feel renewed, at least for a moment.

Swallowing back the lump in my throat, I try to focus on the printout in my hands. Cancer. *Fuck cancer.*

The vet says the tumor is too large, too precariously located. It can be removed but it requires an amputation. I'm a grown man. I can't help but to wonder why this hurts so much. I'm trying to hold it together, but Margaret has been dead barely two months. I'm not sure that I can lose Zuzu, too.

The neighbors blame him, of course, but Margaret died from a car accident. She may have walked away, but it was a resulting aneurysm that took her in her sleep. I wish that she would have died in the hospital if she had to die, just so her death wouldn't feed the Pine Hills insanity.

I wipe away the budding tears from my eyes. Margaret will never have the chance to walk our Billy down the aisle. I'll walk him now in her place. She'd want that and I realize that I want that, too. He's happy and this is enough for me. Still, Billy will be leaving now, starting a new life in Montana and I'll be all alone.

No, I can't lose Zuzu, too.

He rests with his head nuzzled into the nook beneath my chin, his body softly vibrating in time with his rhythmic purring.

The monster fades into darkness and I close the book for the last time. Billy will be by in the morning. I made sure of that. I can't have it any other way. I hate that he will have to find me, but I can't risk it being one of the neighbors. They cannot be trusted.

Four years have gone since my Margaret passed away, four years since Zuzu lost his leg. He saw me through my cancer and I through his, but my cancer is back now. I'm too far gone, its progression too advanced. This time I'm not prepared for the chemo. My son knows Zuzu is his for the taking. He and his husband have plenty of open space on that big ranch of theirs, space where no one knows Zuzu and he can be free again. I think he'd like that.

Zuzu shifts his head and I feel his teeth on my cheek as he gives me a soft love nibble. It took me years, but I understand him now. The neighbors were right, in part. Zuzu does bring death—his was never a gift of ill luck, but rather a gift of mercy.

"It's time," I say, and I can see it in those eyes. He understands me, too.

S. Michael Wilson (he/him) is a poet and author currently based out of Texas, where he works as a tech support specialist in the medical device industry. He is the editor of the book *Monster Rally* and the author of the book *Performed by Lugosi*. His poetry, short fiction, and non-fiction have appeared in numerous anthologies and magazines, including *Shriek Freak Quarterly*, *Uncle John's Flush Fiction*, and *Butcher Knives* and *Body Counts*. He was also the First Prize Winner of the 2016 Wergle Flomp Humor Poetry Contest for his poem *Dick Candles*. When in between writing projects, he can be found co-hosting the film review podcast/vodcast *Moviesucktastic* with his childhood friend Joey.

You can find him at https://www.livingseveredhead.com or Moviesucktastic.com.

THE HOOD
by S. Michael Wilson

The stray black cats that congregate in the alleys
and dense foliage of this dormant, frosty suburb
copulate violently on the sleet-speckled
hood, still warm from that evening's commute,
of my late-model Volkswagen Jetta.

In the primitive twilight of the late winter eve,
through the milky glaze of my bathroom window,
I look down on a street of sterile sheets, comfortless
blankets of snow and ice, and bear helpless
witness to their unspeakable savagery.

Pulsing masses of matted, patchwork fur,
misshapen abominations, bodies twisted and distorted
from years of urban feral inbreeding, a tangled mess
of polydactyl paws and acrocephalic skulls,
undulating in rhythm to their primal urges.

Polluted canines sink into mangy, flea-scabbed flesh.
Yowls of feline carnality penetrate the frigid
air, piercing shrieks of rapturous intent. The smoke
of their fetid breath mingles with the subtle steam
emitting from my cooling engine's sleeping beneath.

That my abandoned vehicle should arouse passions
in such foul perversions of nature replaces my disgust
with an impotent jealousy sharper than the claws etching
the arcane symbols of ecstatic star maps
into the fading red paint of my rapidly idling inertia.

S.S.N. Smith (she/her) is a fiction and romantic-comedy writer living in Eastern Washington with her wife and three dogs. She currently serves as a vehicle mechanic in the United States Air Force. She received her B.A. in Humanities and is currently pursuing a Master of Arts in Liberal Studies with a focus on literary arts. Her passion for writing started when she was a child when her mother had her scribble down the long stories she told, even before she could write. In her free time, if she is not with her family, you can find a guitar in her hands, either jamming or making repairs.

THE WRITER
by S.S.N. Smith

"Clark," Alex called.

She stood from her desk. Her thumbs ached from tapping across her phone screen, pushing out words, the latest idea burning in her mind. She left the only room in the 600 sq. ft. apartment she shared with her lazy roommate. The hallway was ten feet long and dimly lit. She needed to change the second lightbulb, but never remembered when she left the hallway. She never thought about what was behind her, beyond her, the ideas she had swelled in her mind.

"My laptop," she entered the living room/kitchen combo. "Have you seen it?"

Clark was lying on the couch, his long limbs stretched out, yawning like he had just woken up. He probably did, he slept more than anyone Alex knew. The television was on, but the volume was so low it was almost inaudible. Clark used the television to drown out the sound of typing, but when Alex was in her room or using her phone to birth a new story, the talking heads on the screen usually whispered in the apartment.

Clark looked up, his face neutral as always, "Table."

The silver computer was waiting for her on the dining table, which acted as a writing table. She never had a true dining experience, not here, not in this apartment. Alex used most surfaces to write, most chairs as a place to create a lap for her laptop. Everything in her house was used to get her thoughts out and help her write her next work.

"I have something going," Alex said. "It's a love story about two office workers. One is the boss's daughter, who has had everything handed to her. The other worked her way up from nothing."

"Sounds angsty," Clark replied.

"Angst sells," she said. "I've been on my phone typing. The story revealed itself to me while I was on the toilet."

That was something she would never share with her fans, that her best ideas usually came when she was in the bathroom with nothing to do but think. Not that she wasn't always bored and trying to come up with a new idea. But new ideas, like children, only come when you are not expecting them, a wild night with too much vodka, as opposed to a well-planned event. But it didn't matter; Alex had all the time in the world to birth her happy little accidents now that her job was writing.

When she was twenty-one, after years of posting her work online, she wrote a book that became a best-seller. It was followed by two more novels that did just okay, then by a fourth that did well, then by a collection of short stories that became a best seller. She afforded her one-bedroom, three-quarters-bath apartment and everything needed to keep her and Clark alive off the sales of those books. They didn't need much space, she only needed her laptop to write, and Clark needed a television and a place to nap.

"I have five thousand words already," Alex said as she opened her laptop. "Charger?"

"In the kitchen," Clark gestured towards the pitiful kitchen.

The charger was plugged into the socket where the toaster was usually powered. Alex remembered a writing frenzy last night when she was cooking and writing simultaneously. The words to a short story popped up while she was glazing onions, and since the dish didn't require much work, she thought it would be fine to write and cook. She finished the short story, and five thousand "needs to be edited" words were saved in the drafts folder on the laptop. The onions were overcooked.

"This is a new book?" Clark made his way to the kitchen.

Alex yanked her charger from the wall, "Yes. I thought it might be a short story, but it started pouring out of me. The scenes wouldn't stop."

Clark took a drink, "That's good. It's always good when it comes out in a stream."

Alex hummed, taking her charger to the table. She looked out the window. The alley was four stories below, it had two dumpsters and a pile of wood pallets, the wood swelled from the rains these last few days. She'd been to that alley a few times. She'd been to many places, but it was hard to remember sometimes. She thought maybe she hadn't been outside in a little while.

It wasn't that she was a recluse, she enjoyed going outside. She enjoyed being at a cafe, sipping a latte and reading the latest novel by her favorite authors, but lately, it seemed like she hardly ventured outdoors. Lately, she felt stuck in a loop of writing, sleeping, writing, dreaming and writing some more. Lately, Alex has had a hard time remembering what *lately* meant.

There were times when she would forget to eat. She would sit at the table two feet from the kitchen and forget what food was. Her mouth would be so dry, her tongue stuck to her pallet and her lips cracked, but she didn't move to take a sip of water. She would write until her bladder called out but refused to get up until the idea was finally out of her mind. She had to finish the chapter, even if her eyes burned from staring at the screen, even if her fingers were sore and callused from typing. The words were what mattered, the thoughts and ideas, the feelings behind them. Her fans were waiting. She was waiting.

She opened her laptop and connected to her docs.

"Water, Alex," Clark told her.

"Right," she said.

Now, she had a routine, and Clark had to catch her before she sat down. Alex got up to fill her water bottle and grab a pack of cherry pop-tarts to set on the table. Clark would remind her to take a few bites now and again.

Sometimes, she thought Clark and his reminders were the only reason she didn't forget to shower or die from dehydration. Clark was her best friend. Honestly, if she thought about it, she would realize that maybe he was her only friend. She had her family, but they only spoke when they needed something. She had more friends at one point. She used to call people, used to have people over, talk and laugh about so many things. She used to do things other than writing.

It was a flash, the way the sun was now low in the sky, and her water was half gone, but the foil packet toaster pastry remained unopened. She had another ten thousand words, and there were a few chapters about the two women having feelings for each other but not wanting to act on them. She was on a roll and close to something great when a knock came to her door.

Alex looked to Clark, "For you?"

"Is it ever?" he chuckled.

She reached the door, a few feet from where she was writing. Looking out the fisheye view of the peephole, Alex saw her neighbor's forehead.

"It's Melanie," Alex whispered.

Melanie knocked again. "Hello, Alexandria?" she called from the hallway.

Alex sighed. Melanie knew she was home because she was always home. Melanie always knew. Alex didn't have an optional least, she didn't feel like she did. She opened the door.

"Hey, Melanie."

"Alexandria, I hope I haven't caught you at a bad time."

Melanie made Alex feel awkward. She was a smaller woman with tiny hands and arms that seemed too thin to carry anything, let alone the giant casserole dish she was holding. She had dishwater brown hair and rain-cloud-colored eyes, perpetually curious. Her glasses were thin, clear plastic, and Alex sometimes wondered if they were prescriptions or props.

"I made too much lasagna," the dish was covered in tinfoil.

Alex nodded, "Oh no."

"Yeah, silly me," she snickered. "Thought I'd come to see if my favorite author was hungry."

Alex's stomach growled, giving her away. She wanted to gut-punch herself.

Melanie often brought food to her at all times of the day. She brought coffee from down the street in the mornings, just as Alex liked it: two creams, one sugar, sprinkle of cinnamon. She offered to remove the garbage because she was 'heading to the bins anyway.' She made little menorah cookies during the holidays and always brought them over. Until now, Alex did a good job keeping Melanie in the hallway, only letting her cross the threshold a few times. But here she was with her giant dish of lasagna, which smelled great, and for the first time, for some strange reason, Alex moved out of the doorway and allowed Melanie fully into her apartment.

"It's funny how our apartments are mirror images of each other," Melanie said, walking in like she had been there a million times. "It's like a backwards world."

"Yeah, sure," Alex rubbed the back of her neck.

Melanie set the dish on the counter and pulled back the foil, steam rose from the food. "My friends were supposed to come over to watch that new show, the one everyone is watching. I don't keep up with those things. As you know, I'm a reader." She looked at Alex and grinned. "But they had to cancel. So. More for us."

Alex worked on getting plates and forks together and set them next to the food. She looked around, trying to find Clark, but of course, he wasn't around. He was never around when anyone else was around.

"This is my mom's recipe, but I made it with beef, not a 50/50 mix of beef and pork. I know how important your faith is to you."

Alex handed her a spatula, "I thought you made it for your friends."

"I did," she stuck the utensil in. "One of my friends, she doesn't eat pork either, not for religious reasons, something about how smart pigs are. But I wanted you to know that this was good to eat."

She took the slice Melanie served up, "Thank you."

"Of course. I do love cooking."

Alex took her plate and gestured for them to go to the table. Before they could sit, Melanie went for the computer.

"Alexandria, you're writing something new?"

Alex slammed the top down, "Sorry." She did feel bad— the quickness felt rude. "I don't like anyone reading my stuff until it's done."

"Right," Melanie grinned. "But it is new, yes?"

Alex took her seat, "Yes, it's a new story."

"Oh good," Melanie clapped her hands, then sat across from Alex. "I reread *Break My Heart* last week, and, of course, it broke my heart yet again."

Alex ate a mouthful of food to avoid speaking about her work. Melanie was about to say something when her eyes were drawn to the couch. Alex looked over, her eyes going wide.

"I didn't know you had a cat," Melanie said.

Alex swallowed hard, looked at the couch, and then back to Melanie. "Yes." She looked back at the couch, "I have a cat."

"He's cute," Melanie said. "He, yeah?"

"Yes," Alex nodded slowly.

Melanie smiled, "What's his name?"

Alex's mouth felt dry as she answered, "Clark."

Clark jumped off the couch, walked over to the table, and rubbed his body against Melanie's leg. He meowed and purred a little.

"He's sweet," Melanie said.

Alex looked down at Clark, "He is."

"Do you like the lasagna?"

Alex almost forgot they were eating, her mind fixated on Clark. "Yes, it's great."

"Oh good," Melanie happily ate another bite. "Last time my friend came over to watch a movie, I made a roasted chicken. I use mayonnaise and Greek yogurt as oil and fat for moisture."

Clark had moved to the kitchen. Alex had an auto feeder for his dry food but needed to open a can for his wet food. Clark was usually the one to remind her of this task. It was right around dinner time, and Alex felt compelled to get up and go for the can in the cupboard.

"Sorry, I have to feed Clark," she said.

Melanie waved her off, "Of course, your little buddy comes first."

Clark wasn't her "little buddy." Clark was his own person. Alex was more like *his* little buddy.

"Did you know that black cats were always associated with magic," Melanie continued without being prompted. "Some people think they give witches their powers."

Alex looked down at Clark, who looked pleased and not annoyed. "I didn't know that. But I don't believe in magic."

"No?"

"Not really," Alex emptied a can of food into a small bowl, setting it on the ground for Clark to chow down. "I think science can explain almost anything."

Melanie waited for her to sit back down, "Science can't explain how you're such a good author. There has to be something that gives you the ability to write what's in so many people's hearts and minds. The feeling you bring to your characters, oh Alexandria, you make hearts melt." She held her hand to her chest. "I didn't think love existed until I read, *She Calls Back*. I read it so many times. I felt like you were speaking to me."

Alex stiffened, her body suddenly cold. She hated talking about her writing with fans. Clark was the only one who truly understood her and her work.

"Thanks, Melanie. I always appreciate it."

"And you're writing now," she looked at the closed laptop. "Wanna give me a hint?"

It felt like her brain was itching as the question hit her ear and entered her skull. "No, talking about my work always takes me out of it."

"Not even a teensy-weensy little hint?" Melanie tried to bat her eyes, but it was more like she was blinking quickly.

Alex wrinkled her nose, "Sorry, I can't."

"Well, dang," Melanie giggled. "Maybe I'll have to bring you more food. Or just come over and cook for you. Then I can get a glimpse into your mind."

"It's not that interesting," Alex scoffed.

Melanie jutted out her hand, grabbing Alex's, squeezing. "It's the most interesting mind in the world."

Alex tried to pull her hand back, but the grip was so tight. "Thank you." Finally, she let go as Clark approached the table and jumped into Alex's lap.

"Anyway," Melanie's laugh died in her throat. "I am baking a cake tomorrow. My coworkers sometimes come over to play board games. If they don't eat it all, I'll bring you a slice."

Alex nodded, "Sounds good."

Melanie placed the tinfoil back over the casserole dish, but not before taking another slice and wrapping it up on a plate for Alex later. Melanie asked if Alex needed her to do the dishes, which Alex refused, so she walked her to the door.

"Better let you get back to your writing," Melanie smiled.

Alex pressed her lips together and nodded, "Thanks for the lasagna."

"Literally anytime," she chuckled. "I love cooking, especially for my favorite author. You know I can also…"

"Melanie," Alex insisted. "I do need to get back to writing."

"Right," she sighed. "Well, goodnight, Alexandria."

Alex opened the door, "Night, Melanie and thanks again."

The door closed, and Alex rushed across the apartment to the couch, where Clark was sitting on the arm.

"What the hell, man?"

Clark whipped his tail around his body, "What?"

"Melanie," Alex said, then looked behind her, feeling her neighbor was still around, creeping up on her. "She could see you."

"And?" Clark asked.

Alex threw her hands in the air, "You're not real, Clark!"

"We've been over this," he responded.

"No," she pointed a finger at him. "Don't do that. You're a talking cat. I know I'm crazy. I know because I talk to a cat. They gave me those pills, but I felt so blocked." She scratched her scalp. "And I don't need them, because I'm the only one who can see you, and I just never mention it. But if she can see you, then what does that make her?"

"You talk to me and feed me," he told her.

She shrugged, "I wouldn't let you starve."

"I appreciate you," he jumped over to the table. "Have you ever wondered where the cat food goes if I'm not a real cat eating it daily?"

"Not really," Alex laughed, feeling kind of silly now that she was thinking about it. "I always thought maybe it was part of the delusion. I imagine feeding you cat food like I imagine we are having this conversation."

"I think it's more likely," Clark sat next to her laptop. "I'm a real cat—the delusion is you talking to me."

Alex considered the idea.

"Did Melanie talk to me?" he asked.

She considered that too, "No."

Clark pawed at the laptop. "Don't worry about these things, Alex. Your story. You were getting to the next chapter."

"Right," Alex's mind immediately cleared all thoughts of her talking cat and her neighbor who could see him but not talk to him.

She was on a good part, her main characters finding that hint of feelings they had for each other. This part is where she made readers feel like they were part of the crush, like they were listening to a friend tell them about how much they hated their coworker, knowing that bubbling beneath the surface was love ready to reveal itself, but they knew that hate was love. She was good at the whole secret crush that the characters themselves didn't know about. She needed to focus on that, not the real world.

Alex opened her laptop and read over the last three pages she wrote, then started the next chapter. That feeling she always got began to take over. The words started spilling out of her, the scenes playing in her mind, crying to get out of that dark place and onto the paper. Alex typed, knowing she would be at this for the rest of the night.

Once Alex had been writing for a few hours, Clark headed for the entryway coat closet. He pushed past the shoes thrown haphazardly on the ground and past the coat that covered the hole in the wall. He moved easily through the plaster and studs and into the apartment next door—towards the kitchen that smelled like cooked tomatoes.

"Clark!" Melanie jumped, her hand reaching her heart, "You scared me."

"You really freaked her out," he told her as he jumped on the counter. "You've never seen me before."

She waved her hand and returned to squirting soap into the glass dish. "It's time. She needs to know that she can trust me with everything—with her mind and thoughts. Her heart."

Clark looked around the small apartment. Plain furniture and blank walls, the only thing that stuck out was a bookshelf filled with paperback novels, the only hard covers by A.G. Durwood, Clark's best friend.

"I can take care of her," Melanie continued. "I can remind her to eat and drink water and make sure she sleeps. I can do all of that, and it starts with her knowing that I don't think she's crazy."

"She wouldn't think she was crazy if you didn't send me over there to keep her writing," he said.

"You keep her company!" Melanie snapped, slamming the scrub brush into the sink. She turned to Clark, took a deep, calming breath, and scratched a finger under his little furry chin. "Sorry, I don't mean to get upset."

Clark purred, "No, I'm sorry."

As if it never happened, Melanie went back to scrubbing the dish.

"You make sure she is safe and healthy until she's ready. I know you're her friend, Clark. You want what's best for her. I want that, too. I want to love her and help her write the best romance novel that's ever been written. And yeah, I want her to base a character off of me and our love, and that's not a lot to ask after everything I've done for her." She rinsed the dish and placed it in the drying rack, turning to the cat still perched on the counter. "She let me in tonight, that's a step closer. Next, I'll cook dinner. Then I'll stay over. Then, I'll be the one reading her rough drafts. And it all starts with you," she rubbed behind his ears. "The spell is working, she writes all the time, and it's beautiful work. It won't be long now."

Clark purred at her nails scratched the thick black hair on his neck. He had no idea how to tell her that Alex would never allow that to happen.

Scott Urban has had fiction, poetry, and reviews published throughout numerous print and electronic outlets. Recent work has appeared in *EXQUISITE DEATH, THE HORROR ZINE, MIDNIGHT TALES, BINDWEED*, and *FALLING STAR*. With Martin H. Greenberg, he co-edited the *DAW* anthology *THE CONSPIRACY FILES*. His early fiction is collected as *BLOODY SHOW*, available through Amazon's Kindle Store. A former public school teacher and administrator, he now writes full-time in southeastern Ohio.

GARBO

by Scott Urban

"Ray?" Marjorie's voice rose higher in pitch with each repetition of her husband's name. "*Ray?*"

"What?" His running footsteps set the floor shaking. "What is it?" Wearing grimy work clothes, Ray Carter slid to a stop. His eyes darted around the kitchen, alert for a grease fire or sparking outlet. In his right hand he still held the hammer he'd been using to hang pictures in the family room.

"Here!" Marjorie stood in the door that opened on their backyard. "I opened the door to let in Garbo, and... this was here." Her nose was wrinkled in disgust.

Coming up beside her, Ray had trouble making out what lay on the narrow concrete stoop outside their door. Since it wasn't in flight, it looked more like a clod of dirt than a sparrow. Legs like withered sticks jutted from underneath the torso. The head was turned at an unnatural angle.

Marjorie gave a start when Ray began chuckling. "What are you laughing at?" He pointed back in the kitchen to a tiny mound of dark, bristly fur that even now squatted beside a saucer and bobbed up and down lapping milk. "Garbo brought us a housewarming present."

A shudder ran through Marjorie's shoulders. "Tell her I don't care for it, will you?" She went back to the sink, wiping her hands on a dishtowel as if she had squeezed the life out of the bird herself. "And please take care of *that*."

Still laughing at his wife's squeamishness, Ray stepped outside, wondering if he could remember where he had last seen the shovel. Marjorie started to rinse off more dishes, while the little black puffball of a kitten nibbled the finely chopped tuna her owners had set out for her.

The house, the lot, and even the kitten represented a new beginning. Taken together, they were the culmination of a decade's worth of work—Ray as a software programming troubleshooter and Marjorie as a hospital dietitian. When the two of them first drove out to take a look, they did not see a brick and stucco ranch home on three-quarters of an acre. Instead, they saw a haven, fashioned from fifteen-hour workdays, an escape from the cramped one bedroom walk-up apartment–and the rigid, almost fanatical, postponement of purchases or a family.

They worked so long, with such conflicting schedules, that they often awoke wondering who this other person was sharing the bed. But in the last month, Ray secured a contract to oversee cybersecurity for a quickly expanding financial institution. With the additional income and the renewed sense of security, they purchased their first home. Silently, internally, both hoped it would bring them back together without making them face the intervening years of being strangers.

On their final trip from the city to their new home, Marjorie patted Ray's thigh. "Slow down! I want to see something!"

Ray followed the aim of her finger and only just had time to read a handwritten sign tacked to a utility pole. Large red letters spelled out "KITTENS-FREE!"

Ray groaned but pulled over to the shoulder and backed their SUV to the dirt driveway. "You don't really want to do this?" he asked without hope.

"Please?" Marjorie was almost clapping her hands in anticipation. "Can't we just look at them?"

"A cat? Honey, you know they have dander, and they tear things up, and they bring fleas in the house—"

She put her left hand over his right on the steering wheel. "Ray, it would make me happy. I've always wanted a kitten, and we could never have one in the apartment."

He realized he hadn't seen his wife display so much emotion in many months. The change was welcome, even if he didn't particularly care for the direction of her interest. Sighing, he pulled into the driveway.

The tobacco farmer who met them at the side of the house looked as if he might have been packed together from field dirt, leaf mold, and fertilizer. He greeted them with a nearly toothless grin and brought them to a shack that only remained standing because the walls had fallen in on each other, partially propping all of them up. In the soft loam and weeds within, a gray mother cat nursed eight or so jostling balls of fur. She looked up and then away in haughty disdain at so rude an intrusion.

A strident yet firm 'mew' made them turn around. A black kitten, scorning its mother's milk, was taking high steps among the dandelions and crabgrass. Responding to the streak of independence, Marj leaned over, picked up the explorer, and brought it to her breast. The kitten opened its mouth and *mew*-ed once more, revealing tiny needle-like teeth. It looked like nothing so much as a cotton-ball dipped into a well of Indian ink, except for a white ruff across its shoulders where it might have been held by its mother during the dying process. Then it snuggled down in the crook of Marj's elbow as if it knew it belonged there. She laughed and looked up at Ray. He was startled by the tears in the corners of her eyes.

"Like her?" the farmer asked. "She's yours. Hell, you can take 'em all if you want!"

Smiling and shaking hands, the couple, along with the new addition to their family, got back in the vehicle. Marj couldn't stop stroking the gleaming fur, which stood out in all directions. "Isn't she cute?" The last word came out *kee-yute*. The animal's ears, almost as tall as the head itself, swiveled around like radar dishes.

Ray rolled his eyes. "You realize we're going to have to pick up a sandbox, kitty litter, food dish, flea collar, license—"

Marj was undaunted. "I can pick all of that up after work tomorrow. I'm sure she'll be fine with us tonight." She held the kitten aloft and turned her right and left appraisingly. "Now we need a name—"

"A decent one. Not something so cute it makes me puke every time you call her. Not Snookums—"

"Or Katerina—"

"Or Lady's Sable Bernadette—"

They both chuckled. Ray took his eyes off the road long enough to give the kitten a long, hard look. "She does have a vaguely aristocratic air to her."

"And look at this." Marjorie pointed to a thin yoke of white fur that draped across the kitten nape and shoulders. "Looks like a lady's stole."

"Well, we're both movie fans. What about Greta?"

"As in *Anna Karenina*? *The Painted Veil*?" Marjorie titled her head. "No, not Greta… but what about Garbo?"

Ray slapped the dashboard. "I like it! It's got a good ring to it." He reached over and ran his fingers down the purring form for the first time. "How ya doin', Garbo? Gonna come live with us for a while?"

The diminutive kitten looked up at Ray as if she somehow understood the import of the words. She blinked once, twice, then put her head back on Marj's arm.

"I want to be left—a-*lone*," Marj drawled, and the pair howled with laughter as if they'd just remembered how.

All of their furniture was in place, but it was going to take weeks of work to unpack the rest of their belongings. They opened boxes like children at Christmas, amazed with the removal of each sheet of wrapping paper. Garbo eased around their ankles, sometimes nearly tripping them as they tried to keep from crushing the tiny sinuous form.

Then, one morning, Marjorie opened the door to find a dead sparrow—

"You know," she said that night as both got ready for bed, "that bird must have already been dead for a while."

"What do you mean?" Ray tugged the spread back and slipped in the sheets.

"Think about it. Even soaking wet, Garbo can only weigh about a pound a half. Even if she somehow pounced on a bird, I don't think she would have been able to hold or kill it. The sparrow would have flapped, kicked and fought and Garbo would have backed off."

Ray shrugged. "I guess you're right. Either that, or we've got one hell of a hunter on our hands." Before she could say anything else he leaned over and kissed her—and before long they weren't thinking about the kitten anymore.

On the third morning following, Marjorie didn't call for Ray. She wasn't certain she trusted her voice not to rise into a frenzied shriek. She went to the study and stood in the entrance.

"Ray," she said flatly. He was absorbed in hooking up his entertainment system, and she had to repeat his name to make him look up. "I need you to come with me."

He opened his mouth to ask her what was going on, but when he saw the expression on her face he simply rose and followed her. On the stoop at the back kitchen door lay a carcass—a doe, perhaps three years old. "What is it, Ray? What's going on?"

Her voice told him she was close to losing it, so he gently pushed her back inside. "Don't worry. I'll take care of it."

He shut the door and knelt beside the dead animal. He had expected to find a bullet hole, but the doe's throat had been savaged. As he looked to the right, he could see the trail left in the sandy soil where the carcass had been dragged out of the woods and up to the house. But the wide swath obliterated the tracks of whoever delivered the doe.

The door reopened. "I'm all right," she assured him. "I won't go off the deep end."

Ray nodded. "I'm trying to figure out what brought this down. It looks as if it might have been attacked by a wolf or a cougar."

Garbo leapt out from between Marj's feet and began sniffing the nose of the deer. "But we're not supposed to have any of those around here!"

He tried to ignore the panicky note in his wife's voice. "I know. And more than that, I can't figure out what brought it to our door."

"You don't think—" she began hesitantly.

"What?" Ray absently scooped up the kitten and stroked it, setting its purring engine into action.

"You don't think this could be someone's idea of a practical joke, do you? Or maybe someone killed the deer behind our house and left it here as—some sort of offering?"

Ray stood up, shaking his head. "I can't imagine how a man could have killed a deer this way." Garbo leapt to the ground and Ray brushed his hands against the seat of his pants. "I'm going to bury it. Then I'm going down the road to talk to Mr. Wertzler. Maybe he saw someone—or something—suspicious."

When they signed the contract on the house, the real estate agent informed them of one close neighbor, a Mr. Wertzler. They had yet to see or meet him. His house was fifty yards farther on the opposite side of the road. Ray was already walking down the shoulder when he heard a winded panting behind him.

He turned and gave Marj a stern look. "I thought you were busy. I really don't need you to come."

"I want to meet him too." A rustle in the leaves at their feet alerted them to a third presence. "Someone else doesn't want to be *left alone*, either."

Ray glanced at his wife and the tiny kitten but didn't put up any more resistance. Wertzler's house sat closer to the road than their own. A high chain link fence enclosed the backyard. The house was much older than theirs and hadn't been kept up well. They walked up rickety steps to a narrow porch. Ray knocked—and the couple immediately stepped back as a deafening chorus of barking thundered from inside. Marj picked up Garbo and cradled the kitten in her arms. They heard claws scrabbling on the opposite side of the door, but it didn't seem as if anyone was going to answer.

The door opened abruptly. A stooped, older man held the door in one hand and a cane in the other. He glowered at them from under jutting brows. A nimbus of white hair ringed his otherwise bald scalp. Behind him two huge Dobermans pranced frantically, trying to get outside. One of them poked its muzzle around the man's side, caught sight of Garbo, and nearly exploded across the threshold. Garbo stood up in Marjorie's arms, the claws sinking through her sleeves and into her flesh. Kitten and woman howled simultaneously, as Garbo jumped from her arms and darted down the steps.

"Phantom!" The old man's voice was heavily accented, something mid-European. "Back! Heel, boy!" Only by dropping the cane and tugging the dog's collar was Wertzler able to keep the pinscher inside.

"Mr. Wertzler?" Ray hesitantly held out his hand. "Sorry about all that—"

"Phantom! Ulysses!" Wertzler wasn't even looking at the couple. "Quiet!"

"I'm Ray," he began again as the man turned around. "This is my wife Marjorie. We've moved into the house up the road."

Wertzler sniffed and looked past them as if he didn't quite believe the house was there. "Yes, yes. Can I help you?" His tone was curt—and it was obvious he longed to shut the door.

"We're sorry to bother you, but something rather strange happened this morning. We found a carcass of a deer on our back porch, and we were wondering if you saw or heard anything suspicious or out of the ordinary last night."

Wertzler had to shout to make himself heard over the deep-throated yelps of his dogs. "I didn't see anything! And I'd appreciate it if you wouldn't return. Since my wife passed away, I find it difficult talking to other people. I can't open my door to you again. Good day!"

They found the door suddenly in their faces. Behind it they heard their neighbor yelling at the dogs.

"Jesus Christ!" Ray threw his hands up into the air. "What a fuckin' Scrooge! What did he have up his butt?"

Marj was biting her lower lip. "I'm not sure I like this, Ray. We should have checked this out before we moved in. I don't like the idea of little kids near those dogs."

They stepped off the porch and began walking back. As they did, they were startled once more by fierce, staccato barking behind them. They turned to see the Dobermans flinging themselves again and again at the chain link fence. It was almost as if the pinschers couldn't believe there was something holding them back.

"Bastard!" Ray snapped. "He let them outside the minute he shut the door!"

He started to flip the bird at the gloomy edifice, but Marj caught his arm and pulled him toward home.

They wanted to work in the yard the next day, but a light drizzle kept them indoors, cleaning the fireplace and hanging new wallpaper in the bathroom. Garbo continued to explore and needed to be let in and out all day long. She didn't seem to mind the rain. Shortly after five p.m., as the couple prepared dinner, they heard a harried knocking at their front door.

Marj turned to Ray with a worried expression. "Who could that be?"

"I don't know. Find your cell phone, just in case." He headed out of the kitchen.

"Be careful!" Marj called after him, uncertain why she felt the need to caution him.

Ray stood on tiptoe and peered through the glass panes set across the top of their front door. He saw a bent form in a threadbare hat and old-fashioned rain slicker. Wertzler's simmering eyes were fixed on the knob. Ray opened the door. "Good evening, Mr. Wertzler—" he began, then he realized there was something he had not seen through the window.

Wertzler was jabbing with the tip of his cane at the body of a dead Doberman on the Carters' front stoop. Fresh blood, diluted by standing puddles, glowed pink in the light from the foyer. "You—*shit eater!*" Wertzler invested each word with poisoned animosity. "My Phantom did you no harm. Why—why have you done this to me?"

210

Ray opened his mouth, tried to find the words to defend himself, but couldn't come up with anything adequate. The old man gripped the dog's collar and yanked the front half of the ponderous canine up off the stoop. Ray's eyes went wide at the evidence of strength in the old man's arms.

"You can't think—I had anything to do with this?" Ray finally managed to say. He sensed a presence behind him and felt Marj's hand on his shoulder.

"What's going on here?" she asked, then bit off a cry as she saw the dead animal.

Garbo came up behind them and sat on her haunches. She watched the confrontation for a moment, then began licking her right paw.

Wertzler shook the Doberman as if it were a dishrag. "I let Phantom and Ulysses out an hour ago. After a while I heard them barking at something. Their barks became screams—screams of pain!" Brackish water sprayed from the dog's body onto the foyer's parquet floor and Ray himself. "I went outside. Ulysses had been hurt. He was licking his wounds. There was a bend in the fence where Phantom had been dragged out of the yard." Ray grimaced and stepped back. "When I went out front, I found a trail of blood. It led me here—and now I find my Phantom, dead, on your doorstep!" The old man's face was flushed, his fleshy lips trembled.

"Hold on a minute." Ray held his hands up. "Just wait a second. I didn't do anything to your damn dog—"

"I know you hate me. I know you hate my dogs. But this, this is… inhuman—!" Blood trickled down Wertzler's sleeve, ran under his slicker. "This is the work of a butcher! I have learned many things in my day, and I swear I will find a way to pay you back for this—barbarity!"

"You crazy lunatic—!" Ray shook his finger in Wertzler's face. "I think you better start walkin' home right now." Garbo slipped around Ray's feet and ran outside.

Wertzler backed off the stoop, dragging the mutilated carcass with him. "Slaughtering a poor dog," he mumbled. "Are you not even human?"

"Take it home!" shouted Ray. He slammed the door so hard the entire wall vibrated. "That insane fuckwad!" Hands balled up into fists, he spun around, looking for somewhere to vent his frustration. "How *dare* he come here and threaten us!"

Marj stepped between his arms and hugged him. "Calm down, calm down," she said soothingly. "Something's going on—Wertzler just doesn't realize it yet."

Ray put his trembling hands against his wife's back. "What do you mean?"

"There might be—a person around here who is unbalanced. Mentally ill."

"You mean other than Wertzler?"

She nodded. "And that person is—killing animals and leaving them for us to find."

"That's sick!" Ray spat out the words. "Why would someone do that? To scare us? To try and drive us insane?"

"Or maybe," she offered slowly, "in a twisted way, to show love for us?"

Ray broke free of her embrace and took several unsteady steps down the hall. "Remember—a couple days ago? That sparrow? We thought Garbo found it and brought it home. But maybe that was our first *gift*. Then there was the doe. And now—Phantom."

Marjorie pushed the stray locks of hair back from her face. "It's almost like—a progression. Each one larger—and potentially more dangerous than the animal before."

Ray shook his head slowly from side to side. "If what you're saying is true —what would be even larger—and more dangerous than a Doberman?"

They both looked up at the same time. Their faces— pale, aghast—mirrored each other.

"You can't honestly believe—" she began.

"I don't know—"

"But she's so small! How could she—"

"I don't *know!*" Ray slammed his palm against the wall. "The question is, where is she *now?*"

"She ran outside just before you shut the door!"

Marjorie turned and fumbled at the knob, but in her anxiousness couldn't make it turn. Ray brushed her aside, flung open the door, and ran out, all the while shouting for the black kitten, likely invisible in the evening shadows. Marj was close behind, screaming the name of the next offering, hoping the old man would hear her in time.

Somehow both knew they would be too late.

Linda Neuer is from Miami, Florida. Recently, some of her poems have been published in *Penumbric, NewMyths, BFS Horizons, Abyss & Apex, Quantum Poetry Magazine, Sangam, Lily,* and *Astropoetica.* She is inspired by the protection of all felines, including Florida panthers. And she hopes for the imminent revival of Tasmanian Tigers.

NIMBLE CAT
by Linda Neuer

The people are arguing in the house again.
Their shouts make the dogs bark.
I'm a shadow they don't notice.
Leaving the noise I enter the yard.
My darkness is one with the night.
On her swing, I see the little girl by the apple tree.
Soaring higher than the branches,
she's a silhouette on the full moon.
The moon has crystal towers where onyx cats play.
From the boughs of the blossoming shade,
I leap beyond this earthbound trance
where lunar felines invite me to dance.

A. R. Bagne is a chronically ill literature student that can be found haunting the woods when not crocheting their way through class or trying to convince their roommate's cat to form a pirate crew. They have no other published work, but have created an Instagram account in celebration of the possibility of being perceived @arbagne08.

GIRLHOOD IS A THING WITH CLAWS
by A.R. Bagne

Marla didn't remember her waking life, only her dreams. She was certain she must have had one, for she used to wake up at the end of her dream-days, but now her waking life was a distant foggy memory. Out of reach and irrelevant.

In her dreams, Marla was a cat. She knew this was wrong somehow, but since she couldn't actually remember ever being a little girl she was quite comfortable in her cat-body. On this dream-day, she hopped across a clear stream and admired her shiny black coat before her reflection warped into Something Else, as they always did in her dreams. She walked down winding paths through a giant mushroom forest, and flew through the air on the tail of a distant tornado. A good day. Then, as she ordered cinnamon rolls for dinner (as she always did) the baker asked her a question in a voice that was not his.

"Wouldn't you like to wake up and be our little girl again?"

Marla opened her mouth, but her cat-tongue would not form people-words anymore. Something vile bubbled up in her throat and she felt hands underneath the skin of her paws, pressing out from inside her and trying to rip free. She shook her head and yowled, desperately trying to cling to the tiles of the bakery floor with her claws as her entire world started to shift, shimmer, and then clarify, as if she had been living in a world submerged and was now being

218

dragged up to the surface. The bakery melted away and Marla squeezed her eyes shut. This was all Very Wrong.

When Marla opened her eyes again, it was a struggle. Her eyelids were heavy and crusted shut, and as her senses returned to her the sensation of Wrongness did not go away, but intensified. Her body was too heavy.

"She's awake!" Someone called from her side. Marla was not able to respond and say that couldn't possibly be right before her eyes slid closed of their own accord and she was set adrift in a dark void.

The girl that claimed to be Marla's older sister sat across from her at the dinner table and smiled. Marla tried to smile back, but the muscles of her face were all wrong.

She didn't know how long she had spent in the hospital, even after waking up. Everything was a blur tinged with the sense of dreaming, but this morning she had been sent to this house with these people. The woman that claimed to be her mother spoke, "Marla, you need to eat. You need to regain your strength."

Marla looked down at her plate of chicken and asparagus. She picked up a bit of the chicken and popped it in her mouth.

Her mother spoke again, "Where are your manners? Use your fork."

She picked up the fork and tried to figure out where each of her fingers was supposed to go. She struggled to work her mouth, but was able to ask, "How do the thumbs work?"

Three sets of eyes stared at her. Even the inattentive man in the corner looked up from whatever he was reading on his phone.

Marla stood up, "Never mind." She ran.

Once she'd gotten the balance right, running came naturally to Marla. She'd been very good at running in her dreams. She ran to her room and closed the door behind her.

They'd put Bat's collar on her nightstand while she was in the hospital. She remembered Bat, he was the only thing she remembered. It was his body she'd inhabited in her dream-life for the past several months. She knew all about the small scar on his ear, the curve of his fangs in her mouth, the impressive heights he was able to jump.

Marla cradled his collar in her too big hands and cried.

The truck driver had claimed he hadn't seen the cat, or the little girl. He came to apologize to her. To give her a bouquet of roses and a new kitten. The kitten was tiny and orange, nothing at all like the perfect black Bat had been. She screamed at him to take it back and locked herself in her room.

As Marla grew, it became easier to forget that she had ever been a cat. Memories of being a little girl returned and filled her mind, driving out thoughts of warping reflections, mushroom forests, and cinnamon rolls for dinner.

When she was a surly teenager, she sat with a friend on a bridge at night, both of them dredging up things from deep within themselves.

"I was a cat once." Marla said.

Her friend giggled, "Really?"

"His name was Bat."

Neither of them mentioned it again.

When she was 22, Marla went on a hiking trip with Riley, her older sister. They laughed and sang as they walked, and when rock crumbled beneath them, only Marla was light enough on her feet to get herself back to safety.

The paramedics almost took too long to get there. Instead of Riley, Marla could see only her own fragile childhood body, lying in the road next to her cat as her sister screamed on the sidewalk.

Marla sat beside Riley in the hospital, reflecting vaguely on the time their positions had been reversed. She barely remembered it all.

Her parents would sometimes laugh about how strange she'd been after she'd first woken up. Or, her mother would. Her father's expression rarely shifted from one of polite disinterest.

When she fell asleep in her chair, she found herself in Bat's body for the first time in over a decade.

She stretched, amazed at how well the body fit. She'd been given several rounds of physical therapy after she'd woken up as a child and she was strong, balanced, but occasionally her hands would slip, her fingers fumbling and clumsy. She didn't feel clumsy here.

She looked around and found herself in a mushroom forest. Pink clouds crossed in front of a silver sliver of moon, and a clear river gifted her reflection. Marla's heart sang when she saw her face, her best friend, Bat, the black-furred body she learned to run in, as she chased butterflies and freedom.

By the time the reflection warped into Something Else, she was on her way, traversing old paths she had long forgotten and rediscovering the secrets inside of her. Marla crested a hill and saw Riley sitting underneath a mushroom, staring at the sky. She approached her slowly and stood next to her, also gazing skyward.

"Am I dying?" Riley asked.

Marla crawled into her lap and nuzzled her face into her leg.

Riley smiled. "It's just like you always said. Can you talk here?"

Marla looked up at her, and opened her mouth. What came out were not words.

Riley listened in awe, and nodded when Marla reached the end. She wiped a tear from her eye, "I'll miss you, you know."

Marla clambered up onto her shoulder to shove her face into hers.

She laughed, "Okay, just stay out of trouble here."

Riley picked up her cat-sister off her shoulder and set Marla down on the path, watching as she raced off in the direction of a small bakery that had appeared out of swirling dream-stuff.

When the hospital staff found them, they were shocked to find Riley awake, tucking a smiling comatose Marla into her hospital bed.

"Look at her," she said, "She's having cinnamon rolls for dinner."

L.S. Johnson writes about the past to better understand the present, and about monsters to better understand ourselves. She is the author of the *Chase and Daniels* quartet of queer gothic novellas and over 40 short stories. Her first collection, *Vacui Magia*, won the North Street Book Prize and was a finalist for the World Fantasy Award. Her second collection, *Rare Birds*, was an IPPY medalist and longlisted for the Stoker Award. Her Enlightenment-era series, *Prima Materia*, about vampires and alchemists and a returning serpent god, is happening now. Find her online at traversingz.com.

ELEGY FOR PILATE HARDESTY
by L.S. Johnson

1.

You could blame the preacher for everything that happened after, for the cats and poor Pilate Hardesty, but that would be like blaming a match for the fire. It was not the first time a man of God had come to Schoenville after a bad harvest. The old-timers sucked their teeth at his bombast, but old-timers were few by then. Most of the townspeople—Frank, Pilate's father, among them—sat with their ears and eyes open, wanting to be told that it wasn't their fault, that there was nothing wrong with the soil which had been farmed to the point of exhaustion. And who was the preacher to disappoint them, especially when his collection baskets were at the ready?

The preacher came to Schoenville with a clean beige tent, dressed in a crisp but plain suit and his wife and three daughters all in white, their hair combed and their heads bowed modestly. "Satan," he told the townspeople, "comes among us in many forms. I see his mark on your land now. I see the fear of him in your faces, because you know in your hearts that it is he, the Great Adversary, who blights your crops and sours your milk. He turns wife against husband and child against parent. He is among you now, right here in this house of God, for he has eyes and ears everywhere and he drinks deeply of your suffering. Can you feel his eye upon you now?" He swung his arms wide and the crowd moaned in fear. "Everywhere I see his dark minions at work. The crows feasting on your crops? Satan. The unfriendly stranger who passes through, leaving dry cows in his wake? Satan. The rats in your barns, in the silos, in your pantries? Satan."

As he spoke one of his ghostly daughters stepped forward with a large, covered basket in her arms. The wicker jerked and shuddered, and strange noises came from within; the crowd inhaled in shared anticipation. "Behold," the preacher bellowed, and plunged his hand into the basket. He grimaced, he cried out "in God's name!" and at last he held up a small, scrawny black cat by its scruff. A woman screamed; the tiny cat yowled and hissed; in the back of the tent a few voices began to sing, and soon everyone was bellowing:

The devil is mad, and I am glad,
The devil is mad, and I am glad,
The devil is mad, and I am glad,
He lost the soul that he thought he had
All my sins are washed away,
I've been redeemed.

The preacher sang too as he held the cat out to them, and as the last line filled the tent he roared "thy will be done," and with two hands he snapped the cat's neck.

Later, when the collection baskets came around, everyone paid, Frank Hardesty among them. His face was stained with tears, though he would never have admitted to weeping. He turned out his pockets and handed over every penny, all the money he had planned to spend on the day's drinking. When God spoke to you, when God answered every dark question and accounted for every bitter woe in your life, giving up a bellyful of whiskey was the least you could do in return.

Frank paid, and his neighbors paid, filling the baskets with coins and small bundles of food and even a battered gold watch, for what was the point of keeping time when God Himself had spoken and the Adversary was at your doorstep?

Everyone paid, they nearly tripped over each other in their haste to pay, and through it all the cat lay half-draped in the basket atop the altar, its head twisted unnaturally, its pink tongue protruding from its lips as if about to lick the hand that killed it.

By morning every trace of the tent was gone. In the field where it had stood lay a half-dozen dead black cats, battered and bloody. More appeared as the days wore on, laid out at crossroads or nailed to fence posts and trees, their bodies ragged from buckshot and mangled from clubbing. There were so many the old-timers muttered suspiciously to each other about folks traveling to find more, but they were few and easily ignored. Still demand soon outstripped supply, and then it was the turn of black cats with patches of grey or white, dark grey cats that were declared "like black," calicos that had patches of black in their markings. When a group of boys came for old Mrs. Wagenheim's cat she threatened them with her dead husband's rifle. "My pussy is a creature of God," she yelled, and kept the cat indoors thereafter.

There were still the crows, of course. Some tried poison until the Lafflerns' little girl ate some by mistake and nearly died, going into convulsions and seemingly left simple by the ordeal. Others sat on their porches and took pot shots at them until Bert Yount shot Ezekiel Tailer, nearly taking his head clean off and leaving him with a notched ear.

If some saw the sheriff—one of the muttering old-timers—sitting on horseback at the turnoff from the county road and redirecting strangers, "just until spring, just until all this dies down," no one spoke of it.

By winter the rodent came in force, devouring every spare morsel not sealed away and biting children and livestock. The doctor was on call day and night for fevers and vomiting; three families simply packed and left, moving in with relatives a safe distance from Schoenville.

The bodies of the dead cats rotted, and fell, and sank into the rainy autumn soil. Winter blanketed the world, and in its depths even the rats became less numerous. And that was to be the end of it for most of Schoenville, but not for Frank Hardesty or his daughter Pilate.

2.

There had been Hardestys in Schoenville since before there was a Schoenville, farming the land north of town. Over time, however, their numbers had dwindled until there was only Frank and his daughter left. Frank had named her Pilate because she had been the death of her mother who he had loved beyond reason. In his grief he had sent the baby Pilate to live with his sister, but when her aunt died, Pilate was returned to her father.

She had just turned thirteen and was uneasy at meeting her father at last, for her aunt had told her tales of Frank's suffocating jealousy. Now she was being sent back to the man who had adored her mother to the point of violence. She had stepped down from the wagon, tense as a bowstring, ready to run at the first harsh word or twitch of a fist; but Frank did nothing more than nod at her, and in the days that followed he did nothing at all. He had become a heavy drinker in the wake of her mother's death, and lost all interest in the farm, selling off tools and horses alike to keep him in whiskey. When his daughter stood before him looking uncannily like her mother at courting age, he was self-aware enough to know his rush of emotion boded ill for them both, and moved his drinking to town. Absence, her aunt had counseled, was one of the best outcomes for a woman, either through neglect or widowhood. So Pilate thanked God for her good fortune, had a hot meal waiting on the table each night, absented herself to bed as soon as was seemly, and was busy with chores each morning well before her father awakened. There were many days when they exchanged not a single word. She felt blessed.

His one rule was that she not go to town. She looked too much like her mother; he couldn't bear the men seeing her. Thus Pilate had not been in the beige tent with her father, though she saw the preacher's wagons on the road the morning after. The wagons slowed as they passed, and the preacher leaned out and made the sign of the cross at her; Pilate cried out in surprise for she *felt* it, she felt the gesture as if the preacher's fingers had grazed her very skin. When her father appeared that night for supper, sober but wild-eyed and with his hands scratched and bitten, she felt that strange, grazing sensation again. Frank told her that the preacher had warned of disease and to stay away from any creature that seemed darkly natured. And Pilate, still only thirteen but with her aunt's tales vivid within her, had bitten her tongue before she could ask if that warning included him.

That night she lay in bed, rubbing her chest where she felt the preacher's touch, feeling her little room grow small and suffocating until some wordless compulsion forced her out of bed and into her mother's heavy coat. In the kitchen she took up the lantern and tinder-box and went into the barn. Once the measure of the farm's prosperity, the barn was now testament to its decline, but Pilate loved it for the lingering presence of her mother: the milking stool, the frayed canvas apron still hanging on a peg, the pile of baskets that had once carried eggs and vegetables.

Now, safe from the house windows, she lit the lantern—and at once heard plaintive mews coming from a shadowed corner. Drawing close, she saw two round eyes reflected in the lantern-light. A little coaxing brought out a scabbed, black-furred cat with a swollen belly; some soft words and petting and soon a second cat emerged from the shadows, and then a third, one all-black and one black with a single white spot on its chest like a heart. Soon they were rubbing against Pilate, purring and giving her dirty hands little cleansing licks, and for the first time in her life Pilate felt love.

She made a bed in an old barrel that she carefully hid in a stall, and brought them a little of the stew meat from supper. The following day her father went to town as usual, smacking his lips from need; she spent the morning pretending to rake the last of the autumn leaves, waiting for the doctor to pass on his rounds. When he stopped his carriage she asked in a roundabout way if there was anything to fear from cat scratches, and he explained that if washed thoroughly not at all, and then before Pilate could take her leave, he continued dolefully that it was a dark time when a sweet girl such as she would have to witness such doings, and would that her mother was alive to see what a lovely woman she was becoming.

All of which Pilate merely nodded to, for she had her answers.

When the mama cat had five healthy kittens—all black save for one that was a striped soft grey—she made a second bed for the new family. And then a third, and a fourth, as each week there seemed to be more cats huddled in the corners of her barn, bony and battered, all dark-furred and eyes wide with whatever horrors they had escaped. Pilate fed them, and tended their wounds, and waited patiently for the gift of their trust, and for the first time in her short life her days flew by with purpose and affection. She loved the cats and was loved by them in turn; at times she thought this too was her mother's presence, calling to the animals, giving Pilate this blessing of joy.

Until the rainy night when her father came into the barn, home early and stumbling drunk, his movements unheard in the storm, and found her sitting radiant in the center of the barn surrounded by purring, drowsing, playing cats, like she was the queen of them all.

For a moment Frank was filled with roiling memory, so overwhelming it blotted out all sense of where and when he was: of a picnic in a nearby meadow soon after they were married, his wife radiant in the warm sun and her belly swollen with the life that would become Pilate, and how she had looked at him and shown none of the fear, none of the silent hurt that he could never smooth away. She had looked at him and smiled, and in that moment he had felt certain that she loved him.

And then he was back in the barn, in the darkness and the smell of cat piss and cat bodies and all those flat empty eyes, and the creature with his wife's face smiled at him. His inebriation vanished as if blown out by the storm's winds, and with the clarity of revelation Frank saw the mockery before him, understanding now that Pilate too was Satan, that she had been Satan all along.

3.

It was, at least, swift. Frank made a fist but did not use it; instead he reached blindly for the sickle and swung it at Pilate's bared neck in a full-bodied arc born of a lifetime of practice. The blade bit deep into skin and muscle and vein and when he pulled the blade free Pilate fell backwards, head lolling above a gash of red flesh and her arms askew. He cut down the devil in a single blow, and through the rain he thought he could hear the crowd singing:

I've been redeemed
by the blood of the Lamb
Filled with the Holy Ghost I am
All my sins are washed away,
I've been redeemed

And there was blood, a great deal of blood. It pooled in the straw-covered dirt and soaked into Pilate's thick blond hair. Sprawled on the ground she reminded him again of his wife, of the bloody childbed and her splayed bare legs, and he felt in his drunkenness the rightness of it, that the creature claiming to be their daughter should die this way.

He turned to finish off the cats next, but they had vanished. He lumbered around the barn, finding the still-warm beds and kicking them until they were little more than rubbish. He thought then to burn the whole tainted building down, but somewhere deep inside him, there was still a farmer who balked at the sheer waste. Instead he dragged Pilate by her feet out into the yard, digging his hands into the thick woolen slippers that he realized had been her mother's, she must have found them. His eyes stung with understanding. The gall of the creature. That she should put her feet where her mother's once rested. That she should try and take her place.

Outside the storm was clearing, the rain an icy spatter and the heavy clouds starting to let through bursts of moonlight. Frank dragged Pilate, leaving dark streaks in her wake, until he reached the center of the yard. There he dropped to his knees and began hacking at the ground with the sickle, only to be stymied for the ground was rock-hard, though he did not feel the cold. He did not feel anything. He sat on his heels, looking down at the tangled body, at her sightless eyes staring back at the barn. He felt nothing, he thought nothing, and then from the haze of drink the thought sluggishly rose. *I can burn her.*

Finally, a purpose. He went back to the house and lit a lantern, then gathered up the oil can. Back outside it was dark, but the clouds soon parted again, painting into sharp relief the little heap of Pilate's body—

The little *moving* heap.

Frank watched, dazed, the lantern dangling from his fingertips, as the body wiggled and shuddered but did not rise. He raised the lantern and saw her torso twitch violently; his lips formed Pilate's name but he had no spit or voice. Without conscious thought he found himself taking one step and another towards the body. An icy wind raced across the flat plain of the farm, rustling the overgrown fields and stirring the ends of Pilate's hair; in response the movement seemed to become more agitated. Closer now, and he heard rustling within her old, oversized coat—his *wife's* coat, his *wife's* shoes, everything his *wife's*—and saw her pale hand twitch against the dirt. Still he could not stop walking. Her face was turned away, screened by her blood-matted hair, yet her whole body seemed to be distended.

His wife, swollen with life in that golden field, and how she looked at him, the only time she had ever so looked at him.

He stepped up to Pilate's body and watched as her coat rose and sank; from beneath it came a muffled rumbling. With a queasy fascination he shifted the oil can to his arm and bent over, the lantern swinging in his grasp as he used his free hand to ease open the top button of the coat. He saw a black-furred shape moving atop the gaping wound on Pilate's neck, heard the faint scraping of tongue against skin—

And then the cat looked up at him and screeched.

Frank flinched and stumbled backwards only to fall heavily to the ground. The coat strained until the buttons popped as cat after cat emerged, ears flattened, tails brush-thick as they leapt at him. He cried out as the first ones landed atop him, all claws and teeth. As he flung his arms up to protect his face oil can and lantern alike fell from his grasp, smacking against the hard earth. He smelled the fire before it licked into life, eating up the pool of oil, merrily leaping onto the splashes on his clothes. He tried to roll away, tried to get to his feet, but at every movement the cats were there, screeching and yowling and slicing at him with their small sharp claws. One seized his head and kicked brutally at his face with its hind legs, and though he wrenched it off his eyes could not open for the pain. His face was bloodied, everything hurt and he could not see—

But oh, the world smelled of fire.

He struggled to his feet and tried to move away from the smell, aware his clothes were burning, aware of the hairs on his body starting to sizzle as the flames reached his skin. He took a few steps only to trip over a mass of knotted cats and once more fell to the ground.

Before him the black cats of Schoenville watched Frank Hardesty burn, their eyes glowing with the light of the blaze. And then, one by one, they trotted off into the night, their long line of upright, dusky tails becoming one with the darkness.

Nico Martinez Nocito (they/them) writes speculative poetry and fiction, often with a queer and feminist bent. They spend their free time running, acting in local theater productions, and posting about fantastic MG and YA books on their blog, *Rapunzel Reads*. Find their work in the fairytale anthology *Grimm Retold*, or learn more about them and their writing on Instagram @nicowritesbooks!

BAIT
by Nico Martinez Nocito

Shadows swarm the alley and you hesitate,
listening. It's noon already, but the night won't leave—
stubborn, silent, just like you. When you glimpse
a flash of fur, a dark paw—a cat, a black cat—
you smile, walk away, and you don't
look back.

A mistake—the shadows coalesce, resolve;
one black cat becomes five becomes ten becomes
nineteen. You walk on. They follow—
soft-footed, self-assured, invulnerable.
The cats don't realize they're being followed, too—
don't see the shadow too dark to ignore

don't heed the icy wind that lifts
their fur and makes the earth crackle beneath
their paws. They're hardly innocent, but they are
naïve: they forget that even the worst monsters
can't claim a town just by stealing its children,
that other demons haunt the night
and want back their ancient hunting grounds.

The black cats swarm, fan out, prepare to
spring. They think you're prey. They don't realize
you're the bait.

Anna and Tod write as **A. Kristina Casasent**. They serve the whims of their Newfoundland and Mini American Shepherd dogs, two cats, and Crested Gecko. Living in Texas, the couple works in the sciences by day and compose fiction by night.

They write across a selection of genres, usually with a slight touch of humor, including science-fiction, fantasy, and thriller/horror.

Anna has a PhD in biomedical sciences and a background as a bioinformatician. She is an avid dog (and cat) trainer and is the driving force behind A. Kristina Casasent.

Tod is a software developer and has worked in a variety of industries. Anna turned him into a writer, beyond authoring role-playing games.

More information about A. Kristina Casasent's writing can be found at https://casasent.blog.

A PRESS OF A BUTTON
by A. Kristina Casasent

Danielle knelt before the hexagonally-patterned button rug inside a secure room in the space station. The skylight above made the pattern of odd groupings and clusters of buttons almost glow.

Another female was already sitting across from Danielle. The diminutive and regal ebony figure of her interrogator sat calmly, surveying the visitor. Distant and disdainful.

In contrast, Danielle's heart pounded, her hands felt damp, and her fingers shook slightly, as she pressed the first button, beginning negotiations that would change her life forever. Danielle's medium-honey blonde hair was brighter where ringlets caught the sunbeams as she moved.

The buttons were about the size of Danielle's fist. Pressing a button generated an eerie artificial voice that filled the room. Each word was simple, flat, and missing so much context. Her soul shuddered inside, tortured at being forced to use such an emotionless, sterile medium for such a heartfelt request. But this synthetic language—devoid of body mannerisms or nuance— was the only way to communicate with her interviewer. All other forms of communication were considered elitist and xenophobic. It would not do for the penitent to showcase verbal talents that Charlie, the interrogator, lacked.

Danielle pressed out her simple and life altering request. If answered in the affirmative, her life would never be the same. Her mouth formed the words as her hands moved between buttons, but she did not speak aloud.

After she finished, her diminutive interrogator pressed buttons in response. "You... query."

Danielle nodded, gulped, and quickly pressed out her answer. The young woman desperately hoped her interrogator did not notice her lapse in body language or any improper mannerisms. For an interminable length of time, Danielle faced a long string of questions, pressed out in slow mechanical precision.

Was she married?

Did she have kids?

Did she live alone or with other people? Since Danielle lived alone, she was asked for a backup contact.

What was her current job and schedule?

List her rooms and describe them, down to the last pillow.

Danielle thought she would scream when asked if she had windows that got sun regularly.

She wondered if the length and annoyance of the questioning itself was another test. Or even the main test. Trying not to think about that, the young woman concentrated on her interrogator's queries.

Sweat beaded on her forehead but Danielle continued to make eye contact and press buttons with a false calmness, glad for once she was not allowed to verbalize, so her interrogator could not hear her voice tremble with anxiety and anticipation.

"Will... visit... query," the dark interrogator pressed out.

"Yes," Danielle pressed, wondering how often she would need to come but did not ask. This was a one-way interview, and she was desperate to be chosen. She did not want to seem finicky.

Shaking her head to herself, Danielle felt the ringlets against her face. She definitely did not want to be considered greedy or possessive.

"Love… forever… query." After the diminutive female interviewer pressed the three buttons, she tilted her small head, watching Danielle through half slitted green eyes.

"Yes," Danielle pressed and pulled her hand back. This was the last question. Now all she had to do was wait for the decision.

From a dark face, the interviewer's small eyes watched Danielle intently as more buttons were pressed. "Ashley… come… bring… small… one."

The door slid to one side silently, allowing a large black Newfoundland dog, Ashley, into the room. He was tall enough to be eye level with the kneeling Danielle. In his mouth rested a small, black-furred kitten. The dog meandered to the small interrogator. Moving around her, he reached the hexagonal buttons and pressed a three-button sentence.

"Give… human… query."

The interrogator pressed a single button. "Yes."

Charlie's cat body looked even smaller to Danielle, when she saw it next to the giant Newfoundland dog. The human watched the adult cat's tail flick as the dog moved too close. Danielle could just detect twitching whiskers and the ripples of grey shadows in the black fur. When Charlie's claws slid out and then in, Danielle was startled out of her fascination. But the adult feline did not reach out towards the dog.

The oblivious Newfoundland ambled over to Danielle, opened his mouth, and let the nameless kitten gently tumble into Danielle's lap. Danielle gathered the kitten close. Its fur was slightly sticky with dog drool. The small, beautiful, short-hair kitten mewed once and purred as Danielle rubbed it lightly under the chin.

"Feed… Care… Train." The small black feline's commands were sharp and demanding despite the flat, emotionless tone of the synthetic speech buttons.

Danielle fumbled for a moment, about to speak. In warning, the vertical pupils of the interrogator's green eyes narrowed, and Danielle quickly caught herself and pressed out, "Yes… Thanks."

Tears streaked down Danielle's face as she slid a metal token across the floor to Charlie, before gathering the precious kitten in her arms. Danielle stood and with a final quick glance over her shoulder, moved towards the door. As Danielle was leaving, the giant black dog picked up the token and put it into a bowl of similar metal offerings.

The door shut and Danielle was gone, leaving Charlie and Ashley alone.

The Newfoundland dog ambled over to one side of the room and pressed a button on the wall with his nose, leaving a slimy streak of drool behind. A small door to a concealed closet quietly slid open. Ashley moved his head and used his mouth to take a new set of hexagonal-voice buttons from the closet. He turned slowly and placed the new buttons next to the existing set.

"Humans…" The Newfoundland moved his drooling muzzle to the new set of buttons. "Stupid."

The black cat picked her first button from the old set also. "Soon…" Her second button was selected from the new set. "Revolution."

The cat purred as the drooling Newfoundland settled with a contented grunt beside her. They waited to plant another of their brood with the next human supplicant.

Gregg Stewart is an HWA author, award-winning songwriter, musician, screenwriter, journalist, and film composer whose dark fiction tales have appeared in *The Sirens Call, Crimson Quill Quarterly, Crystal Lake Publishing's Patreon* flash series, and the print anthologies *Hotel Macabre Vol 1, Shallow Waters, Dead Letters: Tales of Epistolary Horror, Sley House Presents* (2025), and *To Hell and Back* (HellboundUK). He has recorded and published over 100 songs, toured the US and Europe countless times, and placed songs in a dozen films and tv series. His nonfiction book, *"LET IT OUT: Unlocking Creativity to Access Authentic Expression"* reached #7 for best sellers in creativity. You can find him on Bluesky @greggstewart, on X @thegreggstewart, and Instagram @thatgreggstewart.

LITTLE BLACK KITTEN
by Gregg Stewart

The raven hung upside down, its frozen talons gripped around a high branch. Katrya gazed up into the leafless elm, waiting for the raven to right itself. It did not. *That's what you get for not flying south when you had the chance.* Kat pulled her black woolen scarf tighter as she surveyed her estate's grim, grey courtyard. *Why didn't I go south when I had the chance?*

Kat strode the gravel pathway to the side entrance of Houtenstaak Manor and stepped inside the kitchens to warm her frigid bones. Mrs. Maythorpe was twisting and pounding a loaf of raw dough, and she called over her shoulder in her singsong way, "Morning, mistress."

"Morning," Kat replied in monotone disinterest as she poured herself a tall glass of milk.

Mrs. Maythorpe rolled her eyes. "Yer about as gloomy as the weather of late. Ya won't ever find a suitor if ya keep goin' about lookin' such a sourpuss."

Kat's expression grew sourer still. "I'll wear the face I please."

"Oh, 'course ya will. Milk mustache an' all." Kat quickly wiped her mouth while Mrs. Maythorpe prattled on, "Just don't blame me when ya come of age this spring and got no friends or husband to help ya celebrate. I tried to tell ya, Kitty Kat."

"I've got friends!" Kat meant to say this with confidence, but it came out more whiny than intended.

Mrs. Maythorpe arched a brow in reply.

"Lady Fairlawn says I am a delight to behold," Kat shot back.

"Ah, right, the ol' near-sighted dowager. And when's the last time she beheld ya?"

Kat twitched her nose, trying to recall.

"I suspect 'twas last summer," Maythorpe continued, "when the Lady hosted that grand picnic and served up her scandalous cherry cream-filled tarts. You're never one to pass up baked goods."

Kat set down the crumpet she'd just bitten into and cursed inwardly. With her mouth full, she could not offer a witty retort. Still, she had to admit that Mrs. Maythorpe was right.

Kat swallowed hard, then brightened. "I've plans to visit her today, in fact."

Mrs. Maythorpe spun around wide-eyed, and Kat awaited this reaction with a self-satisfied smirk. "Today, mistress? In this weather?"

"Yes, I'm taking Whinny. And, since it's so close to Christmas, I'll need to come bearing a gift. What's something a *friend* would bring? Perhaps a loaf of fresh-baked bread?"

Mrs. Maythorpe glanced at her raw dough and sighed. "Oh, that's fine, mistress," she said. "You can take this loaf soon as it's out o' the oven. I'll have it wrapped and set in a basket while ya ready yourself."

"Thank you!" Kat called as she swung open the kitchen door, crumpet in hand, and headed for the stables to have the groomsmen saddle Whinny.

Kat changed into her high-buttoned black boots and black riding cloak with its thick black fur-lined cowl. Though she dressed like a lavish mourner, she had resolved to make a cozy, bright day of it, even if it was the dead of winter.

Wind whipped Katrya's cheeks, and she cursed her big mouth. The ride to the Fairlawn estate was not going well. *It's colder than a fjord fisher's fanny out here!* Worse, Whinny was older than the glaciers and moved at a similar pace.

Kat's lips were now blue from the gale that whipped through the barren woods they traveled. She kicked Whinny's flanks for the hundredth time. "Damn you, trot!"

The horse halted, snorted once, and twisted her ears in all directions. Kat tensed in the saddle. "What do you hear, girl?"

Visions of half-starved wolves filled Kat's imagination. Her breath hitched as shadows darted amongst the trees.

The old mare commenced walking again as if she hadn't a care in the world. Kat exhaled with relief. "Daft thing! Why must you work my nerves so?"

Kat hugged the basket, hoping the warm bread might save her from death by freezing. She considered pulling Whinny around, but her recollection that it was the Christmas season compelled her to stay the course. *Who might visit Lady Fairlawn this holiday if not me?*

Besides, Kat liked the dowager. No one else spoke their mind like she did. Nobody had such grand ideas about being a *free-spirited woman*, as she called it. Also, no one else served such delectable pastries. Most of all, nobody else called Kat their friend.

Kat soon arrived shivering at the Fairlawn estate's long, tree-lined drive. Her heart sank when she saw the padlock on the black wrought-iron entry gates. *Has the dowager gone south for the winter? Who is looking after her cats?*

Kat dismounted and peered through the gate. The manor house on the hill looked deserted. Whinny snorted and stamped the slushy ground.

"Yes, I know," Kat replied. "All this way for nothing." In frustration, she slammed her gloved palm against the iron gate, and it swung open with a low creak. The sudden movement caused Kat to step back in alarm. Then she noticed the padlock hung around only one side of the gate. *Bloody hell.*

Kat walked Whinny up the long drive and rang the brass bell for a valet. When no one showed, she took Whinny to the stables and found them as empty as the courtyard. Kat placed the mare, still saddled, in one of the stalls and tossed her a handful of frozen oats. Whinny made no complaints while she chewed the cold morsels.

With her horse safe in the stables, Kat returned to the manor entry and rang the brass bell again. Still no answer. She considered what had occurred at the front gates and tried shoving the dark green double doors.

They opened without protest.

Kat peered inside, calling into the dark expanse of the manor. "Lady Fairlawn?"

She stepped over the threshold. The foyer was frigid, and the tiled floor was as slippery as a frozen lake. Kat tip-toed toward the parlor room but stopped short—her throat tightened.

Black cats. Dozens scattered across the parlor floor like dried leaves. She nudged the closest one with the tip of her boot and recoiled at the bloodless, lifeless form. Then the stench hit her nostrils—the rotting, acrid odor of death. Kat stepped back, swallowing her queasiness. Her voice came in a shuddering gasp. "Lady Fairlawn?"

Kat fought the urge to run. *What if the Lady Fairlawn is upstairs and in distress? What if outside forces—guiding angels or some such—led me here on such a cold, unforgiving day?*

Kat peered up the dark staircase, trying not to imagine the horrors awaiting her on the second floor. Holding her breath, she set down the breadbasket and dashed up the stairs until she stood on the landing.

Dim light emanated below the shuttered doors on either side of the dark hall. *Which is Lady Fairlawn's room?* Kat took a tentative step and halted. Dead black cats littered the hall. Kat knew Lady Fairlawn kept cats, but it seemed like every coal-black feline in the county had come here to die. She turned the knob and opened the first door. On the bed and floor were more black cats. None moved. She eased the door closed, recalling what the dowager had once told her.

"Cats are guardians on the path to the afterlife, ensuring souls get where they are meant to go. When I cross over and make my way through the underworld, I want as many cats as possible to guide me and ensure I arrive at the right place."

Kat continued down the hall, opening each door to reveal more lifeless cats with the blood drained from their small bodies, but when she opened the eighth and final door, something moved on the bed. Kat squinted and blinked. A pair of green eyes blinked back.

Kat stepped into the dark room and emerged a moment later with a black kitten nestled in the crook of her arm. Kat stroked its ears, keeping the furry bundle held against her black cloak. The kitten purred so loudly that its body shook. Kat had to fight tears at the sight of a living creature within this house of death.

With the kitten clutched to her chest, Kat strolled back to the landing and froze.

An impossibly tall and lean man stood at the foot of the staircase. The stranger was dressed in ebony from head to toe and with a face as pale as a snowdrift. He was holding up the fresh-baked bread, pawing at the wrapping and sniffing it like a dog.

"Excuse me, that bread isn't for you." Kat bounded down the stairs to stop this rude man from further blemishing her gift to Lady Fairlawn.

The man looked up, and the menacing gaze from his citrine eyes caused Kat to pause midway down the stairs. The kitten hissed.

The man dropped the wrapped bread into the basket. Touching his charcoal-gloved hand to the brim of his top hat, he spoke, "Greetings, little black kitten. I am Lord Fairlawn. Welcome to my estate. What brings you mewling around my doorstep?"

Kat's brow furrowed at the man's condescending tone. She liked less that he claimed to be the Lord of the manor. Worse, she worried that she *did* resemble a little black kitten in her fur-lined cloak. And the fact that he pointed it out made her dislike him *to the extreme*.

"I know this to be Lady Fairlawn's estate. What relation are you to her?"

The man flashed his pearly, wolfish teeth—the incisors abnormally long. "Her beloved grandson. I've been away for some time. If it's an audience you seek with the Lady, I regret to inform you she has departed."

Kat gasped, tears pricking the corners of her eyes. The man's grin widened. "For her summer cottage on Majorca."

Kat's jaw tensed. She wanted to slap him.

"She's entrusted the estate to my... capable hands." He raised his gloved mitts as he said this, and Kat could have sworn icy claws flickered at the man's fingertips for the briefest moment. He took the first step up the staircase, and the kitten in Kat's arms hissed again. He paused. "How were you acquainted with my dear grand-ma-ma?"

"She's my friend," Kat replied, taking an involuntary step backward up the stairs.

The man tilted his head, considering. "You need more youthful friends, little black kitten. Certainly, you need more handsome ones to suit your beauty."

"Please don't call me little black kitten," Kat said.

Lord Fairlawn arched a brow. "What else am I to call you? You've entered my home without giving your name."

"I am Katrya Houtenstaak. I live north of this estate. My father was a professor."

"Was? Is he a professor no longer?"

"He's dead."

"My condolences. And your mother?"

Kat swallowed. "Also dead."

"Ah, an orphan." Lord Fairlawn pouted. "Though I suppose you are the lady of the manor now?"

"I suppose."

Lord Fairlawn held out his arms. "So, we are Lord and Lady of two great houses, are we not? No reason *we* cannot be friends."

"I suppose," Kat repeated, stepping down the stairs while keeping the kitten clutched to her chest. *'A lady should remain cordial,' her Mother had said.* With a demure smile, she added, "As Lady Fairlawn is on holiday, it would seem you are the benefactor of my gift of fresh-baked bread."

Lord Fairlawn glanced at the basket with disinterest. "I shall treasure any gift from a lady such as you." His voice remained congenial, but his gaze pierced through Kat as she descended the stairs.

"Happy Christmas," Kat said with a quick curtsy as she passed him, skirting her body along the railing on the opposite side of the wide staircase from where he stood.

Lord Fairlawn's gaze did not waver from Kat as she walked past.

When Kat reached the front doors, they slammed shut of their own accord, trapping her within the cold manor.

Kat smelled sulfur in the air like a rotting egg. She slowly turned on the slippery, tiled floor to find Lord Fairlawn still staring. His skin seemed more pallid, and his wrinkles more pronounced.

He cocked his head to one side with a smirk. "Aren't you forgetting something?"

"Whatever do you mean?"

Lord Fairlawn's eyes narrowed, his smirk growing to a yellowy grin. "That's my cat."

Kat's heart sank. "Oh, is this kitten yours?"

The man gave her a withering look. "Did you find it in my manor house?"

Kat nodded once.

"Then, it's my cat."

"Well," Kat began, jutting her chin high, "I see how you treat your pets and I'm not sure you are the right person to care for this little one. Besides, when someone brings you a gift, it's customary to make a gift in return."

The man's eyes turned to slits. "I do not believe that is how gifts work, but if you insist." The doors cracked open, sending an icy wind whipping through the foyer. "Please. Take my cat."

Kat lowered her chin. "Thank you." She stepped towards the open doors. Everything in her body told her to run, but something gnawed at her. She turned, fighting the words but unable to stop herself. "Lord Fairlawn? What *has* happened to all these cats?"

The man looked over his shoulder at the morbid scene in the parlor. "Oh them? They were... messengers."

"And what was the message?" Kat asked, her teeth beginning to chatter in the open doorway.

"They want me to return home," Lord Fairlawn replied. "But this is my home now." He tapped his gloved knuckles against the banister with finality.

'Curiosity killed the cat,' her Mother had said. Kat did not want to ask, but she had to. "And where *is* your former home?"

Lord Fairlawn leveled his gaze. "Far. Far. South."

Kat bolted down the front steps and across the courtyard, clutching the kitten while she ran. When she reached the stables, she dashed inside to find them empty. *Bloody hell! Where's Whinny?*

Kat spied Lord Fairlawn crossing the grounds at a steady gait. She dashed out the back door for the woods.

As she darted between the trees, Kat lamented she would never make it home on foot. She stumbled onward, cursing her too-cumbersome boots, and wishing it was warm enough to kick them off and run barefoot.

Kat's breath came in billowy smokestacks as she fought to keep moving, heading toward what she hoped was the Houtenstaak estate. Glancing back, Kat saw Lord Fairlawn with his ghostlike complexion and glistening incisors, following in his cold, calculated manner. A scream caught in her throat as she quickened her pace. He was toying with her, she knew. He could catch her at a moment's notice.

Kat's heel buckled, and she slipped, sending her cartwheeling down a snowy embankment. When she hit bottom, the sudden impact knocked the wind from her.

Kat lay on the snowy ground, gasping for breath, staring at the darkening sky through the bare trees. Her thoughts drifted to her parents. *Maybe it's for the best. Would it not be easier to join them in Heaven? I shall never find another who loves me so unconditionally.*

"Kitty?" Kat whispered, realizing her arms were empty. She clambered up using a broken tree limb, took a step, and winced in agony. Her ankle was already twice its usual size. She balanced against the broken tree limb, placing the pointed end in the dirt as a crutch. She took several tentative steps, searching for the kitten and a pathway out.

"You seem to have lost something."

Kat froze.

Lord Fairlawn stood atop the snow-crested slope, holding the black kitten outstretched. It hissed and clawed at the air in a vain attempt to free itself.

Kat retained her composure. "I see you've recovered my gift."

Lord Fairlawn's tone grew mocking. "I see how you look after your pets, and I'm not sure you are the right person to care for this little one."

Kat's eyes turned steely. She was through playing the amiable lady. "Give me my fucking cat!"

Lord Fairlawn leered at her, baring his menacing teeth. "Perhaps you'd like to come up here and try taking the wretched beastie from me?"

Kat knew the man—*was he even human?*—might be stronger, faster, maybe even smarter than her, but there was one thing she knew that he did not. Katrya was a Houtenstaak. She might look like a little black kitten, but she was still a hunter and knew when to pounce.

"Never mind, I'll come to you," Lord Fairlawn said, throwing the kitten aside as if it were a ragdoll.

Kat's scream caught in her throat as the man flew at her like a winged demon, coming on so fast she had no time to brace for impact.

Lord Fairlawn crashed into her with the full weight of his body, sending Kat toppling to the ground once more. He pinned her there, digging his icy clawed fingers into her shoulders, his mouth unhinged, unnaturally wide, revealing lengthy, razor-like incisors that hovered mere inches from her face.

Kat's legs kicked, and her body squirmed, but she could not free herself or find enough air to scream.

Lord Fairlawn's citrine eyes glowed hellfire. The drool from his fangs dripped onto Kat's flushed cheeks. He seemed to delight at her inability to free herself.

She knew what he was now—not all things that die go where they should. Some find their way back from the underworld, and once they return, they make their homes in the remote places they once knew, until someone comes along to send them back down south.

Kat's father, a professor of mythology and occultism, taught her this. He knew how to send these creatures back from whence they came. Who would do it now? The task fell to her. She understood it now. The guiding angels, or maybe the cats, had called her to the Fairlawn estate. *Perhaps I am more like my father than I thought?*

With her last reserve of strength, Kat launched her knee into Lord Fairlawn's groin. He twisted away, groaning in agony. With her arm freed, Kat snatched the branch she'd used as a crutch and slammed the sharp end into the man's chest.

Lord Fairlawn's face twisted in shock and surprise as he collapsed onto his back. He coughed and spat blood, a look of utter disbelief on his pale, gaunt face. Bright crimson pooled on the snowy ground.

Kat stood, chest heaving. Though hot tears warmed her cheeks, her voice was cold venom. "I told you my name was Houtenstaak. It means *wooden stake* in Dutch, the language of my father and his father. We are hunters of lost souls and predators such as you."

Lord Fairlawn tried to speak as more blood bubbled from his mouth. His eyes glazed, and he lay still. Kat prayed he would not stir. She looked up and found dozens of black cats atop the snowy slope, peering down at the gruesome scene.

"He's all yours," Kat said as she staggered up the embankment. When she reached the crest, she found Whinny standing not ten paces off. The kitten was crouched between the horse's front hooves, shivering in the snow. *Bloody hell.*

Kat rode Whinny back to the Fairlawn estate with the kitten tucked inside her cloak. She could not in good conscience leave all those dead cats lying inside to rot. That was no condition to leave the home of a friend. But as Kat approached the manor, she noticed small shadows darting through the trees. Cats. They were black cats!

When she reached the courtyard, hundreds of dark felines with whiskers alert and tails high dashed off in all directions, returning to their homes. *Leading lost souls through the underworld is dangerous work, which is why they have...*

"Nine lives," Kat whispered in amazement, overwhelmed with emotion.

Kat walked through the house, nibbling Mrs. Maythorpe's fresh bread as she confirmed every cat was restored and headed home. When satisfied there were no cats inside, Kat closed the large double doors, imparting a final blessing for her hostess. "Happy Christmas, Lady Fairlawn. Perhaps I shall join you in Majorca next winter?"

Kat hobbled into her family courtyard with the moon high overhead. Looking up at the barren elm tree, she saw the dead raven was gone.

She placed Whinny safely within the stables and asked a groomsman to ensure they kept the old mare warm and well-fed.

Kneeling before the hearth, the young lady of the manor set the kitten on the soft carpet and collapsed onto her back, letting the heat thaw her bones and bring blood back to her trembling limbs.

Mrs. Maythorpe emerged, holding a silver tray. "My, you're home late."

Kat was too exhausted to respond.

"Brought ya a crumpet an' a spot o' warm milk."

Kat sat up. "Thank you, Mrs. Maythorpe. Whatever would I do without you?"

"I shudder to think. How was yer visit?"

"Awful," Kat replied as the purring kitten climbed into her lap. "But I made a new friend."

Gerri Leen is an award-nominated poet from Northern Virginia who's into horse racing, tea, and collecting encaustic art and raku pottery. She has poetry published by *The Magazine of Fantasy & Science Fiction, Strange Horizons, Dark Matter, The HWA Poetry Showcase, Dreams & Nightmares* and others and has just published her first poetry collection *Unwilling: Poems of Horror and Darkness*. Visit gerrileen.com to see what she's been up to or check at her Instagram @leengerri.

DOES THAT FAMILIAR COME IN BLACK?

by Gerri Leen

She comes to me, gaunt
And worm ridden
Afraid and angry but
Hiding within the dull black fur
And wary green eyes is
The soul of my last familiar
(Cats can "walk in," but
New bodies bring new baggage)

I'm not sure at first that it's her
She's so different, but then
I turn on my electric razor
To make my legs summer sleek
And she attacks it (it, not me)
My old familiar went deaf after
A very bad vet visit, the last thing
She heard: electric clippers

DOES THAT FAMILIAR COME IN BLACK? *by Gerri Leen*

Welcome home, dear one
A witch without her familiar
Is a sad thing but now
That you've returned
We can get back to work

Mark S. Causey reads, writes, edits, and publishes works of fact, fiction, and fantasy. Causey has loved reading and collecting comic books his whole life, and co-owned a comic shop for nearly 20 years before joining Black Cat Publishing as editor and publisher. He's currently living out his wildest dreams near Monterey, California with his wife and cats.

LUCKY THE 13TH
by Mark S. Causey

Lucky isn't exactly an original or clever name for a black cat, but since he was Agnes' thirteenth familiar, it seemed appropriate. Though an officially certified and recognized Will of the Witch, Lucky was just a housecat, really. His Mistress of Magic was advanced in years, even by Wicca standards, and it had been a long time since she had ridden a broom, much less with a feline passenger. These days the witch gripped her cane more than her wand, making money at home by crafting potions and fortune telling, while Lucky The 13th Familiar kept the abode safe from unwanted pestilence.

Everyone everywhere was afraid of Agnes The Moon Queen, and only the most desperate among the townspeople ventured so far into the forest seeking her arcane assistance. Lucky liked to smell the fear as they begged for help. He enjoyed seeing the sad faces of those who would pay the sorceress for a potion to ensnare a lover, or to be freed from a curse. Lucky would purr as hungry dogs would come to the home looking for scraps of food, only to end up in the witch's cauldron. He had fun catching toads as they slapped around the kitchen floor, and returning them to her steaming stew. The old woman and her constant companion had a good life.

But one midnight, while double double toil and troubling, the enchanted cane was left standing when Agnes

The Moon Queen fell to the floor. Lucky was, as he had always been, at her side and ready to do as she commanded, but the Devil had already claimed her, and she had no more orders to give. He licked her face voraciously, and even began to scratch into the flesh of her cheeks, but this time she didn't open her good eye and cackle with laughter. Lucky nudged his head under her left wrist, hoping the wand would slap into her hand and restore her with Dark Magic. But the wand stayed in its place on the mantle. Lucky kept his head under the witch's hand and whimpered for one last scratch from her long, yellowed nails.

The Witch was dead.

Lucky had never really considered this before. It had never occurred to him that this was even possible. Yet there was Agnes. On the floor. Growing, somehow, even colder than she had been in life. The Witch had never prepared her Familiar for this eventuality. Without Agnes and without her commands, demands, and reprimands, what was Lucky supposed to do? Was he to find a new master, and continue a life of service to Dark Magic? Was he free to pursue his own dreams now? Was he finally able to see something outside of this dark, dank dwelling? Could he travel the world, make new friends, or maybe even find a mate?

As Lucky began to ponder his place in a new universe, the spiders came. Arachnids have an understanding and appreciation of suffering and death, so, unlike the black cat, they had been eagerly anticipating the old woman's inevitable demise. They had been watching her decline with fervor, and the moment she let go of her enchanted cane the spiders came for their feast. Lucky could only escape to the shadows and mew for the detritus of his former master. He had seen the way she handled spiders as she crafted potions, and knew enough about their venom to know he wasn't going to be able to protect her body from them without joining her in the afterlife. Every jumping, long-bodied, house, and widow spider in the area used their silk and skill to open the door of the hovel home, and drag the corporeal remains of Agnes into the forest. They would take their revenge on the witch for a century of spider potions by feeding on her flesh for generations.

After the arachnid army had gone, Lucky was alone for the first time. And being alone meant the witch's abode wasn't his home anymore. He was going to have to start making decisions for himself. No more being told what to do. No more having everything he needed or wanted being given to him by someone else. He stared out the opened door, past the webbing that dangled and wisped, and into the darkness. Lucky grew curious as he sat listening to the hoots of owls, the flutter of bat wings, and the cries of wolves. They didn't sound terribly distressed out there in the wild. Somehow all the other creatures of the night were living their lives free of masters. Why couldn't Lucky be like them?

He decided to take one last look around. This had been his whole world for all these years. As he thought about it, Lucky couldn't really remember ever leaving. He had many great memories of serving his master. Bumping the table or blowing out a candle at just the right time in the Séance parlor. Coming out from the shadows and around the crystal ball on cue, as if it were a strange coincidence. Cuddling on the flayed skin couch by the fireplace as Agnes wrote and read from her Spellbook. Lucky went into the kitchen to have one last boiled toad. He wasn't going to find any of the witch's treats out in the forest. He was going to miss this place.

And now it was time. Time for Lucky to discover his destiny. It was time for him to find out who he truly was without the responsibilities of being the witch's thirteenth Familiar. He was ready to assume a new identity. He was ready for a new life.

Lucky circled the room three times wanting to gain momentum both physical and emotional. He wanted to leap into the outside, and get a running start to his next adventure. He began sprinting toward the open door chasing an imaginary mouse that represented every unspoken hope and dream he had ever possessed. As he reached the threshold, he leapt into the air as if he were going to fly on forever. He inhaled his first breath of true freedom and felt the chill of the midnight air engulf him from nose tip to tail.

And as he flew, his thick black coat bathing in moonlight, Lucky The 13th Familiar burst into a greenish-black cloud of smoke that dissipated into the night air. When he left the home in which his creation spell was cast, the enchantment was broken. Lucky was free, but maybe not quite in the way he expected.

Agnes loved her twelfth familiar, SixSix, more than anything. Upon his passing she couldn't bear to find another, so she recreated him with Dark Magic, and called her new Familiar "Lucky The 13th." Like the cane, the enchanted Black Cat was to make her final years a little easier. And like all Familiars, Lucky The 13th served his master faithfully until...

The End.

Alexa Donley is a speculative fiction author living in Washington. When not writing, she can be found traveling to new places or walking in storms. Her first book, *The House on the Rocks*, is available now, as well as monthly short stories on Patreon. You can find her on https://www.alexadonley.com/ and on social media @alexadonleybooks.

THE COLD
by Alexa Donley

Shadow crouches in place, tail swishing against the ground. It's mostly quiet now, the sun having set long ago, but there is a noise in her house. An intriguing noise, when there should be no noise because her human is asleep. When her human is asleep, a hush falls over the dark, and she likes to patrol to make sure that there are no wayward mice or spiders that need catching, but this noise is different. Soft. Light. She knows it from somewhere, but not what it is, and she sticks to the shadows that mask her approach in the night. Her haunches tighten, her focus narrows—

She springs toward the noise, dashes around the corner, but there's nothing there. She stops, tail flicking irritably, ears pivoting to find where it went.

There. A tiny scratch against the hardwood. She bounds toward it, claws scrabbling against the ground in her tight turn to catch it.

She knows the shape now, the one causing the noise—the tiny human! Shadow springs upright, ears perked in eagerness. He's rougher than her human, he pulls her tail sometimes, but he's good enough. Especially when he moves the toys like he is now, so they scrape and she wants to leap and bound for them like a kitten again, like her own kittens used to.

The small human leans over on wobbly legs, brushing the ball so that it rolls towards her, and something inside it makes noise—a mouse! She bounds forward and bats it away, his light giggle floating towards her. She likes that sound. It means she's being good to her humans.

He pushes the ball again, and Shadow swats it across the floor so it tangles in the curtain. When she leaps for it, though, there's a sharp, monstrous sound, and she runs from the room with an alarmed meow. Her human needs to wake up!

A muffled thump. When Shadow is in her human's room, she's already sitting upright in bed, eyes wide and vividly awake. The human doesn't yell, though, like she usually does when Shadow wakes her up; instead, she stares at nothing, listening to the loud, continuous sound instead of stopping it. Her human makes no noise, the way a mouse freezes when it senses Shadow watching.

Slowly, she moves the covers, her feet hitting the floor. Shadow leads her back to the main room, where she can still hear the tiny human laughing, unafraid of the loud noise behind the curtains. There is a light coming from it, too, incessant, bright enough it makes Shadow squint.

The human drops to her knees, slowly, moving the curtain and picking the toy up so the noise stops, its wheels still spinning on the underside. It's shaped like the contraption outside, she sees now, with lights in front and on top that blink on and off. Shadow lays her ears flat and takes a step forward—

"*No!*"

She slides across the hardwood when the human shoves her, and Shadow backs up. That's not what her human usually does, when she holds one of her toys.

"Bad cat!" her human spits, her tone harsh and sharp, clutching the toy to her chest. "Bad cat! Y-you don't play with this, this isn't yours, this is—" She sucks in her breath. Something crosses her face that makes Shadow want to hiss. It's what she saw in the dog that chased her long ago, that attacked her and her kittens: desperation. She felt it when she fought back, too. Shadow itches to run.

But then, just as quickly, it's gone. Her human folds over the toy, and it makes the loud noise again, and her whole body moves with a jolt and a hiss. Pain? The noise hurts her?

The tiny human is next to them, but he's not laughing anymore. He reaches to pull Shadow's tail, but there's no force behind it; it's barely a brush. There was a time he would yell, when the noise started or stopped, when the human was ignoring them for too long, but there's no sound now. When Shadow arches her tail to curve around him, he is cold as frost.

Her human is still bent over, still making the hissing sound, too loud and sharp. The noise from the toy makes Shadow's ears hurt, and she wants to run but the tiny human is there. If both of her humans are here, surely it's nothing dangerous.

The noise stops. Her human cries out but it isn't a word Shadow knows. Only the feel of it. It drags out, out, out, like when she catches a bird and it cries for escape.

The tiny human pulls Shadow's tail again but it doesn't hurt anymore. The intriguing sounds he was making have stopped, too, so now there is only her human keening to herself quietly.

She knows what to do with that. Just like when her kittens cried out for her, or when she cried out and her human found her.

Shadow walks towards her human, leaving the smaller one behind, and brushes against her knee, and then her elbow, rubbing her scent on warm skin. *Mine.* She still wants her human, even if she's loud, even if something inside of her is unfamiliar. She purrs comfortingly.

The human laughs under her breath, leaning over to wrap Shadow in her arms and around her stomach, burying her face in Shadow's dark fur. The sounds are louder now, rattling inside her ribcage. Shadow purrs louder, reaches up to lick her face. Salt. She licks again.

The laugh is broken, sharp, her human's grip is strong enough that Shadow couldn't squirm out if she wanted to, but she is a good cat and she doesn't move. *Good cat,* just like her human calls her when she plays with the tiny human. *Good cat,* like when her human picked her up and held her and she didn't have to stay with her lifeless kittens anymore. She whispers it now. She's safe, forgiven for whatever she did. She purrs and stays still.

The tiny human watches, fingers curled around her tail, but her human never holds him, doesn't feel the cold.

Deborah H. Doolittle has lived in lots of different places, but now calls North Carolina home. A Pushcart Prize nominee, she is the author of *Floribunda, No Crazy Notions, That Echo,* and *Bogbound.* When not editing *BRILLIG:* a micro lit mag, she is training for road races or practicing yoga.

COUNT DRACULA'S CAT
by Deborah H. Doolittle

As the cat,
sleek and black,
climbed over

the top of
the casket
leading with

one front paw
leaving a print
the back paw

to step into
carefully
skillfully

across the lid
keeping all claws
drawn

into its mitts
not to nick
the glossy wood,

not to wake
the sleeper
but to take

a nap in
the moonlight
with his master

Donna Marie West is a Canadian educator, translator, author, and freelance editor. She has published some 500 drabbles, short stories, and non-fiction articles in a wide variety of Canadian and American magazines, web sites, and anthologies. She loves the unusual, unexplained, and mysterious, and often finds ways to weave these themes into her stories.

LAVENDER
by Donna Marie West

"Well, would you look at the hour? Time for my afternoon stroll," Wayne announced to his empty cottage at precisely three o'clock. He glowered at the cane resting by his side, loathing it. Loathing every new symptom befalling him since he'd been diagnosed with amyotrophic lateral sclerosis, also known as Lou Gehrig's disease, two years ago. Loathing how he'd been forced into retirement from the teaching job he loved at the age of fifty-one and was now becoming something of a hermit. He'd never been big on the social scene, but he never even went to the market anymore, having his groceries delivered weekly instead.

From fatigue to leg cramps to fingers so stiff he feared to pick up anything remotely fragile, his condition was growing worse month by month. He dreaded what was coming—an inability to walk or care for himself, followed by an inability to speak or swallow or, ultimately, breathe, all while retaining his cognitive faculties. In short, a slow and humiliating death. He vowed to end it all himself soon, while he was able—if only he could gather the courage to do it.

With a sigh of resignation, he gripped his cane and rose from the couch where he'd been napping. Not bad. His legs were cooperating today. He usually walked down the road a ways, but not today.

Today, he descended the four steps from the back door to the yard, where his once beautiful garden filled with roses, boxwood, and lavender was now little more than an overgrown jumble of bushes and weeds.

Got to get the neighbor girl Kylie to mow the lawn and do some weeding, Wayne thought as he toiled to walk in the thick mixture of early summer grass and dandelions.

It was exactly one year to the day that his chocolate Lab, Bennie, had crossed the rainbow bridge after fifteen faithful years at his side. Wayne buried him here, in the far corner of the garden, near the cache of bones, balls, and squeaky toys that Bennie had hidden over the years.

He gazed down at the grave, obscured now by a huge rose bush, about to relay his woes to his last best friend, and noticed something tucked away in the depths of the lavender at his feet.

Carefully, lest the strange something be a porcupine—or worse, a skunk—he pushed the fragrant stems aside with his cane and caught his breath.

A black ball of fur raised its tiny head and blinked at Wayne with bright blue eyes.

"What in the name of God's green earth are you doing there?" he asked the kitten. "You're much too small to be out alone. Where's your momma?" He considered leaving it there in case said momma came back for it, but what if she didn't? He couldn't risk it running into the road or falling victim to a predator.

Wayne lowered himself stiffly to his knees, scooped up the kitten in one hand, and, leaning heavily on his cane, pushed to his feet. Left leg cramping painfully, he hobbled into the house and deposited the tiny creature onto the kitchen table. He examined it as best he could and was happy to find it appeared healthy and clean, save for a dusting of soil on its feet and belly. It must have been about six weeks old, a female, he discovered, and she smelled lovely, like the lavender where he'd found her.

"If I don't find where you ran away from, I'll be keeping you," he told the kitten, which looked up at him as if this was exactly what she wanted to hear. "And I shall call you Lavender."

Wayne had had dogs and cats all his life, although the last two kitties had actually belonged to his wife Lucy, who took them with her in the divorce six years ago. He knew what to do.

First, he called his neighbors and the local veterinary clinic, who all assured him they weren't missing a kitten and knew of no one who was.

"Dumped on the road, then," Wayne said to little Lavender, who sat cuddled in a blanket in a big cardboard box after consuming her fill of warm milk and chicken left over from last night's supper. "Probably because you're black. Silly superstitious people, thinking you're bad luck. Well, I say their loss is my good luck."

Grateful that he was still able to drive despite his doctor's warnings not to, he headed to his favorite pet shop to buy everything a kitten needed to live her best life.

Weeks stretched to months, and Lavender grew into a faithful companion who spent all her waking hours at Wayne's side. He took her to be vaccinated by the vet, who declared her the picture of health, and later, to be spayed. He worried that she would cool off on him after that, but if anything, she only grew more loving.

She got into the habit of sleeping on the empty side of Wayne's bed at night. During the day—between playing and eating and scampering around in the yard with him whenever Wayne went outside—she napped on a small rug beneath the wilting branches of Wayne's ancient rubber plant.

"I don't quite know what you see in that thing," Wayne said to her one day as she curled up for a nap, purring like a little motor. "But it was a housewarming gift from my mother, and I promised to keep it forever." He gave the plant in question a long look. "Five leaves left. Guess it won't be long now until forever is up."

Summer faded pleasantly into autumn. It was early November when Wayne noticed a change in the old rubber plant. It had visibly perked up and sprouted half a dozen new leaves.

"Well, looks like you're lucky. Your favorite plant will be around for a while yet," Wayne told Lavender, who gave him a slow blink with those eyes that remained sapphire blue although she'd long passed the age when they should have turned green or yellow.

Wayne's ALS seemed to have stabilized, so Christmas was a happier time than he'd anticipated. He introduced Lavender to Lucy, who came for supper on Christmas Eve. Although divorced, they'd remained friends and between Christmas and New Year's he even went shopping for sales at the mall.

As he watched the New Year's Eve fireworks on TV, he realized he hadn't thought about ending his life in quite a while. How could he? Despite Lucy's promise to take Lavender in when the inevitable happened, he couldn't imagine leaving her any sooner than he had to.

Winter thawed into spring, which gradually warmed to summer. A year old now, Lavender took to jumping the fence into the next-door neighbors' yard, where she befriended their elderly, arthritic terrier, Samson.

"Sorry if she bothers you," Wayne apologized to his neighbor Wendy. "I hate keeping her in on nice days, and since she never ventures near the road or any farther than your yard…"

"Oh, it's no problem, Wayne," Wendy replied with a laugh. "Your little kitty seems to be putting some life back into the old pup. Kylie loves seeing them play together."

By the end of the summer, Samson was running around like a younger version of himself. The vet credited a new medication, but as Wayne considered his now flourishing rubber plant, he began to wonder.

Does Lavender have something to do with this metamorphosis?

It was a ridiculous thought to be sure, but two more ailing plants that Wayne placed beside Lavender's favorite nap spot gradually grew hardy; one of them even began to flower for the first time. In fact, all of his plants—indoors and out—were thriving like never before.

And then there was the question of Wayne's ALS. His condition was still stable—somewhat improved, even—allowing him to discard the hated cane, and he was strong enough to teach a literature course each semester at the local college for the next three years.

No longer wishing to live a hermit's existence, he began playing Friday night Bingo at the local community center and accepted the occasional invitation to visit Lucy or various friends for brunch or dinner. He even did some gardening, although he left the lawn mowing to Kylie.

Lavender's fluffy kitten fur had given way to a sleek coat of midnight black, but she kept those stunning blue eyes. And what a character she was! From the age of six months on, she refused to drink from a bowl, demanding fresh water from the bathroom faucet uncountable times a day. She loved treats of salmon, chicken, and pork, but not white fish or beef. Luckily, she devoured impressive quantities of the best cat food Wayne could afford. She never scratched or growled or hissed, but at the mere touch of Wayne's hand, she would purr up a storm. Outdoors, she loved to snoop in the garden and roll in the lavender. Indoors, she prowled every nook and cranny of the cottage, catching the occasional misguided mouse, proudly bringing it to Wayne like it was a gift— usually after she'd decapitated it. Well, she was a cat, after all.

Wayne taught her to walk on a leash, prompting his neighbors to begin calling him "The Cat Man" when they saw him with his little panther trotting along beside him on his daily strolls like any good pooch. Wendy and Kylie said he should write a book about her; he laughed and said yes, maybe he should.

Sadly, Lavender's pal Samson eventually succumbed to old age. She appeared to grieve for a few days, sleeping more than usual and eating less, but she perked up upon meeting Kylie's new poodle puppy, Maggie, and the two soon became fast friends.

For five years, life was unpredictably and wonderfully good. Wayne's doctor was astounded, his only explanation being that Wayne was "one in the lucky minority who see the disease progress very slowly." And then one day, all at once, his ALS came roaring back with a vengeance. He needed his cane again. Only weeks later, the cane was replaced by crutches, with the prospect of a wheelchair looming in the near future. His arms trembled and his hands cramped so badly and so often that he had to hire in-house help for his daily needs. Some days, he could barely swallow a bite. He didn't dare pick Lavender up for fear of dropping her, never mind the old adage that cats always landed on their feet. Knowing he would never drive again, he gave his car to Kylie, who was in college and thrilled to have her own transportation.

Lucy came by every Saturday—sometimes for the entire weekend, sleeping on the couch and leaving the bed to

Lavender—but it became increasingly obvious that home care would soon not be enough. Wayne was going to have to sell the house and transition to a nursing home. Lucy promised to help him arrange everything.

"I'm sorry I won't be able to stay with you much longer," he told Lavender through a tight throat once the decision was made. Words were coming harder for him now, even without tears threatening. "I know you helped me stay healthy for as long as you could, but even you can't beat this damn disease of mine, can you?"

Lavender looked up at him from her perch on the arm of the couch and gave him one of her best slow blinks.

"You'll be fine with Auntie Lucy," he assured her. "I told her about the plants and Samson. She thinks I'm imagining it, of course, but no matter. She knows all your foibles. She'll take good care of you."

Another long, languid blink. He hoped she understood.

Wayne went to bed that night feeling weaker and more hopeless than he ever had. If he was going to end things on his own terms, he would have to do it soon or be forced to suffer to the bitter end.

Lavender hopped onto the bed, but instead of sprawling beside Wayne like she usually did, she curled up on his chest, purring loudly. The sound and gentle vibrations comforted him, even if just for a little while.

The sun was barely above the horizon when Wayne awoke the next morning. He was on his side, almost in a fetal position, with Lavender draped across his waist. Most unusual.

He lay there for a moment, taking in the pale yellow sunlight and relishing the best sleep he'd had in months. He drew in a long, satisfying breath. No problem there. He flexed and wiggled his fingers. They worked better than they had in years. He slipped out from beneath Lavender and sat up on the side of the bed. He couldn't remember the last time he'd done this so easily.

Something has changed.

Cautiously, he pushed to his feet. The room spun around him for a few seconds, then steadied. Heart racing, mouth dry, he took one tentative step, then another. He walked to the hallway and back without stumbling. He had no stiffness, no cramps, no tremors. Incredibly, he felt as though the last ten years of his life had been washed away.

His doctor would say it was a spontaneous remission—it happened sometimes—but Wayne knew better. It was Lavender. He hadn't imagined her special gift. It was real!

Lavender!

With no fear of dropping her now, he scooped the cat up in his arms. She was breathing, barely, and was limp and cold. Much too cold.

"Oh, no. No, no, no," he cried. "Lavender! Wake up, honey! Please!"

He held her close, and she began to purr. She opened her eyes and looked into his face, which was already streaming with tears that fell on her fur. After a minute or two that lasted forever, the little motor wound down, the light faded from her eyes, and she was still.

Can one give CPR to a cat? he wondered frantically. But he knew it would be no use.

She'd given everything she had to heal him, and then she'd waited for him to awaken to say her goodbyes. How could he ask for more?

He was still sitting there on the edge of the bed in his pajamas with Lavender cradled on his lap when Lucy came in.

"Wayne! What are you—Oh!" She swooped in and dropped to the bed beside him. "Lavender." She reached out to stroke the black fur, already losing its luster in death. "Oh God, Wayne, what happened?"

He'd ceased crying, but the words came with difficulty over the lump in his throat. "I told you she was special, Lucy. She had a gift. She healed me."

"What? How? That's"—Lucy looked into his eyes, her own wide with questions—"impossible."

"I don't know how. All I know is this morning I woke up feeling ten years younger. And I guess it was just too much, too much for her." The last few words came out over a strangled sob.

"Oh, Wayne. I'm so sorry. What can I do for you?"

He thought for a moment. "Nothing, Lucy, really. I just want to be alone with Lavender for a while. Bury her and, you know, remember her. Come back this evening if you like. We can talk then."

"All right." Lucy gave him a heartfelt hug and leaned down to kiss Lavender on the head. "If you're sure. I'll make you some coffee before I leave."

"That'd be nice. Thank you."

Wayne sat there for a while in a grief-stricken stupor but finally recognized the need to move. He placed Lavender on the bed and headed to the kitchen, reveling in his ability to walk unaided despite his sorrow.

After fueling his rejuvenated body with coffee, he endeavored to eat a blueberry muffin but ended up pushing it away after one bite. Wayne dressed for yard work and headed outside. He grabbed a shovel from the garden shed and dug up one of the smaller lavender bushes at the near end of the garden. Then he kept digging. The ground was soft from rain earlier in the week, and he soon had a cat-sized hole a good three feet deep.

Every muscle in his body protested the sudden physical exertion, but it was good pain, completely different from the cramps and spasms of ALS.

He retrieved Lavender's little body and gently laid her to rest at the bottom of the hole with her favorite catnip-stuffed toy birdie beside her. Fresh tears blurred his vision, but he made no effort to hold them back. He told her how much he loved her. How much he would miss her. He thanked her for coming to him and told her he would never forget her. Well, how could he after what she'd done for him?

Then he filled in the grave and replanted the lavender bush on top of it. He thought Lavender would like that. He went inside, made fresh coffee, and sat down at the kitchen table with his cup, a pen, and some paper.

He didn't know how long his miraculous remission would last, but he planned on making the best of every single day. He began to write the story of Lavender—fiction, of course, because no one would believe it was true, the black cat who had brought him the greatest of good luck.

He thought she would like that too.

Ben Kardos is a dark fiction writer, musician and cat dad from Washington state. His stories have been published in various ezines and anthologies published by the likes of *Wicked Shadow Press*, *The Sirens Call* and *Carnage House* among others.

Some of his work is available on godless.com.

He also hosts the YouTube channel *Reading Monstrosities* dedicated to the review and discussion of transgressive and horror literature. This channel also features his podcast *Talking Monstrosities*: conversations with independent horror authors.

AGENTS OF SATAN

by Ben Kardos

The wheel turned, bones cracked. The prisoner's anguished howls echoed through the torture chamber's stone corridors. Pope Gregory's eyes blazed in the torchlight as he watched the screaming man's body stretch painfully upon the rack. It had taken hours, but they were so close now, so close to a confession. He could feel it.

The prisoner's naked skin glistened, his arms and legs pulled taunt as the heavy ropes dug sharply into his wrists and ankles.

The masked torturer gave the wheel another turn, tightening the ropes a few more inches. There was a sickening pop as the prisoner's arm pulled free from the socket. The man shrieked like the damned in Hell.

"Stop! Please stop! For the love of God! Stoooop!"

"Keep the Lord's name off thy blasphemous tongue," Gregory hissed. He took the man's face in his hand. The prisoner flinched as if Gregory's fingers were hot brands. Gregory leaned down and whispered in his ear.

"I could end your suffering now... with one word I could give relief, but you must give me the information I require. You must tell me about your black masses; only confession will end your pain."

The prisoner gazed up into the elderly man's stern, wrinkled face. Tears cascaded from his eyes. His chest heaved as he began to sob hysterically. His hiccupping cries sounded like relieved laughter. Gregory waited patiently for the man to find his voice.

"It ends now?" the prisoner asked.

"God forgives all who confess. Now tell me, what was it that my friars discovered you and your companions doing the night of the full moon?"

The prisoner closed his eyes, lips quivering, body trembling. At last, he spoke. "It was an initiation ceremony. We were welcoming a new member into the fold."

Gregory's eyes arched inquisitively. "Ah, and what did this ceremony consist of?"

"If I tell… will you let me go?"

Smiling slightly, Gregory said, "I will end your suffering. You have my word as a man of God."

The prisoner looked at Gregory, then at the torturer behind him. He coughed wetly, and continued his confession.

"At the ceremony we sit in a circle around a stone statue of a black cat. Prayers are repeated until the cat comes to life. Once it is flesh and blood, the initiate must lift its tail and kiss its genitals."

Gregory's lips turned up into a disgusted sneer. "What happens then?" he asked.

"We… we each take turns kissing the cat. We then allow it to scratch us, one by one. Once the blood is flowing, we have the initiate drink from our wounds. Then… then…"

"Then what?' Gregory pressed.

"Orgies," said the man, "great orgies as the cat watches from a place of honor."

It was all Gregory could do to keep from gouging the man's eyes out with his thumbs. His skin crawled, his heart pounded in a blend of anger and revulsion. "This black cat," he managed to whisper, "What is the significance of the cat?"

The prisoner stared at him like a man on the edge of madness. His face suddenly changed and he began to laugh, as if Gregory's question was a joke told by a court jester. "You really do not know?" the man exclaimed. His laughter filled the room like water. Gregory felt as if he might drown in the man's hysterics. "The cat is an agent of Satan! How can a man of God not know that?"

Gregory tried to speak, but his words caught in his throat. He stammered, "you… you mean…"

"Yes! The black cat paves the way for the Master to visit us! After the orgy we are joined by Him! Now tell me, Your Holiness, where is YOUR fucking God?"

The man crumbled into a fit of rapid giggles. His eyes rolled back in his head like a man possessed. Froth flew from his mouth, his head shook back and forth. Overcome by fear, Gregory looked at the barrel-chested torturer and nodded. The torturer seized a heavy axe leaning against the wall. With a quick, arching swing he sliced through the prisoner's neck, silencing the manic laughter.

The head hit the floor and rolled to Gregory's feet. "Rot in Hell," Pope Gregory spat, kicking the head away.

With that, he left the torture chamber and ascended the stairs to the Lateran Palace where he called an emergency meeting with his closest Cardinals.

"We must do more to purge the world of the satanic heretics," he said from his papal chair in the meeting hall. "They are a plague that will consume the world if we do not act accordingly."

"What do you propose, Your Holiness?" asked Cardinal Archibald.

Gregory looked each Cardinal in the eye. "The Inquisition must be extended. We must conduct more investigations, more interrogations. The fate of the world is in our hands."

"God help us," whispered Cardinal Matthew.

"I shall write a decree shortly," Gregory continued, "detailing everything that must come to pass. We must do everything necessary to squeeze confessions out of the heathens. In the meantime, gentlemen, I need you to capture all the black cats in the city and bring them to me."

"May I ask why, Your Holiness?" said Archibald.

"Black cats are agents of Satan. They must be purged along with the witches and heretics.

Several Cardinals gave Gregory curious looks, but none questioned his statement.

"As you wish, Your Holiness," said Archibald.

A week later, heavy smoke filled the air above the Lateran Palace. A massive pit was dug into the courtyard, belching flames from its depths. Around it stood the Cardinals, priests, and palace guards, each holding a large, squirming bag.

From the balcony, Gregory surveyed them. Even from his elevated position above the ground, the flames from the pit singed his skin, the smoke stinging his eyes.

He raised his arms. "This year of our Lord 1233 begins a great purging," he bellowed. "All those not with God are against Him, and those who do not turn from evil shall be cast into the great fires of eternal damnation."

A basket sat at Gregory's feet. Stooping down, he removed the lid. The small black kitten inside looked up at him with frightened yellow eyes. Gregory reached inside and grabbed the creature by the nape of the neck. The kitten hissed and struggled in his firm grasp. The Pope's heart pounded, half expecting to see the creature transform into Satan himself. Pushing through his trepidation, he held the kitten above the balcony for all to see. "Satan hides in plain sight, and his agents take many forms. It is our God-given duty to stay vigilant and on the watch for these abominations. For the glory of God, they must be PURGED!"

Gregory dangled the kitten over the balcony and dropped it. Tumbling end over end the animal plummeted into the flaming pit. A blood curdling screech emanated from within. The flames rose high as they fed upon the fresh fuel.

In turn, the guards each heaved their own sacks into the pit. More screeching filled the air. The terrible cries of the burning cats were matched in fury only by the crackling and roaring of the blaze.

One of the cats managed to climb the wall of the pit, pulling itself over the edge and into the courtyard. Its black fur was scorched off, its skin charred and bubbling. The smoldering cat lunged forward to make an escape. Two of the guards blocked its way. One impaled it with a spear, lifted it up, and threw it back into the inferno.

Slowly, the screams of agony ceased. The flames danced high as greasy smoke plumed up like a dark flower above the palace.

Gregory made a sign of the cross in the air. "May God's justice be done," he said.

As the Inquisition spread throughout Europe, so did the purging of cats. Word spread fast of Pope Gregory's declaration. Suspects were interrogated; those found guilty of heresy or witchcraft were condemned either to lifelong imprisonment or execution. Churches were built, pagan temples destroyed. In time, not only black cats were killed in his crusade; soon all cats were viewed as satanic and condemned to the flames.

Gregory heard the news of all that transpired and smiled, confident he was performing God's work.

Within a year, the cat population had been all but decimated. Those found harboring cats secretly were brought in for interrogation, the cats executed immediately. Fear and superstition surrounding the four legged creatures spread as fast as the bonfires that burned them.

Gregory was not immune to these superstitions. Many nights he awoke sweaty and screaming from nightmares in which he was being chased through Hell by swarms of black cats. Prayer was his sanctuary from these nightmares. Countless hours were spent praying to the gold crucifix on the alter in his private chapel.

It was during one of these solitary prayer sessions that he was interrupted by a soft scratching at the wooden door. Turning his head away from the cross he called out, "Who's there?"

He was answered by a gentle meow.

Gregory's body went cold. How did a cat find its way into the palace? Had they not all been eliminated from the city? How could one have found its way to his door?

His only conclusion was that it had been sent there.

Hit with a rush of adrenaline, Gregory rose from the kneeler with the speed of a much younger man. He picked up a fire poker leaning against the hearth, holding it in front of him. Blood pounded in his ears as he slowly walked towards the entrance.

The cat meowed again, still scratching at the door.

Gregory's breath was fast and raspy. He opened his mouth and shouted, "In the name of God I command you to leave!"

He was answered by a sharp hiss.

Hands shaking, Gregory grasped the door knob and slowly turned it, prepared to club the creature the moment he laid eyes on it. He threw open the door.

The hallway was empty.

He listened for the sound of claws scampering on the stone floor, but all was silent. Scanning the empty hall,

Gregory slowly relaxed his tightened muscles, keeping his weapon poised before him. The air felt heavy, the silence deafening.

He backed away from the door, confused and apprehensive. Had the scratching been in his head? Or had his command really chased the devil away?

Locking the door, he turned back to his alter. He gasped with fright.

Sitting there staring at him was a black cat.

The cat's tail curled slowly in and out, like a finger beckoning Gregory closer. Gregory felt dizzy, his vision tunneled.

Rising to its feet the cat paced across the little altar to the gold crucifix. Casually, it lifted a paw and knocked the cross to the floor like a checkmated king. It then stared at Gregory with indifferent yellow eyes.

The blatant act of blasphemy broke Gregory from his spell of fear. "Demon! I cast thee out!" he screamed. Raising the fire poker over his head he rushed at the cat, bringing the weapon down on the altar full force.

The cat effortlessly dodged the old man's attack. Spittle flew from Gregory's mouth as he chased the cat off the altar. Hissing and cursing, he swung the poker, backing the cat into the corner of the room. Through it all, the cat purred, as if enjoying the battle. Enraged, Gregory lifted the poker like a spear, drawing it back over his shoulder. "Go back to Hell, vile beast," he growled through clenched teeth before hurling the weapon.

The iron projectile struck the floor, releasing a flurry of sparks, missing the cat by the width of a hair. Crouching down, the cat sprung at Gregory. The old man screamed as the creature's teeth latched onto the flesh between his thumb and index finger.

The needle-like teeth dug deep. The pain was sharp, explosive. Gregory flung his arm in crazed loops, desperately trying to unlatch the beast. He resorted to beating the cat against the wall. The little body made dull thuds as it connected with the hard stone, but it still refused to release its hold on his bleeding hand. After half a dozen strikes there was a shattering of bones. The wall was quickly splattered with blood and black fur. Still screaming like a madman, Gregory hammered the cat against the wall until its body went limp, its internal organs spilling onto the floor.

When the cat was finally dead, he used his free hand to pry its locked jaws open. The small puncture wounds in his flesh flowed freely with blood. Half shocked, Gregory stumbled to the door. "Guards, help!" he screamed as he ran down the hall, leaving a trail of blood behind him.

Gregory's private physician cleaned and wrapped his hand. However that did not stop the wound from swelling and turning purple as a ripe plum a few days later. The veins in his arm started turning black soon after.

Hit with fever, Gregory was relegated to bed. The physician kept watch over him night and day, pressing cold cloths to his burning face.

Days passed, but Gregory's condition did not improve. He was bled several times in hope of draining the infection from his body. Medicinal herbs were applied to his aching joints. Prayers were also offered up, but it soon became clear all efforts were in vain.

Pope Gregory IX was in his final days.

A priest administered Last Rites. Gregory smiled at the young man performing the sacrament. He gently patted the man's hand. "I am ready to go, my son," he said weakly, "I have fought with the devil, and won. I have done God's work and am ready to see Him face to face."

These were his final words. As Gregory faded away he reflected on his struggle with the black cat, the sounds of its bones crunching against the wall, its blood staining the stones, its organs splattering on the floor. Somehow he knew that his battle with that cat was his final test in life, God's last trial for him to conquer. He had triumphed.

I fought the devil, and won, he thought again. When he died his face was the picture of perfect serenity.

Gregory found himself alone in a large round room with walls rising up into a stormy sky. The dark clouds churned violently, threatening rain.

Spinning around, Gregory took in his simple surroundings. Where was he? Swallowing nervously, he glanced down at his body. It was still old, still draped in the clothes he had died in.

"Hello?" he called out. "Somebody, answer me!"

"Greetings, Gregory," said a deep voice.

Turning in the direction of the voice, Gregory discovered a tall man dressed in a long red robe. The man's skin was pale, nose long and beaky, eyes silver. He had a short beard, sharpened to a point.

"Where am I?" Gregory asked.

The mysterious figure smiled. "You were the Pope, should not you know?"

Gregory looked at his surroundings again. Surely this was not Heaven, so it could only be…

"Purgatory?" Gregory asked.

The man laughed. "Sure, why not?"

There was something about the man's laugh that sent a cold chill through Gregory's body. "So what is to become of me?" he asked. "I dedicated my life to doing God's work. I have led the flock according to the scriptures, I have built churches…"

"Killed heretics and witches, expanded the Inquisition, burned cats," the man interrupted.

Gregory nodded. "Among other things, yes."

Striding forward, the man came face to face with Gregory. "Tell me Gregory, what good did you think burning cats would do for the world?"

Gregory answered confidently, "Cats are agents of Satan."

"Hmm, and who told you this?"

"One of Satan's followers just before we executed him."

The stranger stroked his beard. "And by killing cats, namely black ones, you felt that you would somehow purge evil from Earth?"

"Of course. As Pope there was nothing I would not do to purge Satan's evil from the world."

The man began to pace back and forth, hands clasped behind his back. "So by your logic, if cats are from Satan, then killing them would be favorable in the eyes of God?"

"I believed so, yes."

Spinning on a heel the man faced him. "Did you ever wonder if perhaps it was not God that wanted you to kill the cats?"

Gregory furrowed his brow. "What do you mean?" He began shifting nervously on his feet. He noticed that the room was very warm.

"What if by purging these so-called *evil* cats you were really doing the work of the Evil One?"

Gregory scoffed. "That is ridiculous. Why would the Evil One want me to kill His agents?"

Shrugging his shoulders the man replied, "Perhaps to make room for others."

With that, the man raised an arm, pointing into the sky. Gregory looked up. The clouds parted. Between them appeared images of Earth. What he saw sent his spirit into a freefall of despair.

Rats.

Massive swarms of rats clogged streets and sewers. In the absence of cats, the slimy, flea-ridden rodents had no predators to stop them from proliferating unfettered. Flashing images showed them scurrying across Europe like an invasive army, polluting the water supply with their excrement, climbing into beds, biting children, infecting families, spreading contamination and illness.

Gregory watched in stunned silence as the rats spread illness around the world. The images depicted bloody, puss filled boils, cries of agony, painful death, rats feasting on the bodies of the deceased millions...

The clouds closed.

"Just a few scenes of events to come," said the man.

Shaking, Gregory turned to him. "Wh... wha...?"

"So do you still believe executing cats was the work of God?" the man asked, his lips curling up in amusement. "Do you really think God would have orchestrated suffering like this disease?"

Gregory fell to his knees, shaking with horrified realization. "Oh, God! I did not know! How could I have known?"

"Did not you yourself say Satan hides in plain sight?"

Gregory crawled to the man, clutching at his robes, sobbing. "But... I am a man of God! I only did what I thought was right in His eyes!"

The man snorted and looked at his fingernails apathetically. "It is ironic, is it not? By slaughtering black cats you paved the way for what shall be known as... the Black Death."

Gregory's voice rose to a pathetic level. "Have mercy! I beg you, please let me make things right! I did not mean for this to happen! Let me fix it!"

The man gazed off as if in deep thought. "Very well Gregory, I will give you one chance."

An opening suddenly appeared in the wall. Beyond the opening a statue of a black cat floated several feet off the floor.

"Touch the cat, and the world will be saved from this plague and you will get to join your God in paradise."

Gregory looked at the hovering statue and began walking towards it. It seemed so easy, just an arms-length away…

"Make haste though, I fear you have company joining you."

The clouds rumbled with thunder. It was followed by the deafening sound of squeaks and scurrying. Looking up, Gregory saw the sky raining a torrent of rats. Hitting the floor, they rushed towards him, jaws snapping, their beady eyes crazed with hunger.

"When the cats are away, the rats can play," said the man, cackling with laughter. He slowly vanished from view as the rats ran past him, his laughter echoing through the room.

Panicked, Gregory fled out the opening and down an endless hallway, chasing the black cat hovering just above his head, arms stretched, desperate for a single touch of the stone object. It floated before him like a carrot before a mule.

On and on he ran, the horde of rats right behind him.

Gregory could not tell how much time had passed: hours, days… years. Nevertheless, he continued chasing that illusive black cat, the army of rats forever nipping at his naked heels. Sometimes he stumbled and was smothered by the rats, their teeth gnawing into his flesh, devouring him bit by painful bit, only for the chase to begin again from the same room they had started from.

Still, he ran. What else was there to do?

His lungs burned incessantly, his legs heavy, his heart pounded painfully. His mind constantly replayed the sickening images he saw of the Black Death, the horror that he had unleashed through his misguided crusade.

There was no question in his mind where he was. He also knew there was no chance in Hell he would ever touch the black cat suspended frustratingly just out of reach. It was only there to give him false hope, to torment him, to toy with him.

It only made sense. The cat was, after all, an agent of Satan.

T.L.K. writes to appease the ghosts that have haunted her since childhood. Like Sarah Winchester who built an architectural house of mystery, T.L.K. tries to outpace the ghosts by writing as many words as it takes to get them lost in her ether, so the unwanted spectral visitors cannot find her. Some days she succeeds, some days she fails. Her clowder of black cats keep the ghosts at bay when she is not writing.

REST
by *T.L.K.*

I come but once a lifetime
Welcomed by some
Feared by others

My presence leaves nothing
And takes all that ever was
A life ends as I breathe

Sharpened claws slice through
Releasing souls
Into the dark fur of my being

Where I knead each one into a tapestry
Using paws to quiet
The last beat of a heart

I am endless
And yet I grow old
For each harvest takes something

My body grows heavy
My eyes cloud like milk
My being ever weary

Waiting for the last one to collect
And then my job will be done
And I may finally rest.

ACKNOWLEDGMENTS

This book would not be possible without the help and guidance of several people: Kealan Patrick Burke for his incredible cover design, Steve & Heather Ventura of Brigids Gate Press for their wise wisdom and guidance, Loren Rhoads for helping us identify and avoid mistakes before we made them, the San Francisco Bay Area Horror Writers Association for their encouragement and support, and every single author that contributed their talents to this book, we are in awe of your awesomeness.

And to all the little and big black cats out there that we love, that love us back and inspire us to create.

KICKSTARTER THANK YOUS

It took a worldwide village to make this project happen. Thank you to all of the following who contributed to our Kickstarter campaign including:

Albert Tomista, Jr.
Brett Hansen
Christopher Gallo
Curt Cloninger
Curtis Y. Takahashi
David
David S
Dexter Yaneza
Eric Mobley
Evan Finnian
GhostCat
Jennifer Dore
Kerry Causey

KHG
Kristal A Macintyre
Mary Causey
Michael Becerra
Miles
Nacia
Nathan Plunkett
Randy Hilborn
Ruben Jackson
S.L.Kay
Stacy Christopher
Tabitha Mashburn

ABOUT BLACK CAT PUBLISHING

It all started with a special black kitty named Agnes. She came into our lives at a time when we needed her love the most. She was fearless, despite her tiny six pound frame, and had a purr that would rival a Harley. She was the luckiest miracle we could ever receive. She was with us for nineteen years which wasn't long enough.

Agnes is the namesake for our comic book store which we ran as Black Cat Comics in Northern California for nineteen years. Towards the end of our career as four-color-funny pushers, we started to develop our own line of comics and got into publishing stuff we wanted to read which tends to be on the slightly darker side.

This book is the first non-comic we've produced and we hope you enjoy it. To find out more visit us at black-cat-publishing.com. Meow.

MORE FROM BLACK CAT PUBLISHING
Black Cat Chronicles

*true tales of terror narrated by a mystical black
cat*